THESE PRECIOUS DAYS

BY

No Sweat

Old Seventy Creek Press 2012

Published in the United States
by Old Seventy Creek Press
Rudy Thomas, Publisher
P. O. box 204
Albany, Kentucky 42602

ISBN-13: 978-0615609898
(Old Seventy Creek Press)

ISBN-10: 0615609899

Introduction by Guy Davenport

621 Sayre Avenue • Lexington Kentucky • 40508

11 February 1985

Dear Mr. Robbins:

I've been reading your manuscript a few chapters a day since you brought it over. I apologize for taking so long, but it's a long book and I'm a busy man.

You have enormous talent, that's for sure, and a wonderful way with words. I've enjoyed all the doings in the book, which reminds me of Elizabethan fiction: boisterous, cheeky, wildly energetic, outrageous, and a bit crazy. For a parallel (remember that I'm a professor) one would have to go back to Spanish, German, and Italian literature of the early Renaissance. Something out of Mother Courage and the Hundred Years War, or rogue literature of the Spanish. I find the book engaging and grandly readable. You have an ear tuned to the speech of your characters, and you have the Appalachian sense of general mumpery, disaster, and shittiness. Grimmelshausen is what your text is like: rogues, poverty, the Law, custom, a hypocritical religion, and moral rot.

So. My opinion is worth precisely nothing. I'm very much afraid that the fancy boys at the New York publishing houses will jump on you to revise, shorten, change. I don't know how you feel about such tampering. Maybe they won't. I think the book has a chance, and that you should try.

telephone conversation intervenes here.

EDITORS:
> Write each and ask permission to send the manuscript, saying that I advised you to.

Irene Skolnick
Harcourt Brace Jovanovich, Publishers
757 Third Avenue
NYC 10017

Robert D. Loomis
Random House
201 East 50 St
NYC 1002

Jack Shoemaker
North Point Press
850 Talbot Ave
Berkeley, CA 94706

Harry Ford
Atheneum Publishers
122 East 42 St
NYC 10017

Allen H. Peacock
The Dial Press
1 Dag Hammarskjold Plaza
245 East 47 St
NYC 10017

I'd add New Directions except that I don't think they could print so long a book, and I wonder if it's James Laughlin's kind of book.

Write everybody at once, and sit back and see what happens. I can't "act as your agent" as I know very little about the business, and am not in New York. My kind of writing (limited to like eleven readers) had to wander all over the place before I got connected with North Point. I've done 5 collections of short stories, and have a novel in the press. Each got published by a wild stroke of luck, without an agent. But I'm only an amateur scribbler, who writes for the fun of it.

I have a feeling that you're a real writer. Getting started is always hard (good for your character, adversity). I won't hand out advice (except for those double adjectives); you know what you're doing. As writers, we're as opposite as orange and blue, but there are infinite ways of being a writer.

So, congratulations on having written a novel of great energy, and spirit.

I'll signal again, when I've got to the end.

ad interim

Guy Davenport

FOREWORD
BY A PROFESSIONAL THERAPIST

To Whom It May Concern:

It is with pleasure I write to you of Mr. Robbins'
original and compelling book, *These Precious Days*. It
has been my honor to be witness to its development
and conclusion.

First and foremost, his distinctive expository style
grabs one's attention from the outset. Terse, bare-
bones and powerful, his voice rings with the
authenticity of native experience combined with
seasoned compassion. This is his world sung in the
clipped jargon so distinctive to the region, an
intimate and outrageous journal of a man stitched to
his heritage but standing observer to the wholly
unavoidable cycles of his lifetime. The author has
stripped his soul to its basic components, allowing
the reader to slip inside his skin, peering out
through his heart's eyes.

The No Sweat quotes and comments that lead into
each entry are simply marvelous. I laughed. I cried. I
shook my head in amazement. His use of family
dynamics as background is superlative, richly
confided with no apology. Mr. Robbins' philosophy of
life and its mysterious interweaving are encapsulated
with such lavish cynicism and wry with that I
savored them like a fine appetizer to the main
course. Pithy and acerbic they sway to the genre of
poetic essay and social commentary in the infamous
style of Mark Twain; yet, expose a warm nature and
generous spirit unmarred by aberrant events.

His characterizations are superb, particularly the
hilarious nicknames that summate these unique
personalities with a decisive zing. These are people

7

struggling on the bottom strata of the local social order, belly-crawling at times, but with a ferocious dignity. It is the story of survival at its basest levels, not just a meager getting by, but outwitting the system using its own indignities and absurdities to mock it, provoke it and occasionally defeat it while living on the wicked edges of morality and legality. His actors are not elaborate analyses, rather they blithely hint at folks whose coping skills are jungle-acquired, whose adaptations are made to bizarre, unforeseeable twists of fate. Each player possesses several faceted attributes of the composite complexity of the author, and when taken as a totality produces an intriguing, fully-developed profile of the Eastern Kentucky good-ole-boy persona: a marijuana grower, pigeon breeder/deep-sea diver, law defying and touchingly poignant, a devoted family man and loyal friend marrow-deep.

Perhaps the standout feature of this novel is its extraordinary dialogue. Mr. Robbins is a master of this deceivingly difficult aspect, with his dialect hot-n-spicy and stropped razor sharp. His ability to convey the symbolic meta-meaning with brutal (often monosyllabic) brevity is beyond remarkable. To say it is evocative is an understatement. With practiced expertise he sets each scene with the somewhat anticlimactic off-handedness of just-another-day-down-home, only to render the reader surprised, and often shocked, at the outcome. The verbal punch is delivered with a visceral banter that says as much between the lines as outright. His 'Black Hole' is heart-wrenchingly relevant in scope and one of the finest psychological sketches I have seen in popular print. Their repartee brims with mutual admiration and terrible, doomed camaraderie.

Mr. Robbins has painted a portrait of a man caught in the web of his times, a victim turned survivor, a player in the eponymous reality show of hand-to-mouth grubbing and a victor who has circumvented conventionality and apparent destiny to become a psychical congregate of paradoxical array. More than just being entertained, I learned from this book and felt immersed in its singular culture, as though I had spent years exploring his world. It has the distinguishing earmarks of a masterpiece-vibrant plot, memorable characters, bucolic setting, with the personal touch of the sensitive diarist. H is an intuitive and imaginative author par excellence.

I give this new work by Mr. Robbins my highest recommendation, both as a licensed therapist and voracious reader. I look forward to seeing future offerings by this exciting new author. Thank you for the opportunity to discuss its merits.

Sincerely,

Sara L. Griffith, LMFT
Eagle River Alaska
May 1, 2007

Review of *THESE PRECIOUS DAYS*, by Earl Lowell "Robbie" Robbins, Jr.

Unlike his first novel, *NEFARIOUS*, or the more recent collected short stories, *BLACK BLUEGRASS*, Earl Lowell "Robbie" Robbins Jr.s' *THESE PRECIOUS DAYS* (TPD) is styled as a two-year chronicle of an eastern Kentucky writer's (NO SWEAT) existential observations during this period of his waning youth. Like most writers of the American South, there is inescapable bleakness, sometimes laid bare such as in the pseudonyms given to those that form and flaw his reality (e.g., Black Hole, mentor, Dark Star, best friend, Black Widow, beautiful temptress, etc.). Even the luminous names given to the family he loves (e.g., Sensi, Bright Eyes, True, etc.) are darkened by a troubled and often tragic dynamic.

Set in the hills of eastern Kentucky, the town of Aoephh is spatially, temporally, and culturally isolated; however, the author selects events from his many colorful adventures to demonstrate that it perfectly represents the human condition in all places and in all time. Unlike the typical self- aggrandizing reflections made in the safety of cosmopolitan salons and cafes, it is Aoephh's isolation that allows Robbins to better probe the "essence." During this period, 1981 to 1983, No Sweat (NS) begins to confront his past, present, and future through the struggles of his mentor, Black Hole (BH). BH is a West Pointer who requested a rare change-in-service upon his graduation to eventually become a Cold War B-52 pilot, and finally Air Force Academy professor and troubled intellectual who lost himself in what Eliot called the "shadow" separating abstract ideas and reality. Emotional pain and psychological darkness feed BH's demons, ultimately giving way to a lonely self-inflicted demise. NS's struggle, although never explicitly admitted, is the same. Like BH, NS leaves Aoephh at every chance, but always returns. No one escapes Aoephh (or life), but for death.

Although Robbins' has undoubtedly been influenced by many of the great writers, he has crafted a writing style that is unique. He keeps the dialog short and focused, but still manages to accurately capture the local dialect without distraction. His wordsmith distills and concentrates the characters and their circumstance. The senses are captured in a grand impressionistic manner, and the reader is led through the entire bandwidth of emotion, whether it is comedy in the banter related to a moonshine purchase in the mountains or tenderness and sorrow evoked by his mother's illness. Whatever the emotion, TPD is an implicit and explicit reminder of the pain-of-living each of us endure, but to our detriment often bury in the chaos of daily affairs. Robbins challenges the reader to examine the fragile relationship each of us have with our own demons, and through his well-crafted diary provides a measure of

11

contentment in their pheromones and long sinuous tethers.

Sincerely,

Edward W. Woolery
Associate Professor Geophysics

For my wife, Ruth Chesteen (Hall) Robbins,
Nancy, Matt, Lance, Barrett

And

Charles "Lindy" Yeager, Guy Davenport,
Sarah Griffith, Eddie Woolery, Dave Cox,
Howard Farris, Charlie Harris,
Charles Whitaker, Oscar Rucker and
my kind and brave editor, Rudy Thomas.

AUTHOR'S NOTE

Thirty years ago I fell into writing this journal because something drove me. It had something to do with my existence. And something I wanted to leave behind. It was my first attempt at writing more than a short story. I was thirty years old when I put the first words on paper. After four years there were 2,400 handwritten pages. It was a mess. I spent another six months handwriting my first re-write getting the work down to 2,100 pages. Another handwritten re-write cleaned it down to 1,800 pages. At this point I felt strong enough about the work to hire a typist. I lived with her and her sister for nearly six months in an austere room they rented in Richmond, Kentucky. She grew to loathe my presence. I had her constantly changing what she had typed. I pushed her beyond patience. When she finished she said that she never wanted to see me again. I couldn't blame her. But the manuscript, well, it was everything. I gave her $1,000 for the 1,300 typed pages she completed. A year later, I remained dissatisfied and took on the task of typing a new revision myself reducing it to 1,100 pages. Another re-write after this brought the manuscript down to 863 typed pages. For several years the work remained at that length. That was the manuscript that Guy Davenport,

Lindy Yeager and Oscar Rucker reviewed and liked. After they died something again stirred inside me. I re wrote the journal again and again and again. Slowly, it evolved taking on a new face. I had selected so many song titles over the years for various journal entries. In the end I went with songs by Billie Holiday. Nobody could match my mother singing her songs. The title, **THESE PRECIOUS DAYS**, comes from the melody, *SEPTEMBER SONG*. This was mom's favorite and the one I requested at her funeral which my sister sang. I wrote out of compassion, pain and the joy of living life twice. I employed my imagination to the fullest in an attempt to tell the story of a place and time and a heart laid open. Of course, it's all fiction. That's all there is.

No Sweat

October 1, 2011

Insight by the Author

No Sweat's two year journal. You'd think No Sweat meant everything was OK. Guess again. Aopehh? That's some mythical place in eastern Kentucky. It could have been in Tennessee or West Virginia. Any godforsaken place. No Sweat's next door neighbor, Black Hole, is a retired West Pointer and Strategic Air Command Bomber pilot of the cold war era. He says it's a good time to become insane. And that there is nothing to write about. Still, compulsion drives No Sweat to maintain his journal. What you are about to read begins on April 1, 1982 and ends on April 8, 1984, with a new conclusion added to the 103 journal entries on March 2012. Each shadows a time and place and a heart holding on. It's pure fiction.

No Sweat

March 6, 2012

"I'M NOT DEAD, I'M RIGHT HERE."

No Sweat

"If the writing is true it will own a soul."

NS

Journal Entry 1 – **WHERE IS THE SUN?**

April 1, 1982

For the past six months Black Hole had lived in a tiny room off the left of a steep flight of noisy stairs. He had one large window overlooking the Main Street of Winchester, Kentucky. The view concentrated on an old drug store and an unemployment office.

"Yeah, I can get all the furniture in my van," I remarked.

19

"You sure?"

"If I can haul 250 cases of Blue Ribbon I can haul your stuff."

"You'll never realize how much I dread returning to Aopehh."

"I'd be glad to get out of here."

"That's you."

"What's here? Does it remind you of The Point?"

"I only wish it were New York. I am not this place. I don't belong here. Don't you understand?"

Carrying furniture down the stairs I never asked Black Hole why he'd been fired. He had mentioned his cursing God at break time at his job and that such had gone over badly among his co-workers. The V.A. in Lexington had him messed up on prescriptions. He was retreating back to be my next door neighbor in the simple house where he had been born and raised. He was Black Hole. A mystery inside a gone-to-hell fifty year old body. "Now that I've been released from the unemployment office I can't draw unemployment," he said, shutting my van's door. "Three Jews shaped this world. Jesus, Einstein and Freud. It's not what you know--- it's what you don't. The only time I ever saw man up close was from the air."

"After West Point and SAC, how did you wind up at Columbia?"

"Done all the time."

Driving thirty miles we arrived in an area of Aopehh inhabited by retired railroaders. As we began unloading furniture, Black Hole turned on his radio. "Do you know that music?" he asked.

"Beethoven?"

"Do you know what it is about?"

"No."

"It's about death. Death and victory are the same."

All four walls of Black Hole's bedroom were littered with photos. Tolstoy in rags. Joyce with his dark glasses. Wolfe, his brain ready to explode. Tom Merton. Letters from astronauts. And a photo of my daughter. At times Black Hole blamed women for all of man's problems. Had a lot to do with his wife's suicide. His Kansas mother-in-law had taken his two sons never letting him be near. She considered him insane. He had been seeing a shrink every Thursday for years.

I left him alone in his book filled room.

He cried at night.

He cursed God.

He cursed the dawn.

"One eve down on the river a brute cursed Sensi as she carefully backed our boat up to the dock in a perfect manner. There had been no call for the foul mouth. A couple of minutes passed before I busted him in the face six times. Broke four fingers. Nothing phased him. Sensi leaped like a bobcat on his back after the brute and I came fighting down 20 rough cut oak steps landing at her feet. The owner of the dock broke up the fight. The next morning rumor spread far and wide up and down the Kentucky river that the local asshole got whipped by some green beret. I never knew which one was me."

NS

Journal Entry 2 – **If My Heart Could Only Talk**

April 9, 1982

Drunk inside Aopehh's California Cave with a bunch of buddies.

"No Sweat! Will you stop for a second!"

"Give me some help."

"Which way?"

"Do you know where you're at?"

"Here she be."

"What?"

Calm.

"Snakebite medicine."

"Snakebite medicine?"

"Yeah. And your map, if you'd like." Pulling out fat wool sock. My hands slid sock forward. Top half of pint. Jack.

"Thought you had a map?"

"I said, I had snakebite medicine."

"What do you have in those other pockets?"

Pause.

Bottle to lips. Little taste. "That should put us back on the right road." Passing Jack to Dark Star. "Tell 'em, Dark Star."

Grin. Little taste. "Snakes."

Third drink. Lid screwed. Sock shaken. Joint. Lit by a coal miner's helmet flame. Big inhalation. Held. Slowly released.

"I don't know where I'm at. I never have. I sure don't know where I am going. And I never trust anyone that says they do."

Fifteen minutes.

Crawling.

Climbing down a spiral-like natural stairway wrapping around a colossal stalactite.

The bottom.

A pit. A tall chamber-corridor. SOAPSTONE PIT. No Sweat's initials. Dark Star's initials. Old dripped red paint: 1929 GRAY STAR. Dark Star's father.

Stopping. Relaxing. Gazing. Old names. Dates.

Jack whispers.

"We've made it once more to the water hole."

Little taste.

I'd been coming here for over twenty years. CALIFORNIA CAVE. A rocky, sometimes slippery, limestone Swiss cheese hole. In the belly of a mountain located halfway between Dark Star and me. The entrance, near the steep top, hidden, narrow, shaped like California.

Walking.

"Where you going?"

"Up to The Temple."

"Temple?"

"Yeah."

"Temple." Face lifts. "Up there." Dome. Ceiling. The Cave God has to have a flame lit at its alter. Ain't cha read THE GOLDEN BOUGH?"

"The golden what?"

"Never mind."

X-inch worming. Chimneying. Forty feet straight up. Struggle. Shift weight. Pull. Reaching familiar foothold. One inch wide. Six inches long. Looking down. Black. Dark Star's light blinds.

"How's it look?"

Balancing. Glancing. Tan slabs.
Soapstone. Chalklike. Names carved.
"Everything's fine. Come on up."

Dark Star. Long legged. Climbing.

I light candles. Hidden under rock from
last trip. Timeless cavity reflects eerie.
Enchanting. Ghostly. The Temple becomes alive.
Sacred. Cathedral shadows. Ancient cracks.
Dark Star's fingers spider at my feet. Pulls
himself up.

"See if that joint is still here."

"Done checked. Gone. Rats."

"Happy rats."

Below. Five watch.

Leaning out. Void. No holds. Empty black
drop. Light roach.

"Man, you are crazy."

"Thank you."

Climbing. Back down. Soapstone Pit.

"Does this cave have another entrance?"

Head swimming. Light. Easy feeling. "They
say it does. I've never found it."

"Dark Star, No Sweat told me your dad found a plaque dating in the 1700's."

"Yeah. He came here in 1929. Found it in this room." Pointing to the end wall of the box canyon at the end of the hallway. "Found it over there with some guy's name and 1798 written in old English."

"What did he do with it?"

"Put it up. Got lost."

"Y'all ready for some serious crawling!"

"Lead on!"

Squeezing past two rocks. Bellying through mud and rubble. Encountering deadly crevices. Carefully straddle. Wall. Chimney. Back on hands and knees. Crawl. Pass black void. Drop offs. Narrow. Slippery. Ledges.

Breakdown. Car-sized boulders.

Dead end.

"That's it! We're lost!"

"Lost!" Tired. Mock "We're lost!"

"Yes!"

"Did you hear! Dark Star! We're lost!."
Disappearing through hole. Jagged. Blind
tunnel. Can't see. Hands reaching. On belly.
Can't raise. Inch Forward. Heading downward.
Snaking. Hope no bottomless pit. Or rabid fox.
Hole widens. Face first. Sliding. Diving. Dried
stream bed. Sandy shore. Relief. Waiting for
others. Air. Creek passage. Everybody together.
Resting soft. Tired. "That was THE VIRGIN
SQUEEZE."

"No Sweat, I can't breathe!" Breathing fast.
Holding breath. Exhaling. "I can't breathe!" Wild
eyed. Hyperventilating.

"Quit thinking about it. Stick your hat
over your face. Lay in the sand awhile. You'll be
OK."

Five minutes.

"I feel better. How'd-ju know?"

"The Cave God knows all."

Bent over. Stoop walking.

Stopping.

Solid flat. Limestone. Long and as wide as
a football field. Only two feet tall.

Logrolling.

Stopping.

Wasteland.

Time.

Entering new hallway.

Easy walking.

Feels good.

Vertical forty foot.

"ABANDON ALL HOPE YE WHO SCALE THIS WALL." NS

Shining light.

Looking up. At top. Man sized hole.

Stand still.

Silence.

I hear it. Faint. Water. Other side.

Climbing. Finger holds. Difficult. Very. Three fourths the way, wall leans out.

At top.

Secure rope around rock. Can't see the other side. Feel fresh air. Hear rushing water. Holding rope. Tightly. Balancing. Blue clay.

Slick. Top edge of giant pit. Abyss. Carbide lights too weak. Can't see depth.

Raising rope. Lowering on other side. Vertical drop. Wet. 60 foot.

Rope hits ledge.

"You going down?"

"Can't dance."

Pulling rope. OK. Holds my weight. I lean out. Smile.

Descending.

Down.

Down.

Reached landing.

Coffin size ledge.

Looking over. Another sixty foot drop to next small landing. Shine strong light past that. Can't see bottom. Feel weak. Step back. At my feet a skeleton. Bones perfect. Must-a fell. Old. Beaver. Red-orange teeth. Unmistakable.

"You alright!"

"No! Ask Anyone!"

"If you hate someone, buy them a racehorse."
NS

Journal Entry 3 – **BIG STUFF**

May 1, 1982

First Saturday in May. Tulip poplars bloom. Cardinals rejoice. Bluegrass turns blue. The world's greatest three year olds.

The Kentucky Derby.

Last night Johnny called from Harrodsburg. Insisted I drive over. Be there at daybreak. Get drunk. Head for The Derby.

As the sun rose were engaged in his proposals. Johnny's Anchorage life showed. Heavier. Smoking. Pale. He'd escaped Alaska during Nam. Now laughed. Made it big as an Alaskan contractor.

Firing up a joint. Johnny's passive face became bright with anticipation. HOTEL CALIFORNIA was playing. "Is this home grown?" he asked.

"Tenth generation Aopehh."

Brown-eyed Johnny toked again, smiled a dulcet smile, then coughed. The tape blared, YOU CAN CHECK OUT ANY TIME BUT YOU CAN NEVER LEAVE.

"I'll never forget the hundredth Derby," I said."Bob was with me."

"Who's Bob?"

"Aopehh's African. He was sitting on his steps on Back Street petting Rock and Roll, his mutt. Had on his Humphrey Bogart hat and holding two sacks of Julia's fried chicken."

"How old was he?"

"Nobody knows. Looked sixty. Probably eighty. Acted twenty. Was a porter during World War Two. Went from the Atlantic to the Pacific two hundred and two times. Still had his white jacket. On the hundredth he crawled in my car singing, In the Sweet Bye and Bye. You could smell bourbon for two blocks. Kept harping, one and four. Allowed CV Whitney at Calumet wanted him."

"This is good smoke. What would a couple of pounds cost?"

"Three grand."

"After the Derby I may want some."

"You wouldn't know someone wanting a hundred pounds, maybe more, would you?"

"Sinsemilla?"

"Yeah."

"You come up with over fifty pounds, I'll fly down for it. I'll have the money."

Nearing Churchill Downs we drove by houses jammed with the flow of people and traffic. Hustlers with signs advertising space in their yards for fifteen dollars.

At the day's end we'd lost a thousand dollars. Drunk, we searched for where we had parked. In the midst of a hundred thousand people we were lost. Somehow we staggered upon my van, slid the door, making gimlets. I put in ROXANNE and cranked the vibes. As we left hitchhikers jumped in and out. They'd beat to the sounds, take a toke, then bail. For an hour this continued.

Then my van was funneled into forced traffic. ROXANNE blared. Clouds of marijuana streamed. Arms waved. Gimlets spilled. Faces laughed. Nobody knew anybody. My crammed van stayed moving, continuing to an intersection. I had no choice. Steady as she goes.

Standing close before us was The Louisville and Kentucky State Police. Boots. Holsters. Shades. Guns.

Then a miracle.

Instead of getting in cruisers and calling the paddy wagon they flashed smiles, clicked heels. Gave a heroic salutation.

"Drive on!" said Johnny, upping the amps. "No one arrests anyone on this day!"

"I lived under the same roof with my father for nineteen years. He never knew me. Never cared where I was going. He always pretended to be a family man and brave. But on the inside he was nothing. He went to great lengths never to expose such. He used our family callously. Owned no remorse for any cruelties he rendered. I existed to serve him. I never go around him anymore. If you whip a dog enough it will leave."

NS

Journal Entry 4 – **HOW AM I TO KNOW**

May 2, 1982

The sun shined bright as Johnny, Doc, Mike and I headed out into an area of Aopehh called Barnes Mountain. Johnny would soon be going back to Anchorage and needed a gallon of moonshine. We had our shovels, sifters and boots inside the van hoping we'd get moonshine and gain information as to the exact whereabouts of the recently discovered Missing Link.

Aopehh's current newspaper headlined: MISSING LINK FINALLY DISCOVERED AT BARNES MOUNTAIN. The discovery was under a cliff overhang. Shellshock, a man I knew, being not too far distant from his patch and still, inadvertently stumbled upon a human skeleton. Upon close inspection, he saw a coccyx. Immediately the hills were alive with the sounds of MISSING LINK. The probability that it was no more than a forgotten revenuer simply never entered Aopehh's mind.

Pulling off blacktop on to dirt we approached Shellshock's neat farm lying passive at the base of a mountain. In one mowed clover field bordered by cedars were four rows of box bee-hives setting in front of corn rows. Off to the right was a stream-fed pond with ducks resting at the edge of cattails.

Coming to a two story black and white log cabin fronted with red game cocks under pink red buds I parked my van. The porch hound began to earn his keep. Then in the same way one rooster had eyed me I noticed the swaying stiff neck of Duchess, Aopehh's cobra; Shellshock's cautious woman.

"It's No Sweat!" I hollered, smiling.

"Who ya got with you?"

"Doc. And a friend badly needing something."

"Doc's with you?"

"Yeah!"

"Come on in."

Entering the cabin, Duchess was sitting on a couch in the cramped living room. In front of the couch rested a pot belly stove. Behind the stove a concrete wall was embedded with Indian artifacts.

"You and Doc ain't up to bean dusting any more ponds, are you?" smiled Duchess.

"Nah, we ain't fishin' today."

Moving on to the kitchen, Duchess continued. "Y'all come on in. I've got a mess of hickory chickens frying."

"Mmm. Smells good. Ain't had me no mushrooms in ever. But we best be getting on."

"What's your hurry?"

"We're aiming to do some digging up around where you all found that Missing Link. And we're hoping to get some moonshine. You ain't got any, do you?"

"Who's these birds?"

"The laid back one is Johnny. He's down from Alaska. Wants some shine to take back home. The other is Mike.

"They OK?"

"They're with me, ain't they?"

"How much do you want?"

"A gallon."

"Let me go see. You all find you a seat. I'll be right back."

"Returning to the worn linoleum floor in the living room we sat down admiring the stuffed, open winged, red tailed hawk suspended from the ceiling. On the side of a cedar shelf was tacked a stretched rattlesnake hide with fifteen rattlers and a button. Inside the shelf were four shellacked bull frogs sitting around a miniature table in popsicle-stick chairs playing poker. On one wall was a painting of an eagle feathered chieftain. At the bottom of the painting was BUCK, the signature of Duchess' recluse son.

Duchess came back to the open door. "I hollered for Shellshock. He's down at the creek catching crawdads."

"Where's Buck at?"

"Upstairs. Go up and see him."

Climbing a narrow stairway I knocked at a door. Opening the door I entered a large dim lit room alive with the smell of fresh cut wood. Woodchips lay piled in the middle of the floor. Buck sat at a workbench, sawdust in his bushy hair. He owned the same shell-shocked green eyes of his father.

Here at the foot of Barnes Mountain in the middle of this old log cabin labored an Aopehhean artist. His art was tits. Tits of every proportion. Chipped out of sandstone, limestone and coal. Made of concrete. Smoothed in clay. Forged in steel. In brass. Whittled out of every kind of wood. Fat tits. Attentive tits. Pointy tits. Droopy tits. Tits spaced in between. Uneven tits. Dixie cup tits. Odd sized tits. Tits stacked on top of tits. Tits poking out of the corners. Tits lining the walls. Tits back to back. Tits, tits and more tits. Except for one pair attached to a solid walnut, life-sized mermaid sprawled seductively on the floor with her arms surrendered behind her head.

"Buck, you've gone hog wild on tits, ain't cha?"

"You noticed."

"No Sweat. Y'all come down for a minute. I got something to show you. My mountain canary."

Downstairs.

Duchess was setting a parakeet cage on the kitchen table.

"A mountain canary?"

"My baby. Screech owl."

"No Sweat, where you been keeping yourself?" asked Shellshock entering the cabin. He was carrying a skunk. "I just got through de scentin' him," he said.

"How-d ja do that?"

Pulling out a small pocketknife, Shellshock handed it to me. "Open 'er up," he instructed. Opening the stiff blade I saw a fine edge. "She'll shave ya," added Shellshock. He handed me the skunk, taking the knife. Slowly running the blade edge down along one arm to his wrist, shaven hairs accumulated on the blade.

"What do you cut to de scent him?" I asked.

"His nuts."

"You can have that job."

"It's nothing if you know what you are doing."

"You couldn't put a fellar on to a gallon of moonshine, could you?"

"I'm out. But I know where you can get all you want."

"Where?"

"You go about six miles on the main road until you come to The Holy Pentecostal Church. It sits on a grassy hill. Across from it is a road. Go down it. You'll see a building. They've got all you want."

"Where did you find that Missing Link?"

"Do you know Delbert Ivy?"

"I've heard of him."

"You find his place. Park there. Tell him I sent you. He won't say nothing. Go down over the cliff behind his house. Follow it out. You'll see the overhang where we dug. Can't miss it."

Driving down the road we passed scattered shacks. Mike spoke. "Bet there ain't no insurance salesmen working this route."

"Ain't no warrants served up here," chimed Doc.

"Ain't no Jehovah Witnesses witnessing around here, either," I added.

The blacktop ran into gravel a half mile past Shellshock's. Yellow dust boiled behind us covering everything in its wake.

There it was, THE HOLY PENTECOSTAL BARNES MOUNTAIN CHURCH. A white building. Tin roof. Four square parallel windows. And three steps leading to the centered doors now filled with its releasing flock.

"Gentleman, there is salvation," I said. "Look at those happy faces. If Shellshock is right we might be happy, too, in just a bit."

As we turned off onto a dirt road a '60 Chevy having come from the church preceded us. Its bumper stick read: THE TIME IS NOW--GET RIGHT WITH THE LORD."

"Looks like he's gonna get right," spoke Johnny.

About fifty yards down the road we cut up to a dirt hill. On top was a makeshift tar papered shack. Two young men stood looking down at my van. The white shirted Chevy driver had already descended cuddling two six packs.

Walking up the hill we were greeted by Lank. Then his partner appeared, a ground sloth, Grapefruit. I had known him back in Boy Scouts.

"Grapefruit! What are you doing back in here?"

"Taking care of alkies."

"Can you get me a gallon of shine?

"Yep."

Grapefruit instructed Lank to take me to a place. Doc, Johnny and Mike remained drinking beer with Grapefruit. Lank hopped in the van.

"Where we going?"

"Take 'er on out the road."

Straddling ruts for some hundred yards, Lank told me to stop. He opened the door disappearing into the briars returning with two plastic milk jugs. On our ride back, Lank unscrewed one cap handing me the jug. Inhaling the aroma, I took a stout warp. My guts got charcoaled. I had swallowed hell itself.

Pulling up to the shack, Johnny approached. His Bambi eyes were trained on the jug. "Great shine," I said.

Johnny took the jug, downing a mouthful. Then, he handed it to Doc. Doc eyed into the mouth. "What is all that stuff floating in there?" he asked.

"Them's little devils stirrin'. Don't be a-feared, son. Take ya a swig. Drink. They'll make ya slap ya grandma!" informed Lank.

Doc handed the jug back to me. I took another swig. Doc lit a joint and offered Lank a toke.

"Is that marijuana? That stuff will make you crazy." Lank trotted back to his shack carrying the other jug.

Grapefruit leaned into the van, pulled the jug from my lap taking a pull. He lifted his left shoulder to his mouth. Then, drug his arm, elbow and hand across his red face.

"Forty dollars," he said, handing me the jug. Johnny handed him two twenties and we departed.

After driving around in the wilderness for a half hour we found Delbert Ivy's trailer at the end of a ridge. Delbert was that magistrate who ran for sheriff. Got two votes countywide. Even his kin never pulled the lever. Delbert came out of his trailer onto two wooden steps. A dog growled under his feet.

"My name is, No Sweat. We're out huntin' Injun rocks. Shellshock sent us. Told me to tell you. Hope it's OK."

Delbert spit tobacco out of the corner of his unshaven face. Then, motioned his head, stomped the step, shouting, "SHUT UP!"

The growl ceased.

Grabbing our stuff we walked down behind Delbert's trailer stopping at twelve slick car tires. Each was lying on their side some ten feet apart making a semi-circled property line to Delbert's backyard.

"Marijuana. Look. That's marijuana growing in those tires."

"Forget it. Today we are Louis Leaky."

Climbing down over a cliff we came across a pile of empty plastic containers. Mike inspected one. "Doc, these are all prescriptions made out by your mom."

I paused. We had found all we had set out to do. We'd gotten the moonshine.
And found the Missing Link.

"Pigeons are more like us than any other bird.
And one of the few creatures that recognize
themselves in a mirror. Poor things."

NS

"I won the National Racing Pigeon Show in White
Plains, New York in 1974.The youngest person
to ever win the show. The Head Judge was Dr.
James F. Carbone. The following summer Dr.
Carbone paid for my wife and I to stay in Florida
for three months. I paid him back with babies
from my champion. Dr. Carbone was one of
Frank Sinatra's best friends."

NS

Journal Entry 5 – **EMBRACEABLE YOU**

May 26, 1982

Sensi and I sat at a dim table with five of Swallowtail's guests waiting for Ricky Scaggs. Swallowtail was guzzling beer in this hillbilly heaven in Richmond, Kentucky, The Maverick. Ricky was Swallowtail's hero. Music was everything to the young Booneville attorney.

Swallowtail had been my employer the past year working with me on Aopehhean child support cases. We'd struggled to nullify some hundred shale oil leases that would have raped thousands of acres of Aopehh. Beat the oil attorneys. Those oil attorneys had employed local mercenaries to hood wink illiterate farmers into signing complicated leases. We had won the case. But no hoopla came. Aopehheans didn't recognize Swallowtail's devotion at no charge.

I was again out of work because Swallowtail had lost his bid for District Judge over Aopehh to Lips. The reason was simple. Swallowtail had once been caught growing marijuana. Back in the 70's he'd been apprehended growing four marijuana plants in his back yard garden. Such nefarious activity made the front page. In the newspaper photo there was a Kentucky State Trooper and a Lee County Deputy standing on each of his sides holding the cut plants. The caption read: 'When Officer Ward ordered Swallowtail to burn his crop Swallowtail stated: "I don't care to burn it. But I'd like to do it one joint at a time."'

Swallowtail's head swayed in the dark Maverick smoke to an inner rhythm. So did Slowtalk, his third wife. Her drawl, blue eyes and open blouse couldn't help but be admired.

During Nam, Swallowtail had been some sort of preacher. He'd been all over France and Africa. For a number of nude years he'd survived on an island off California dropping acid every day.

Green-eyed Sensi had been with me ten years. Pollyanna. I kept getting drunker looking at her thin frame and maroon mane. Pink stage lights reflected pink images.

There was a force compelling me to write.

I had no control.

What be this strange compulsion?

Sensi sat close while curly headed Ricky tenored, WILL YOU LOVE ME JUST ONE MORE TIME. I was drifting among the good ol' boys.

One street away was the burnt remains of the rat hole liquor store my father had conned a buyer into taking. Once the sucker bought it he found the business was a farce. So he set it on fire. Collected insurance.

Dad didn't care. It was business. And now, well, all that stuff was history

"Guy Davenport wrote me over 400 letters. In
one that was dated March 29, 1985, it began,
'Welcome to the Society of Offensive writers.
Your fellow members include Francois Rabelais,
Henrik Ibsen, Galus Valerius Catullus, Ezra
Pound, James Joyce, William Faulkner, Mark
Twain, Thomas Hardy and Emile Zola.'"

NS

"Dark Star stated that *THESE PRECIOUS DAYS*
would open many doors for me.
Yeah, all leading to the dungeon."

NS

"Nothing so proved that life is an illusion as a
grave."

NS

Journal Entry 6 – **I'M YOURS**

June 26, 1982

Near the end of the day.

I stand gazing up past the pines behind my home. The oaks are green roses swaying in the breeze. A few years ago I carried my daughter, Wide Eyes, on top the mountain. A brown butterfly lit on her forehead, staying there a minute before leaving. At the base of the mountain stands the water tower. A beacon for my racing pigeons. Down from the tower, Black Hole sat in his bath robe in a lawn chair. At his side, a dirty white dog, Boy. Boy is the dog that nobody wants. "You look Florida already," he said.

"We're leaving tomorrow."

"I'm being informed that my heart beats irregular. The heart sees. Not the eyes. They're giving me medication to make my heart beat properly. My God, what a conspiracy. I cannot understand why anyone would want to live forever."

"What do you think happens when we die?"

Black Hole stared into me. He rubbed his hands until tiny strands of dirt appeared. "Freud's mother explained death to him this way. Sigmund never asked again."

"Every day seems the same. I've lost track of months."

"A sign of age. You're thirty, aren't you?"

"Yes."

"A good year for insanity."

"Every day I move around. Nothing is meaningful. Or really accomplishable."

"Most men have to live their entire lives away before they feel that. You are very fortunate at thirty to see that reality. At the end of science lies nothing. Man can't divorce himself from fear. Did you know about Sister Teresa coming to eastern Kentucky? She said, 'And I thought the people overseas were poor.'"

It was almost dark when a SAC bomber broke out sweeping low straight over us disappearing over another ridge toward the remaining light. Black Hole watched. A downcast consumed him. "Like a PS at the end of a love letter," he remarked. "And Freud was wrong?"

"Big words don't make a big writer."
NS

"The year Robert Penn Warren died he told me
that he wanted to help find a publisher for
THESE PRECIOUS DAYS. Aged and upset, he
couldn't because of time. He apologized, adding
that he fully realized that such still didn't butter
parsnips."
NS

Journal Entry 7 – **THE BLUES ARE BREWIN'**

July 6, 1982

"Yonder be a cheap heaven," I said. looking across the inlet. "Over on that island there's more Rolls Royce's than anywhere. When you have everything, you go there. Unless you are John D. McArthur. Sensi and I breakfast with John D. every morning. Feed his ducks our tomatoes. He could have anything. But over here's enough. Last August we made a dive on the day before we were going home. Caught lobsters and busted snook. When we began cleaning we got to drinking. The women wanted to go out to eat at The Crab Pot. Fourteen of us. When we got there we had to wait at the bar. Dad started singing JELLY JELLY. Got up in one couple's face asking for requests. They insulted him, wanted MY COUNTRY TIS OF THEE. When we got seated we were in a glass partitioned room facing the inlet. The women studied the menus. The men ordered drinks. At our table was dad. Mom still thinks he is Robert Mitchum. She was there, drunk, as always. There was Sensi, Wide Eyes, True, Doc, Blackwidow, Larry, Jane and Joe. Larry can't hear and loves trouble. Down on the end of the table was , Kid. Dad knew his dad when he sold Cadillacs in Lexington. Kid had Amy and John with him. Dad got up on the table and crooned Fitzgerald. Was waving his arms when some Fidel seated at another table told him to sit down. Dad shut up. Got all droopy. There must have been twenty Cubans sitting like they owned the place. Nobody said nothin'. On our table was a glass ashtray. Fit my fist perfect. I eased over to Fidel

and leaned over. Mr., I said, that was my father.
If he gets back up and you say a word you'll eat
this. I put the ashtray to his mouth. Nothing
happened. I came back and sat down. Sensi
watched. There was a lot of commotion with the
Cubans. Fidel went to the manager pointing at
dad and I. He strutted back into the dining room
never taking his eyes off of us. Flicked his hand
and his table marched out. Doc gave a giant
salute and ordered six pitchers of Budweiser. In
a while, Doc, Kid and John headed toward the
bar. They mentioned ludes. I never saw them
again. Sensi didn't like the way things were
going. She said she wasn't hungry and took
Wide Eyes back to The Colonnades. A few
minutes later, True cut out. From fourteen we
got down to eight. Black Widow sat in my lap.
Then came the food. Fourteen orders. Ten orders
of all the crabs you could eat floating in garlic
butter. A cavalry charge of waiters brought
drinks. Black Widow ate a couple of shrimp and
a bite of grouper. Then, she and Amy left. Jane
volunteered to take them back. She got Joe and
they left. That left dad, mom, Larry and me.
Larry gave the crabs hell. There was crab shell
and guts all in his hair and beard. We had crab
all over the place. Slung the things. Banked
them off the wall into garbage cans. Gave them
to strangers. Clubbed for an hour. At the stroke
of midnight a waiter handed dad the bill. Dad
asked him if he looked like Santa Claus. The
waiter said if he didn't pay, he'd get the
manager. Dad told him to fetch Jesus Christ
cause he wasn't paying. The manager came.
Then the law. They pinned him against the wall.

Smashed his face. I asked where they were taking him. Riviera Beach Jail. Grand Larceny. Dad's hands were cuffed behind his back. Leg irons around his ankles. Shoved him in the cruiser. His face was bleeding. It was heaven."

"Heaven?"

"Yeah."

"Your dad going to jail, was heaven?"

"No. When the Cubans left. That was heaven. Whatever heaven is, it ain't a place."

"My mother's mother said, dad stood in his own sunshine."

NS

Journal Entry 8 – **NO MORE**

JULY 27, 1982

The three of us sat beside a swimming pool. There's a wooden ramp built at its shallow end for a wheelchair. Near one end of the pool there's an in-ground white, roofless structure about ten feet square, The Bullpen. Complete with a phone. Khrushchev, Sinatra and others have used the structure to tan. Down from The Bullpen along manicured pines bordering 1095

North Ocean Blvd. is a clay tennis court. At the other end of the pool is a lawn of Bermuda grass leading to a sea wall. From the wall to the south is the castle like Palm Beach resort, The Breakers. To the north is The Palm Beach Inlet kissing The Gulf Stream. The ocean breeze disguises the heat of midday.

"Yes ma'am, I'm a writer."

"What do you write?"

"Fiction. It's all there is."

"Denny tells me you are quite the swimmer and diver."

"Yes ma'am, I love the ocean."

"We've always loved the water, too."

"Ma'am, I appreciate your allowing my visit. Denny is an awfully good swimmer. Better than me. Too bad he missed making the Olympics."

"You said you are a writer."

"Yes ma'am."

"Have you ever been published?"

"No ma'am."

"You know, I've done a little writing. Which writers do you most admire?"

"Twain. Tennessee Williams, Poe, Hemingway."

"Did you know, Jack used to fish with Hemingway?"

"No ma'am."

"Jack was with Hemingway when he received The Nobel. Have you read Jack's Profiles?"

"No ma'am."

"Denny, please go to the library. Bring your friend a copy. And bring him, no, us a beer."

"Did you say that you also wanted a beer?

"Yes. I can't remember the last time I had a beer. If ever. But I believe that I would enjoy one with your friend, No Sweat."

"Ma'am, I know a man back home who served with Jack on PT-49."

"Forty-nine?"

"Yes ma'am. The boat after 109. They called it 49. Figured that was when the war would end. The crew loved Jack. They were all

59

older. Still, they called him, Uncle Jack. Near the end of the war the PT boats were converted into machine gun boats. Fifty cals. 49 didn't carry torpedoes. But Jack kept getting his requisition of Pink Lady. Alcohol that propels torpedoes. Shirley King, that's the man I know, made a still on 49. Took the red dye out of Pink Lady. Made it drinkable. Aopehheans ain't good for much. But in most any situation they can locate a drink."

Denny handled us John's small book and two green bottles of beer.

"Would you like to go inside? I'm normally never here this time of year. Two years ago Denny had to wheel me around. But I'm walking again. These bones are about done."

Slowly moving under stucco arches, passing tropical plants, we came to a shaded patio where tiled tables were casually arranged. Pointing to a second story window the aged woman stared. "Joe used to show movies from there. We watched on a wall at the other end of the patio. Watched throughout the winter. Joe owned R.K.O. pictures. Made the Tarzan films."

Finishing our beer we entered the house. The atrium had twelve foot ceilings. A winding stairway overlooked the entrance. Rooms branched off to various nooks.

Passing a dining room with open beams owning Picasso-like figures, we entered a room lined at one end with rows of books. A sink was recessed in the wall. On the right was a framed document; Ted's Democratic Convention Speech. Sketches of Ted covered most of the wall.

"Would you like to spend time here or see more of the house?"

"I'd appreciate seeing the house."

Leaving the library, walking down a hallway, we got on an elevator that took us to the second floor. Stepping out into another hallway there was an even row of doors leading off to eight bedrooms. One corner room had windows overlooking the ocean, pool and tennis court. Two single beds separated by a worm-eaten desk comprised its contents. "This is Jack's room."

Following the woman we came to her bedroom. There was a large pencil sketch of a rose at the foot of her bed. On one wall was a framed verse signed, Caroline. A white terrycloth bathrobe draped a high-backed, pillowed chair. On the robe's back were the large black initials, JPK. The room was quiet. She stood against the double glass doors staring at The Gulf Stream. Then she broke the long silence. "Denny, please bring us another beer."

Denny grabbed two more in the stainless kitchen, so different from than the family.

Only roses bleed.

"I grew up in my grandfather's theater and my father's fruit stand. Mom would bring home the fruits and vegetables that dad couldn't sell; the stuff beginning to rot. She'd cut out the rotten places saving the rest for us. It taught me a lot about writing."
NS

"When I was a baby I was found alone at dawn crawling across Aopehh's Bridge that spans over The Kentucky River. I've been crawling across that bridge ever since."
NS

Journal Entry 9 – **HOW COULD YOU**

July 29, 1982

Rex was enjoying his first summer as a veterinarian at The Stuart, Florida Animal Clinic. Yesterday, he performed surgery on Millie, George Bush's dog. I met Rex while diving the Palm Beach Inlet. He reminded me of Dark Star.

Only luckier.

Rex's wife's rich family had put him through college and vet school. After he graduated his wife made certain he never forgot her bunch had footed the bills. She demanded the best money could buy. Told Rex when he could breathe.

And when he could go diving. Particularly, with me.

Rex's wife was a Spanish hawk. A beak that screeched non-stop. I tolerated the torture because Rex had a small boat. It was impossible to dive the outlying reefs without one. A forty pound lobster was once caught where we were headed. Ten pounders were common. The solo dawn drive north along the coast up A1A from Singer Island had helped me gather peace. She was one of those poor hefty women that didn't have a clue as to what the ocean was about. And never would. The world is full of them.

After listening about Mrs. Bush's dog I learned that Millie wasn't the name of the beast. That was to be the name of her next dog. Actually, this dog was a cocker spaniel named,

C. Fred. Fred had been brought from the clinic as the Bush's were gone and Rex wanted to make certain that Fred got top care. I felt sorry for the dog as I pet it. Such sad eyes. Somehow, it knew that we were leaving it to remain with Rex's wife. Those eyes begged to go with us. "Life's not fair," I told Fred. "Hang in there, you'll survive. Hell, bite her. They can't do a thing to you. Wouldn't dare. Bite the fire out of her."

The thought sustained me.

We loaded our scuba gear in Rex's boat docked in the canal behind his home. Soon we were rooster tailing through mangrove water. Crab traps hung along the waterline near the private docks leading down from the many creamy mansions partially hidden in the distances. As the canal widened, Rex slowed. Near a Tahitian style mansion the canal branched. We went under the structure and close to its guest houses. A pool, helicopter and a sixty foot Hatteras were part of the scene. I reached for my camera.

"What are you doing?" asked Rex.

"Gonna get a shot."

"Put it up."

"What?"

"Put the camera down."

"Why?"

"They don't like pictures. A boat like that Hatteras exploded here a month ago. They make big runs. A friend of mine in the clinic went sailing in the islands. Plane circled him three times. Then, dumped out sealed bales. Over a hundred. Made one last pass and flew off. "

Soon we were in the inlet hitting six foot swells. The water changed from brown to blue. The swells dissipated. The water widened into a calm ocean. The rooster tails behind our boat began cutting through The Gulf Stream. "We better not mess around with the laws," voiced Rex. "I don't want to lose my boat. You don't want to have to buy me a new one, do you?"

I didn't answer. When I came to Florida, all seasons opened. One day I caught 289 lobsters on four dives.

A half mile out our depth finder scratched out a "V" revealing a ten foot ledge in forty foot water. I geared up.

"No BC?" asked Rex.

"Jack Cooster doesn't wear one. Me either," I responded. "Like writing, less is best." Rex was putting out his diver's down flag. "That just homes the law in on us," I informed.

"Fifty dollar fine if I don't fly it."

Jumping feet first I clung to my arbelette. The water was cold. Visibility, poor. Going down I anchored on coral. The ledge was lobstery. A wall rising from the bottom varied in heights from three to twelve feet. Rex soon showed. A few minutes later we came to a high area of the wall. Spiny legs poked from a hole. Seven big lobsters side by side. Antenna followed my moves. On the end, the largest lobster separated from the group to address me. A ten-pounder. Easy to catch. Hard to hold. Rex opened this dive bag. I managed to stuff it in. This continued until there were only three. Then one did a tricky flip to another ledge. The ledge rose some four feet. I swam to it holding still at a small opening counting forty bugs. Swimming back to Rex he had gotten the other three lobsters. I put my gloved hands in his face with my fingers outstretched. I closed my hands re-spreading them three more times. I pointed at the ledge.

He understood.

Swimming to the cave, Rex's eyes held fixed. The lobsters were timid, antenna moving nervously. Rex held up his gauge. One hundred pounds. We surfaced. Our boat was sixty yards south. I left the dive bag with the ten-pounder along with my gun near the lobster cave. We swam back to the boat emptying Rex's dive bag, getting new tanks Returning, the ten-pounder was gone. My dive bag was mangled. Rex had his bag. We went to work. Rex worked one side of the cave and I the other. At one point a lobster pulled that trick flip routine escaping out of the

66

hole. My tank hit against the roof as I slowly backed out of the tight quarters.

I sensed something wasn't right.

As I cleared my head from the hole there was a large form hovering about just above me.

The figure moved.

Square head.

A fifteen foot tiger.

Then, two more.

"I would go down into a concrete block structure in my back yard, one in which I had knocked out a few blocks. The hole left a tunnel that led up behind the gas heater inside my grandfather's theater. I also shoveled out a ditch putting scrap wood over it and covering it with dirt. You couldn't tell it was there. A tunnel that led over to my best friend's yard. Behind that tunnel, if you used your imagination, you could see a large image of Dick Tracy on the bricked wall of my grandfather's theater. Sometimes my pigeons would be scared by a cat and they wouldn't come into the loft. And they would roost high above Dick Tracy. On those nights I'd put my flashlight on the ground and aim it up at them, stationing the light and blinding the birds just so. I'd then go around behind to the Pontiac garage and climb up on some pipes and get a hold on a gutter, pulling up to a roof. Once up on that flat sloping roof, I'd walk upwards to another pipe that stuck out of the roof and stand on it and leap up to a wall that had a toe hold. I'd grab for the edge of the top and pull myself on top of my grandfather's theater. Then, I'd sneak across the roof and go to where I could see partial beams of the flashlight shining along the edges of the roof. I'd pause and would then quickly grab over the edge to catch one or two of my best birds. Once I had them I would slide them into socks and then put them in my shirt and climb back down the way I came up. When I got my birds back in my poor loft I'd go back up the wooden steps that led to the back of my apartment. I'd get my sleeping bag out of the closet and roll it across the pine floor and go to sleep. I remembered before the room that I was in had been built. How the apartment had ended this room short. Mom would fix cornbread in a little tray. The cornbread would be sweet made with sugar and shaped like cupcakes. When I ate supper part of my back would hang out of the back window as I used the sill for a seat. It was my supper seat for many years. But after the room on the end of the apartment got built by my grandfather dad knocked out a part of a wall and put a big piece of wood down that served as our table. After that, I could sit at a barstool in the new room and eat. No longer did half of me hang out suspended twenty feet in the air when I ate. I missed that. But it was worth it to have this small new pine room because it owned four large windows that overlooked the Kentucky River and mountains. Looking out of them you could see the L&N railroad coal cars coming by several times every day. And in a while, I could see, just like I could see Dick Tracy, a herd of giant buffalo along the ridges in the distance. I never told anyone about Dick Tracy or the buffalo. And I never told anyone how mom could sing so perfect. There wasn't any song that Billie Holiday could sing that she couldn't sing better. Mom would sometimes dance when she sang. Danced light and sweet and perfect and sad. She'd sometimes ask me to dance with her and the two of us would be in there in that dull room where the record player was and dance beyond all care. There was an old

skylight in that room that mom put pots and
pans under when it rained, each making their
own music. Of all the tunnels I made, none were
like the one that led to mom."

NS

"Science is a speck of pyrite in a Kentucky coal
field."

NS

Journal Entry 10 – **PLEASE KEEP ME IN YOUR
DREAMS**

August 25, 1982

All last night the rain poured. The first
drops in five weeks. Every farmer gave thanks.
At dawn, camouflaged, I departed for a ridge
Dark Star and I called, The Triangle. Parking my
van near a creek where I found agates I began
walking into the woods with a pack and
machete. An hour later I knelt beside a ginseng
plant. The slope's moist black dirt gave way as I
took it. I rested in the humid silence. Dense
foliage encompassed me. Sweat beaded my
forehead. A gnat whined near my ear. A tick

70

moved up my pants. Moving on, I encountered water-studded cobwebs, a snakeskin, slippery leaves and entanglements before resting. The morning's rays were striking bits of ground when I spotted them.

Verdant angels.

For some time I rested on moss. The perimeter of a patch is special. Nothing not right---good. No movement. No sounds. Aopehhean hide-n-seek. Entering the cleared area surrounded by oaks and hickories I moved to Alpha, an eight foot, budded Mexican virgin. I was here to weed, check for males and hermaphrodites. Many plants didn't have white hairs.

Instead, yellow flowers.

Males.

Thank heavens the flowers hadn't matured. No released pollen. My females were still virgins.

Sinsemilla.

Male leaf brought a hundred a pound. Sinsemillia, fifteen hundred. Cutting thirty males the patch was better spaced. Cutting the males once again at their mid-section I stuffed them into two duffel bags. On last night's news The State Boys claimed Kentucky as the number one marijuana producing state in the Union.

Dark Star and I were helping Kentucky get on the map for something other than clogging, muskrat trapping and Rock Furnaces. Only a few of Aopehh's growers were homegrown. Most Aopehhean growers had drifted in on the run from Maryland, Washington, the Keys and other regions of Kentucky. One rule reigned for all growers. Don't ask questions, I won't tell lies. For eight hours I babied the plants. Hoeing, weeding, suckering and picking the hand sized sun leaves. Many were beginning to die, fading from yellow to gold.

I stopped.

An odd sound.

Possible trouble?

Just two trees rubbing.

Packs stuffed, I began hiking off the mountain. Sweat stood on my face. The thought of the creek below was inviting. I chose a hard route never before traveled. Holding one of the duffel bags as a shield I struggled through head high briars. Hope there's no copperheads. A hundred yards from The Triangle I froze. Newly cut thorn's white edges. Bent grass. I laid my packs down, sitting beside them. Suddenly, there before me, fresh boot prints. I slunk lower. For a half hour I remained motionless. Leaving, I followed the boot prints. They led only in. I was not alone. No squirrel hunter would've went into those briars. Neither would a ginseng digger.

And agate, lay only in the creek.

"It was St. Patrick's Day. Sensi and I were sitting in the back of Lynagh's Pub. The place was jammed crazy with drunks. And wading through the crowd in a cowboy hat was a tall man that looked like Mick Jagger. He came up to our table and saw that we had the only open seat. "Hello," he greeted, shaking my hand. "Would it be alright if I sit with you? My name is Gatewood Galbraith, what's yours?"

NS

"Marijuana increases thought. That's why it's bad."

NS

Journal Entry 11 – **I CAN'T PRETEND**

August 27, 1982

Around three I was headed up to Dark Star's. The law was all over the road. A dozen squad cars. Camouflaged State Boys. I left the nightmare some mile behind before arriving at Dark Star's porch. Rollanotherone sat red-eyed on the steps gazing out across the fields. Black clouds were rising in the distance. Her eyes were red but not from marijuana. She'd quit smoking when she learned she was pregnant. Dark Star paced the porch scanning the skyline. "They've found it," he said. "Aopehh's biggest patch. Ten thousand twenty foot tall sinsemilla plants. Millions of dollars."

"We should've known when our dog, Satan, died things were going to be bad." spoke Rollanotherone. "First it was him getting hit. Then Dark Star hurt his back. He needs an operation. Gray Star died in surgery. Our garden got trampled. Our well is dry. Dark Star can't get another job. When a teacher gets fired that's it. I'm two months pregnant. Now this." Rollanotherone dropped her face into her hands. "Dark Star, you might as well tell No Sweat the truth. Tell him about the signature."

"No Sweat."

"Yeah."

"You know that patch owned by Mrx that I told you about?"

"Yeah."

75

"That's his farm they're burning. He's done for. They've got me, too. Mrx made up a fake lease for that piece of land. The lease has two signatures. People who supposedly leased the place. Below those signatures is my signature. I witnessed their signatures."

"What's their names?"

"John Wayne and William Graham."

"You're kidding, aren't you?"

"Wish I were. It was part of a deal."

"You may not be in any trouble, yet. We better move that ten pounds of leaf."

"There's no telling what the law knows. They could storm up here any moment."

Rollanotheone stood lookout while we loaded the leaf in my van. "Be glad you aren't Mrx. We'll know more tomorrow," I said, leaving.

Traveling back, Dark Star's secret fell in place. Since the beginning of The Triangle he had not shown much interest in our patch. Hadn't been to The Triangle a quarter of the times I had. While I had been in Florida he hadn't fertilized, weeded, or checked for males. The Triangle was a back up. He was counting on Mrx. What scared me was learning how close Mrx's operation was to ours.

At eleven PM I sat watching channel 27.

"A major marijuana bust has been made in Aopehh."

For the next five minutes there was at the site scenes. The State Boys gloated. There was a trailer where a thousand males were hanging to dry. Heaps of green leaves and a fan that was being used in the drying. All bonfired. The law smiled downwind.

"An anonymous phone tip was received leading to the investigation and discovery. Arrests are pending."

At midnight my phone rang.

"Did you see the news?"

"Yeah."

"Have you heard about Maryland Bob?"

"No."

"This afternoon they found him in his patch. Wearin' camo. Shot across the chest three times. Thirty cal. Once up close in the face. Twelve gauge."

"Everybody prays for me. I don't have to waste
time doing it myself."

NS

Journal Entry 12—**ALL OF ME**

August 30, 2007

"Would you take Dark Star, Mrx and me
up to Swallowtail's?"

"Tonight?"

"Yes. And I want you to do me a favor?"

"What?"

"Tell Swallowtail to tell Mrx to destroy the lease. If it's used in court, we're ruined."

Stopping to blink my lights on bright, Mrx hopped out, stomping the heads of copperheads warming on the road to Booneville, Kentucky. There was a drizzle as I pulled into Swallowtail's graveled uphill driveway. Swallowtail sat in a woven chair. Rain tapped his fiberglass carport roof. "Where's Slowtalk?" I asked.

"Inside. Writing poetry."

"Putting out a joint Swallowtail slid on a pair of corduroy house slippers. "Y'all want a beer or something," he asked, moving a lantern to a table.

"Nah. We're here on official business."

"I've never knew that to stop you."

"You're right. I'll take one. I want you to meet my associate, Mrx. He's sixty-two. Married all his life. A God fearing, corn growing, hog slopping, baccer spittin', cow milking man. And, he just happens to be the best marijuana grower in all this nefarious world. The grower's grower. Takes chainsaws to cut his plants. Sometimes, dynamite. Frank and Rosenthal's Marijuana Grower's Guide has a full chapter devoted to him. But, alas, at this tragic hour, sorrow and woe fill our dark sky. All is vanquished. For yonder sinsemilla has been torched and forsaken by the king's men. Now we are all empty with whereforartthous. Or, as honest Abe put it, we are now engaged in a great civil war."

Swallowtail sat in his t-shirt and dress pants looking at Mrx., lighting another joint. Overhead the rain continued tap dancing.

"Four years ago," spoke Mrx, "I didn't know what marijuana looked like. A preacher gave me a dried leaf that he had pressed in the pages of his Bible. A pretty thing. The next year I grew a few plants. They were so beautiful. I fell in love with them."

"That's our angle," I said. "We'll get Mrx. to explain to the jury that he is a wildflower enthusiast."

"How many pounds of those pretty plants did Mrx grow?"

"About a ton of leaf. And a ton of buds. Not counting the thousand plants they destroyed. A few million dollars worth. How many exact millions, I don't know."

Swallowtail straightened up his glasses, leaning into my face. "I guess you expect me to believe this story. You don't think I don't know that you've paid Mrx to put on this performance You really didn't think I'd fall for it, did you?

"You're right, Mrx is an out of work actor from The Barn Dinner Theatre. You saw right through me."

"No Sweat, if I were cast directing for someone inconceivable of growing a ton of marijuana, Mrx would be it."

"He doesn't impress you as a ruthless marijuana baron, does he? Can't see him kidnapping newborns and grinding them up for fertilizer."

"They broke the padlocks off my trailer. Burned my marijuana, heater and furniture. I've been paying the electric bill. That'll look bad, won't it?"

"Yeah. And Maryland Bob's murder. There'll be a witch hunt."

"I'm sixty two years old. Had nothing but troubles all my life."

"Have you ever been convicted of any felonies?"

"No."

"At worst, a five hundred dollar fine. Maybe a year's probation. It takes nine of the twelve Grand Jury to indict. Twelve out of twelve to convict."

As the rain increased, I spoke. "If you still had your crop it would've jumped two foot tonight."

"I was going to make a few million and quit. Would've never done it if'n times weren't so hard."

"Your best angle is to plead innocence. You're just a dumb farmer living at the foot of the cross. Wouldn't know a marijuana plant from a horse weed. Destroy that lease. You've got a chance of beating this if they didn't have a search warrant."

"You're right." spoke Mrx. marking off Dark Star's name.

"Why don't you burn that thing?" asked Rollanotherone.

"I will, later."

"I'll be down on Wednesday," spoke Swallowtail, releasing nefarious vapors.

"Let me know when you are coming. My Dobermans are loose."

"On second thought, I'll call."

"Swallowtail is a good attorney. Everybody likes him. But his reputation may hurt. Least he'll take the case personally."

"During the last year of mom's life dad had a Canadian girl staying in bed with him. Forty years younger. A drug addict. After mom died, he asked what I thought about them marrying. I told him that she had screwed everybody on Singer Island. He defended her saying, Singer Island wasn't that big."

NS

Journal Entry 13 – **SUGAR**

September 4, 1982

Beside Dark Star's outhouse.

"Do you know a State Boy named, Faust?"

"Aint he the one they're saying shot Maryland Bob?"

"Faust and his brother used to live up Cambell's Branch. Mrx practically raised them. He's got a brother that's his opposite. Big into drugs. Especially marijuana. He went hunting on Mrx yesterday. You won't believe what he said."

"What?"

"Asked Mrx if the one patch that made it was his. Described The Triangle perfect. How many plants. How tall. Exact location. Was squirrel hunting. Couldn't believe a patch that good could be where it was. He left it alone. Mrx told him he didn't know anything. Faust said he was going back. After he left, Mrx called me."

"Probably already ripped."

"Probably. Rollanotherone says he'll let the buds get bigger. But won't wait past September."

"She might be right."

"We need to make a trip no later than Tuesday. See if anything's left. If so, we better take it."

"I ain't going without a gun."

"I don't like guns. But I don't want to be another Bob."

Rollanotherone walked over. "I guess Dark Star told you the bad news?"

"Yep."

"My baby will born with nothing to wear."

"We'll know, Tuesday."

"We need to leave before daybreak. Come back after dark."

"Let's dress like we're going caving. Leave the guns. If there's a stakeout we'll have an excuse. California Cave isn't far."

"When I graduated from Eastern Kentucky University our honored speaker was Col. Harland Sanders. He shook my hand and handed my diploma. I didn't wipe the grease off for a week."

NS

Journal Entry 14 – **ONE NEVER KNOWS, DOES ONE?**

September 7, 1982

Dense fog choked the ground as Dark Star and I made our way at daybreak to The Triangle. Wool army pants, packs and pistols. Ants moving up the mountain.

We chose Tuesday.

People were in the woods on Sundays and Labor Day.

It was a Wednesday when I spotted the footprints. A warbler flittered. I put a bullet in the chamber that I had left empty making the climb. If there was trouble we'd agreed to meet back at a certain spot. Cautiously entering The Triangle I gave Dark Star an OK with my hand. It was a few more minutes of silence before we felt better.

Our meat cleaver was still exactly where we had left it.

Laying our pistols down at opposite ends of the patch we began stripping male leaf. One of the females was nice. Buds glistened. Sappy. Purple.

As the fog disappeared the air grew warm.

Ruby Tuesday.

Then a chopper barracuded along the mountain.

We crouched low as it moved closer. Just before breaking to move it veered off. A ruby-throated hummingbird zipped from one small bud to another. For a spell it tasted the nefarious nectar. Flying almost into our faces it landed on a nearby limb. Then, fell and flopped on the ground.

Our packs full. We left. There were circular depressions in the sandy soil just beyond the patch. And a speckled feather.

A grouse's dust bath.

Reaching the dark hollow below, Rollanotherone rendezvoused in the jeep. Driving out onto the sunny Beattyville Road smiles were contained.

Then a State Boy closed on our tail. In the jeep's back were two stuffed duffel bags. Rollanotherone began crying. "Is his lights on?" she asked.

Dark Star sat in the middle keeping an eye glued to the rear view mirror. "No he said. "Rollanotherone, keep cool. Drive normal."

"What should I do with this joint?"

"Eat it."

"No Sweat, he pulled off."

"I've gotta pull over. I'm gonna throw up."

"Man! What a rush!"

"Wish I hadn't swallowed that joint."

"Think what you will. But know I am a writer."
NS

Journal Entry 15– **YOU SHOWED ME THE WAY**

September 9, 1982

Van and Sensi, slick. Lexington. Fleetwood Mac.

Gate Gestapo. Clean.

Inside. 25,000 smoking marijuana.

Loose blouses. Tight jeans.

Rows below, familiar Aops pass joints.

Lights fade. Thousands of lighters. Caterwauls.

By my side some guy in a T-shirt, marijuana leaf on back. MEMBER OF THE COLUMBIAN GROWERS ASSOCIATION.

Fleetwood Mac on stage.

Waving arms.

Nicks. Half bat. Half witch. Tattered shrouds. High heeled boots. Stove-top hat. Scarlet sash. LISTEN TO THE WIND BLOW, WATCH THE SUN RISE, RUNNING IN THE SHADOW, DAMN YOUR LOVE! DAMN YOUR LIES!

Shadow prances. Tall, thin, long hair, painted--jeaned, tiny pocketbook.

Long version. IT'S NOT THAT FUNNY. Primal drummer. Black silk.

Group leaves.

Roars. More!

Twenty minutes.

Fleetwood Mac appears.

SISTERS OF THE MOON.

"Guy Davenport said Aopehh was the only word in the English language that ended with two Hs."

NS

Journal Entry 16 – **SUN SHOWERS**

September 11, 1982

Last night Swallowtail called. Reminded me to show up. Judge a canoe race. An event on South Fork near Beattyville, Kentucky. The Beattyville Kiwanis along with Beattyville's Homecoming and annual Fair was having a race in remembrance of the old Kentucky riverboat days, where the Kentucky River is born.

Arriving at Swallowtail's early, Slowtalk and I got our heads together. Smoked marijuana and drank rum for two hours before locating her husband. At one o'clock Swallowtail and I stood in a small boat tied to SHARP ROCK, a boulder poking forty feet out of a narrow bend. We wore sunglasses. Nobody knew we were stoned. Twenty-one canoes formed an imaginary line from our position to the bank. Swallowtail mega phoned garrulous instructions. On his cue I shot a single barrel 12 gauge shotgun down stream. The five mile race on the musty river began. Cranking up our small motor Swallowtail moved us a few miles down out of sight to stop and drink a few beers and burn a gauger while waiting for the canoers.

"Did I ever tell you about me and dad on The Lower Rockcastle?"

"No."

"We'd canoed about sixteen miles. Came to a spot called The Narrows. A place where the river forms into a canyon. You can't hear anything but a roar. We went through the first two waterfalls OK. Then, we came to two giant rocks. I got out. There was a straight drop. About twelve foot. No canoeing that. I told dad we'd cross over. Try climbing down. Push the canoes through. He got out on the rock with me. I moved the canoe to the place where the water was rushing through. Then, jumped in and hung onto the side working across. The current pulled my legs. All I could do to hang on. When I got to the other side I shouted to dad to be careful. He jumped in. Grabbed for the canoe. But missed it. He screamed for me, then went under. Was pinned. His hands were reaching up. About two feet deep. The river kept pulling him down. I couldn't reach him. It was slippery. If I went in, I'd drown. I screamed. I cried. I couldn't do anything. Dad's hands quit moving. Faded down out of sight. I sat looking at the water. After a few minutes his body came to the surface. Was in a pool below the falls. I dove in and pulled him to shore. Took off his life jacket. Opened his shirt. Laid him on the bank. Put his feet above his head. His eyes were glazed. He was white. Lips blue. No heartbeat. I pushed on his chest then lifted his arms. I rolled him on his side. He began vomiting. I was so happy. I put his head in my lap. His eyes focused. He whispered, he was dead. I told him to lie still. He raised. Said he knew he was dead. He felt being sucked through a cave.

"When dad turned 80 he went on an African safari with his new wife and a buddy that was about the same age as her. They shot the hell out of everything. Had their mounted trophies shipped back to Aopehh for the hillbillies to gawk at. But they never arrived. Dad knew the names of all the strange beast and exactly how he killed them. What he didn't know was the name of my daughter, her birthday, or the names of either of her sons or their birthdays."

NS

Journal Entry 17--**WHAT IS THIS GOING TO GET US?**

September 12 thru 26, 1982

Waking in the backseat of dad's yellow Cadillac. The highway passed fast under me. Climbing over the leather I turned on the radio. 109 MPH. Dad was making miles. He'd been making them all night.

Headed west. Another hunt. He'd been hunting deer and elk for thirty years. Meeker. The county seat of Rio Blanco County. Second largest county in Colorado. 1,500 miles from Aopehh. Always at Keith's ranch. Keith is the County Judge. Had been for twenty four years. The governor appointed him. Keith and his son along with Bill will be our hunting buddies. Bill is the Faulkner flattop game warden.

Glenwood Canyon. Whitecaps on the Colorado River. Loveland Pass. Dad detoured The George Washington Tunnel. We're in the Rockies. My ears pop. Snow. Groves of blue spruce. We park. I stretch in my mother's father's old army jacket. The air is clean. The aspen are going from lime to yellow.

Dad claims rich German ancestry. Actually, he was born in a tent in a coal mining camp in Harlan, Kentucky. When he was a sophomore at Laurel County High School in London, Kentucky, he claimed to have burned down the sheriff's house and then ran away from his divorced mom. He'd brag about his having hitchhiked to New York. Became a busboy in Sheepshead Bay. Met Billie Holiday. Near the end of the war he became a cook in the Merchant Marines. Got torpedoed in The North

Atlantic. When the war ended he came to
Aopehh in a new car and met mom. She was
beautiful, rich, selling popcorn at her father's
theatre. A big wedding. Made the newspaper.
Got arrested for their antics. For a while he sold
insurance. Then my mother's father gave dad a
job managing one of his theatres. We lived rent
free in the apartment over the theatre. Our back
window overlooked the Kentucky river. My front
yard was the heart of Aopehh. No one could have
been born more Aopehhean than No Sweat. I
loved it. The first two children mom had, died.
Dad flushed one down the toilet. Then, me, as
time went by. When I did come into this world I
was given up dead until Doc's mom gave me one
last slap. Mom said that cry was the best
moment in her life. Five and a half years later
she had my sister. When I was a boy dad started
a small fruit stand. For ten years he sold melons
and peaches. I learned how to put the rotten
stuff on the bottom and tip the scales. Then a
railroader came to dad wanting a partner in a
liquor store. In the next fourteen years dad stole
his Aopehhean fortune. Didn't ring up tax
money. Bought stolen whiskey. Turned the store
into a part time pawn shop. After selling the
store he got into used cars. Suited him perfect.
Whiskey brought out a frightened animal in him.
He would smack whatever was near. Took pride
in hurting. Blacked mom's eyes. Pulled out her
hair. Knocked her down steps. Knocked holes in
walls. Flipped tables. Ripped lights from ceilings.
Threw bottles. Smashed chairs. Spoke crude
words. I never saw him apologize for anything.
Always someone else's fault. Drunk or sober he

said he was the most handsome and smartest man in the world. That he did everything for his family. Never tired of saying it. I was on the trip because I was curious why dad spent a month every year out west. I had never seen the west or met Keith.

It was noon when we rolled into Meeker. A sunny 70 degrees. Meeker was akin to Aopehh. Turn of the century square. Keith wasn't at the courthouse. I sat in Theodore Roosevelt's rocker while dad learned his location. A few miles and gates later we pulled up to Keith's home overlooking The White River. Breaking the skyline around back were two piles of rock twelve feet high, monuments to Keith's dad and uncle. Keith's father's ashes had been sprinkled in the river.

Keith was outside, knelt down, nonchalant, working on a fold-out camper. Sagebrush and bear cactus surrounded the area. Below the bluff along the river were blue bottoms filled with black cattle. Keith had a strong build, Hemingway beard, gray eyes and cropt hair.

As the day moved I saw that Keith was gentle. He took dad and I downstairs showing us our bunk bed. The walls were decorated in Indian relics, mounted animals, Winchesters and Colts.

"Did you find that Folsom point?"

"You bet. There was an article about it in our newspaper."

The next day we headed southwest. Billowy sky. Wyoming. I rode with Dale, Keith's son, in a pickup pulling the camper. Dad and Keith drove in front. Beer cans flew. Graveled road. Rattlers crossing. Antelope in the distance. We came into Mabel.

"What do people do around here?"

"Nothing."

Several miles later we met Bill. He was parked with his silver camper at The Little Snake River. We got back on Wamsutter Road. It led to Kinney Rim and Shell Creek, our Sweetwater, Wyoming destinations. We left the brushy mountains to the desolate badlands. Ravines. Gulches. Mesas. A sky I touched. Sagebrush was everywhere. Filled with yellow flowers.

Came sunset camp was pitched. Dale and I relaxed listening to Willie Nelson. HE AINT WRONG HE'S JUST DIFFERENT. The coyotes yelped. I fell asleep.

Dawn found Dale and I in the backseat of Keith's jeep. Keith and dad rode up front. Bill went hunting in another direction.

Flashes of antelope. We stopped to scope.

"An antelope's ear is six to six and one-half inches. If his horns go twice the length of his ears, he's worth dustin'."

We never saw such horns. We stopped to hunt Indian relics in the sand. Rabbits and antelope tracks crisscrossed. Bones. Silence. I felt small.

"Do you like Steve McQueen?" asked Keith.

"Yeah."

"How many McQueen movies can you name?"

"Bullitt. Nevada Smith. The Great Escape. Tom Horn. The War Lover. Papillon. The Magnificent Seven. The Sand Pebbles. Hell is For Heroes."

Keith smiled.

Came dark Keith grilled steaks. "Can you find the North Star," he asked.

"Yeah."

"Find The Big Dipper. See the double star in it?"

"The second one to the left?"

"Yep. That's an old test to see if you've got a shooter's eye. I can't see it anymore." The next morning we ate breakfast before light. When shapes began to emerge there was a slumped figure on a black horse some hundred yards distant. I stepped across the cool desert approaching the image. "Hello, I'm No Sweat."

The Mexican pointed in the distance. "*Ka nahoes*," he said, drawing a pistol, shooting a rabbit. He rode over to the rabbit, got off his horse, tied it to his saddle and disappeared.

That morning there were wild horses of color. Smarter than antelope. I grew tired of scoping and walked into a gulch below the rim, finding a small bug.

"When the Mormons first came west, " informed Keith, "they grew wheat. And those bugs attacked. They prayed for a miracle. Sea gulls came and ate all the beetles."

"What happened to the gulls?"

"The Mormons ate them."

While hunting, we kept our scopes trained for the law. Nobody had a license. That evening we settled down to fried cottontail, whiskey and peppers.

"What do you do?" asked Bill.

"Raise racing pigeons. I'm the national champion. If you really want to know what I do, it's write."

"What do you write?"

"Fiction. It's all there is."

Several days passed. Besides the Mexican there was never another soul. Bill was a Grand Slammer with Sheep. Keith owned two top twenty Boone And Crockett Mule deer. They spotted, tracked, killed and butchered. Waves over a beach.

The last morning's sunrise was a striped sky. Red. Yellow. Violet. Pink. Orange. As we drove out of the desert Dale put in a tape. Charley McClain's *SURROUND ME WITH LOVE.* I thought of dad. Had he always been yellow? Forced yellow? Or had he grown yellow?

The same subtle esoteric wont as does the waning aspen.

"Fightin' Branch. Buck Creek. Barnes Mountain.
Old Pike. Possum Run. Cow Creek. Sugar Holler.
Crystal Creek. Sweet Lick Knob. Cob Hill. Old
Landing. Fox. Rice Station. Turkey Foot. Patsy.
Bear Waller. Red Lick. Spout Springs. Sand Hill.
Poosey Ridge. Patsy. Beattyville Mountain.
Pinnacle. Rudco Ridge. Cave Holler. Crystal.
Trottin' Ridge. Tipton Ridge. Doe Creek. Middle
Fork. Wagersville. Old Pike. Hargett. White Oak.
Gum Springs. Chestnut Stand. Pryse.
Rockhouse. Drowning Creek. Owl Holler.
Wisemantown. Trapp. Granny Richardson's.
Cresse. Muddy Creek. Wild Dog. Ticky Fork. Pea
Ridge.
 Ah-h-h, home sweet home."
NS

Journal Entry 18 – **WHAT A LITTLE**
MOONLIGHT CAN DO

September 27, 1982

Sensi's 32nd birthday.

Pushing 1,500 miles hard straight back to Aopehh.

Calling Dark Star.

"Haven't you seen Sensi?"

"She's not home."

"I'll be down. Rather not talk on the phone."

Five minutes.

Dark Star and Rollanotherone. My home. I give blue spruce and cactus.

"Sensi called today. Swallowtail gave her bad news. The Triangle was ripped."

"Let's go see."

"Can't. We've got supper on the table. Maybe tomorrow evening."

Alone. Vanning. Sunsetting. Chestnut Stand. Having to park in mud a long distance away. Jogging nearly an hour along slippery ridge.

Triangle at twilight. Soaked. Exhausted. Ghostly light fading to black.

Alpha. Queen of unholy convent. Still standing. All seems OK.

No. Not OK.

No buds. No tops. Stripped branches.

Hit. Heart sinks.

Night.

Pulling thirty plants. Fighting black. Bringing to stump where cleaver remains. Roots cleaved. Not donating remaining buds.

I try to pull all the plants across my shoulder. Carry. The walk back, impossible.

Exhaustion.

Hiding plants. Back at first light. Some salvage.

Fighting briars in black. Finally, van. Nearly two days since sleep or food.

Home.

Calling Dark Star.

"Just back. Hit, alright. Hid thirty."

"You what!"

"Couldn't just sit. Lose everything. Gotta be back dawn."

"Wish you hadn't gone."

"I asked you to go."

"And I told you, tomorrow afternoon."

"You said, maybe. If I hadn't gone, we'd've had nothing."

Dark Star was upset. Somehow, he figured, I beat him. I sought a friendship built on trust. Hoped one day we'd rock on the porch telling grandchildren about old marijuana days. He never considered I could blame his laziness.

I was tired.

I was home.

It was Sensi's birthday.

"Somehow, Fred wound up The Bird Curator for
The Mexico City Zoo. Bobby, Editor of
Aopehhean CITZEN'S BLADDER. Every
Saturday night they passed out in our
apartment. They loved mom. And I loved them."

NS

Journal Entry 19 – **I'VE GOT MY LOVE TO
KEEP ME WARM**

September 28, 1982

Emptied duffel bag from west.

Sun soon gone.

Dark Star alongside.

Chestnut Stand.

Parking.

Camouflaging through woods.

"I never thought it would make you mad."

"You shouldn't have gone."

"If I was going to take anything, do you think I would have called?"

Over an hour. Hiking.

Finally, The Triangle.

Dark Star mellows. Thirty hidden "Christmas trees."

Many buds.

Dark Star smiles.

Smiles more. Still many standing buds.

Week old rip.

Quickly work.

Stripping.

Dark Star ruins buds. Jerky yanks. Two duffels and three backpacks filled.

Depart.

Dark Star's attic.

Spread bed sheets. Minty green. Plant decay heat already building.

"A lot more picking down."

"How much have we got?"

"A few thousand."

"We should go back."

"Come get me in an hour."

Home. Fill canteen. Eat jar of artichoke hearts. Feed pigeons.

Dark Star's jeep whines.

One hundred degrees.

Again, Triangle.

Third trip in less than 24 hours.

Filling packs. Half as much as last trip. Hands, sticky black. Hash. Sweat down necks.

Leaving thirty chest-high. Still too young.

Evening.

Rollanotherone, Dark Star and I sat in his attic. Six hours, manicuring, smoking, talking. Guess four grand. Tops in one pile. Buds. Leaf and tiny buds. Leaf.

Relaxing.

Sweet joint.

"I hear Mrx has been acquitted."

"I don't trust him."

"When will you go back to The Triangle?"

"Bout a month."

"Faust will be back."

"Like a homing pigeon."

"The Jesse Stuart Foundation rejected my novel, *NEFARIOUS*. Said the title was a big word that no person could understand."

NS

"Stephen King's literary agent told me it would be a cold day in hell before anyone published my work. I take compliments where I can find them."

NS

Journal Entry 20 – **DON'T EXPLAIN**

October 3, 1982

Midnight Sunday night. Black Hole's. Tea is brewing. The house is a step into the 1940's.

"How was the west?"

"Never knew we had so much wasteland."

"Did you see Denver?"

"Yeah."

"I once loved Denver. You could fly out there. Land anywhere. I made the mistake of changing runs from the mid-west to Alaska. Those mountains there are something else."

"Almost makes you want to live, doesn't it."

"No. Don't you know me by now. All there is, is tragedy. Love is not two people looking at each other, it's two people looking out and seeing the same. Freud said the primary sex organ was not below the waist. Love is two people late into the night, talking."

At the door was Annie, my mixed border collie. Black Hole let her in.

"Come here."

"That dog cherishes you."

"Strange. I never give her any affection."

"That's not strange. That's a typical woman."

"Twain said the difference between a man and a dog was if you picked up a starving dog and helped him he'd be your eternal friend. If

112

you picked up a person and did the same sooner or later they'd turn on you."

"True. They turned on Jesus. Jesus had what's known as, it's alright. When I was in the seminary they didn't sell God as much as they did, it's alright."

"That's all Hemingway. He said everything was true."

"Hemingway killed so he wouldn't kill himself," commented Black Hole turning up his old radio locked on EKU's station. *THE SONG OF THE BLUES* was playing.

"Your generation believe they own the last artists."

"Your generation is laaaid back. You sound like some Dartmouth student. You are full of self hate. But you don't hate enough. You've got a lot to look forward to. See that black robe hanging on the door? Do you see the captain's uniform next to it? See how they hang together? Black and grey. God and country. The two institutions. I flew because I liked the men who flew. Not because I liked flying. You can always spot a married man in the air. The business of the military is death. It's not some social club. When I flew we had orders to refuel and reload bombs in Denmark. Of course, there wouldn't be any Denmark."

"When I was in the Badlands I killed a rattlesnake and cut open her belly. She had six babies."

"Abortionist."

"Not a very good one. I killed the mother."

"Abortionist always kill the mother. A parent committing suicide always murders the children. How was the Kennedy home?"

"Nice. But not that great."

"Aren't they just Snopes? Don't they hire people to take their college exams? Mother always told me, take what you want in life but pay for it. I don't believe you hate Aopehheans for what they are. But because of what they could be. You are what you hate. You hate Aopehh. You are Aopehh. I hate every state in the Union. Except New York. When a man is in love he is insane. Man steals everything he has. Particularly, life."

"How's that?"

"The day you were born you stole life from your parents. Out of death comes life. You've heard about the fatherless child. But you never hear about the childless father? Do you think I speak in tongues? That I am insane?"

"If so, then I'm insane."

114

"You can't afford insanity. You know yourself the least of anything. Your Sensi, next. Husbands and wives are far more distant than any galaxy. There's only one thing before death that is certain. Evil. Evil rules this world. Do you think Hinckley will get better?"

"He'll do better. Not get better."

"The summer has cursed you."

"Maybe."

"The difference in an optimist and a pessimist is that a pessimist is infinitely better informed. If someone comes at you with a weapon, defend yourself. If they come to help you, run like hell."

"It bothers people that I live take trips and don't work."

"People don't know how to live today. They certainly don't know how to die. Pickett's men, that's dying." Black Hole walked to his bathroom opening the medicine cabinet, swallowing several pills "Stuff for my heart. Arrhythmia. Lithium is still a mystery. Doctors don't know it's full effects any more than they do aspirin."

"Or marijuana."

"I was glad to read that lithium is a slow poison. I've had a good life."

"Fruit stand laborer, transporter, hod carrier, carpenter, construction worker, feature editor, photographer, magazine writer, liquor porter, liquor store manager, KIRIS assessment scorer, Kentucky child support worker, used car salesman, substitute teacher, church camp counselor, CSEPP logistics officer, deputy sheriff, chauffeur, surveyor's assistant, homeless shelter supervisor, campaign manager, GE light bulb factory worker, safety diver, video store manager, taxidermist, theater projectionist, session stand employee, Para legal, country ham man, warehouse manager, fencing laborer, oil pipe salvager, Pony Express courier, pari-mutuel clerk, property manager, tobacco farmhand, cattle farmhand, racing pigeon judge and breeder, tree broker, Hemingway-Lincoln-Zane Grey letter broker, agate-civil war--revolutionary war--fossil---Indian relic dealer, inventory

116

specialist, heat plant operator. Some of the
things I've pretended. But I was always just a
poor writer."

NS

Journal Entry 21 – **HELLO MY DARLING**

October 6, 1982

Afternoon. Sun beating. Dark Star called.
Triangle.

Tossed sleeping bag in jeep. Pete
Townsend and joint.

Rattling through Aopehh. Main Street.
Sandstone courthouse. Liar's Bench.

"Did you read about The Golden Triangle
in this month's National Geographic?"

"We're their branch office."

"Branch and bud."

Chestnut Stand.

Fall.

Splashes of yellows, rusts, oranges,
magentas and greens. Leaves float, sway.
Quilting mellow, dying. Collaged pastels.

Parking. Hiking. Crossing over and under dead trees we sawed earlier. Block traffic.

"Think any are left?"

"Fifty-fifty."

"Look, dog tracks."

"Mrx's Dobermans?"

Stopping. Triangle near.

"Look how open."

"Don't see any."

"Me either."

"There's one. They're OK."

Walking to plant.

"Smell. Spearmint."

One, sweet juicy. One, cotton candy. Another, skunk. Two, pepper.

Ten pulled. Roots cleaved. As I lay dying in unzipped sleeping bag.

"Look."

"What?"

"Morphodite."

"Again?"

"Seedy."

"That'll cost."

"Good seeds. Black and beige. Tiger striped. Big as BBs."

Full bag. Zipped. Green devil smiles within. Hope nobody sees. Packing corpse.

Walking.

"Maybe someday I'll write about this."

"Don't mention me."

It was night when Dark Star and I entered into the moldy confines of his black chicken house next to his outhouse. We hammered nails into the rafters stringing twine. Each plant was hung upside down. Someone in a distant hollow was also hammering.

"Somebody hanging marijuana?"

"Future Farmers of America."

"Save every seed. Morphodites make females."

"A lot of males this year."

"Rainfall did it."

"Rainfall?"

"Water helps determine sex. When there is little stress and lots of water, you get more females."

"Survival of the species?"

"Yeah."

"Spoke to a buyer this morning. We can get a good price if we'll go to Florida."

"John Carpenter, Harry Dean Stanton, Patricia Neal, Ashley Judd, George Clooney, Johnny Depp. Native born Kentuckians know all about acting. Government cheese. Government checks."
NS

Journal Entry 22 – **YOU'RE JUST A NO ACCOUNT**

October 11, 1982

Dark Star called. Wanted me to see his labor, an indoor bathroom. We left out walking

to a box hollow where we ate fallen persimmons
and lit a joint. Surrounded by sassafras trees,
we looked at the dried shale creek below.

"If we find a bench we could do a patch."

"We need several patches."

"No one except mushroomers come here."

We walked along the slope. Finally, level
land. Tall poplars. The cliff above was close.

"If we clear the trees and plow, planes
will spot this. We're up too high."

We left. Dark Star's three dogs, two young
collies out of Satan and a young Doberman, Rex,
from Mrx, trailed. Going lower we stopped, back
kicking the leaves, inspecting the black soil.

"It'll take three or four days to clear."

"Plus the hoeing."

"Early one morning I came up on a wreck.
Something awful bothered me as I walked to the
van. Then it dawned, Ed. It was below zero.
When I opened the door the inside was blood.
Brilliant red. He was all but guillotined. I had to
pull his feet out of his wing tip shoes in order to
remove his body. Nobody was such joyous
entertainment. He'd taken dad to Vegas and
Superbowls. At The Indy 500 they roomed with A
J Foyt and Evil Kinievel. The Keeneland race
track and Aopehh's Golf Club were Ed's private
party. Being at his side was any writer's dream.
Even then."
     NS

Journal Entry 23 – **YOU CAN'T BE MINE**

October 17, 1982

Noon. Sunday. Dark Star and Rollanotherone. Jeeping. Cinnamon-apple tea. Headed to Mt. Sterling, Kentucky. County Court Day. Coonhounds. Guns. Heathens.

Ten gauger."

"Ten gauge?"

"I roll 'em the size of shotgun shells. This one took four extra wide JOB rolling papers."

"Fifty dollars in there."

"If you bought it."

Three ham sandwiches devoured. Inner fogged. Gas tank beneath Rollanotherone, leaking.

Laughter.

Nearing destination. Country. Pumpkins decorate yards. Backed traffic. People shuffling.

Parking.

Walking.

Table of shotguns. One musket. 1861 Springfield. One hundred and fifty dollars.

I'm broke.

Walking.

Rollanotherone buys brass toilet paper holder and 25 cent paperback on the Manson family.

Meeting Aopehh's outsider hippies. Counterculture fugitives never looking in eyes. Speak code-like. Gestures. Suspicious. Think I'm a Narc. The guys, overalls, long sleeve shirts, headgear covering long hair. The girls, braless, flowers in long hair, prairie skirts, wool sweaters, boots and sandals.

Walking.

Blaring music. Colossal speakers. The Gospel Echoes. THE OLD RUGGED CROSS.

Aopehh's sheriff's wife.

"Give to the Lord and you will enter the gates of heaven!"

"Once, late at night in a storm at Daytona
Beach, when my uncle and his family and mine
were together in his new station wagon, he drove
straight into the ocean. Nine of us total. Our
parents were marvelously drunk. The waves
smashed over our hood, across our roof. I was in
the very back smothered by older, screaming
cousins. As the water came up around me I felt
a hand grab deep into my arm. Hurting. Pulling
me to safety. That was the hardest mom ever
touched."
                    NS

Journal Entry 24– **MORE THAN YOU KNOW**

October 21, 1982

Dark Star and I.

"Do you think our patch is still there?"

"Yeah."

"A film canister holds a thousand seeds. That gives us sixty thousand for next year."

"They should be good. No more seed begging."

The Triangle.

Thought we'd been hit.

We hadn't.

Some of the plants had flopped over. Top heavy. This last bunch looked like bamboo. Forked sticks. Propping. Mounding dirt.

"What do you think?"

"Another three weeks. Maybe a month."

"Some are about ready. They're turning purple."

"Buds go longer than flowers. If they don't get pollinated they'll keep growing. Send out more hairs. Try to catch any pollen they can. A pollinated female spends all her energy on seeds. If that happens, she'll quit most of her budding.

Some can go three months during budding. You'll lose some sweetness. But you'll get good weight. More THC. Stonier."

"Let's come back in two or three weeks."

"Depends on the weather. The long forecasts say this weather is suppose to hold."

"Frosts won't hurt these plants. Not unless it gets in the 20's."

"Black Hole sat one day in my yard watching me plant a tree. Said that was probably the best thing either of us would ever do in our lives."
NS

"I was unsure if *THESE PRECIOUS DAYS* would put me in my grave or keep me out of it."
NS

"Pigeon lofts are the best churches."
NS

Journal Entry 25—**FORGET IF YOU CAN**

October 22-24, 1982

Louisville. Kentucky State Fair Grounds.
The eleventh National Young Bird Show.
Louisville, Kentucky. Six thousand pigeons.
More racing homers less than a year old than
any show in the nation. The finest in America.
Rows of individual cages. Each entry classed by
age, sex and color.

"Big I, you don't play this game all your
life unless you're a fool. When a speck folds its
wings and falls from the sky at twilight, a hen
that's pushed over 600 miles that day, surviving
every peril imaginable, to be home to protect her
eggs, to keep life going, do you really care what
someone thinks at that moment? Why is it that
showing has to be different?"

"Without organization we'd have no sport."

"Sport? Organization seeks to destroy. Not
create."

"The first time I read one of your articles
in The Racing Pigeon Bulletin I hated you. Over
the years, I thought you'd mellowed. The sport
thinks so. That's why I wanted you to help get
this organization started. But you haven't
changed one bit."

"The best thing I can do is avoid S.H.O.W. I went through this same insanity when asked to be on the U.S.'s Olympiad Committee."

"That cost you friends."

"And kept me, me."

"There isn't anyone that complains louder than you about The National Show. We know New York is politics. Now, I want to try to start something with order and qualified judges. And you tell me, I'm wrong?"

"White Plains had those sentiments fifty years ago. When I wrote *COLOR ME BLUE* I knew I would catch hell. When you lose a race or a show, time and time again with the same bird, what do you do?"

"Pull its head."

"There's your organization."

"Both of the attorneys that ran against each other for Aopehh's District Judge were eventually disbarred for being thieves and liars."

NS

Journal Entry 26 – **TIME ON MY HANDS**

November 1, 1982

A Spartacus Fall Day.

A November Triangle harvest.

Graceful, stretched consciousness.

Enchanting dream.

Jeep vanishes in song. Beaming Dark Star. Eight gauge victory joint. Front porch Rollanotherone cheers.

Nectar. Cotton candy. Spearmint. Juicy fruit. Regal buds. Gilded leaves. Paradise found. Swollen sleeping bags. Holy virgins. Ode to Sinsemilla.

Floating along trail. Autumn leaves. Such magic. Drifting through color.

D-Day. Dope Day. Swallowtail says Mrx is being watched.

Hungry. Messed up. Posing. Camera Dark Star captures No Sweat's soul. Hold still. Got it. My blue bandanna-face outlaws.

Several thousand dollars each, maybe. Regan was right. The recession is starting to give way. NOSTRADAMA. Pink-fragile consuming sky.

Ugly sobriety sneaks back. THC vanishes.

"God is only as smart as man."

"No. God knows everything. Man knows nothing."

"My dad's brother was murdered on his ninth
wedding. He was 61, his bride was 16. They got
married at his car lot while he chugged a quart
of Wild Turkey. He took her to his house in a
nearby subdivision. Her cocaine boyfriend
parked in front of my uncle's, shouting for her to
come back. My uncle got out of bed and emptied
his .357. Two shots got his wife's ex- lover. One
through the door to his belly. Another to the
guy's head. If my uncle hadn't been drunk
he'd've got him every shot. My uncle walked
across his yard in his underwear to the man's
car, looking in. The man he thought that he had
killed was laying in the front seat with a cocked
pistol. Shot my uncle in the throat. My uncle
staggered and fell backwards. The man got out
of his car, stood over my uncle, shot him five
times through the chest. That was the end of
dad's only brother, a man he hated. Jealousy.
That night dad drove down and stole all he could
get his hands on. My uncle was buried next to
my grandmother. Dad never spent a dime. Let
alone any headstone."

NS

Journal Entry 27 – NO MORE

November 4, 1982

134

Fall rains vanquish. Isolated pockets of the golden beech remain defiant.

The blackest time is near.

Walking upstairs in Dark Star's. Mint odor.

The oil lamp continues. An army blanket tacked along the door is moved.

Entering a bedroom. A candle and a lamp are lit. In the center of the floor lays a bed sheet holding a mound of Triangle marijuana.

"Get to picking, boys."

"Roll one, Rollanotherone."

"I'll roll. You pick."

A faded photo of a skinny farmer and his fat wife looms in one corner, Rollanotherone's great grandparents. The purple velvet piece quilt on the bed was made by them. Large cactus surround the walls. Two windows offer views of the hollow. Gallon zip lock baggies await filling. Half pound each. Flickering light. Dark Star takes Rollanotherone's joint.

"I've got the biggest purple plant picked down in a grocery bag. Personal smoke. It won't last the year."

"It'll be tough. Maybe, if you'll cut back to only one joint every fifteen minutes, you'll survive."

Another toke.

"Fetch us a tall drink."

"Tea or Kool-Aid?"

"Tea. And roll us another one."

"I need to wash the dishes."

"Leave the dishes be."

Pale faces with red-squinty eyes look at the new 12 gauge joint as it fires up over the candle.

"The Burning Bush."

Disgruntled Dark Star. The joint unravels, spilling. "Pipes are better than papers. No hassles. Better taste."

Pain. I backed up next to a five foot cactus. Hairy thorns.

"Mom was the last person to check out of The Colonnades Beach Hotel on Singer Island, Florida. Sat there looking out the large window overlooking The Gulf Stream. Said she'd never have that view again. And she never did."

NS

Journal Entry 28—**WHY WAS I BORN?**

November 7, 1982

Black Hole called. Asked me to come up around eight. As I entered the back door of his porch I stepped over FROM DEATH TO MORNING.THE ICEMAN COMETH. DEATH IN THE AFTERNOON. THE MAN WHO DIED. AS I

LAY DYING. DEATH OF A SALESMAN. LOVE IN
THE RUINS. SONS AND LOVERS. NIGHT OF
THE IGUANA. Jazz was coming from his
bedroom. Such a plain house in ruins. Bleak. He
had given me its key. Said, consider it mine. He
was rarely home. Even when he was, he wasn't.
The place was void of everything except books.
Books were waist high in the closets. Stuffed
under the couch and beds. Stacked by the toilet.
Strewn over the floors. He had lost and given
away many times more. He stood at the small
gas stove, barely able to emit a soft flame, with a
bent saucer full of water wearing his gray robe
and torn house shoes waiting for the water to
boil. "You don't deserve a break today," he
spoke. "You only deserve to die."

"Keats believed that conversation was not
to educate. But for its effect."

"Your generation is on the retreat. You
seek sanity when there is none. Isolation is not
the solution. Give me New York every time. She
is Rome. Her religion. Her madness. There's
sanity."

"In grad school I did a paper on the
predictability of war and its relationship to
population. Population rises had little
correlation. Maybe Eliot was right?"

"Did you and Dark Star get in your crop?"

"Yes. I'll roll you a joint sometime."

138

"That stuff doesn't affect me."

"You've probably been smoking male leaf. Very little THC. I'll roll you some sensi. You'll whistle Dixie."

"Then I sure don't want any."

"Why?"

"If it feels good, don't do it. If you feel depressed seek something to increase your depression. Your generation smokes because liquor is too tough. When are you leaving for New York?"

"Thursday. Be back Tuesday."

"That pigeon stuff of yours is complex."

"Not really. It's simple."

"Audry didn't believe."

"Maybe she wanted you instead of God."

"You would never understand. I didn't want the children. She didn't either. I was up sometimes for two weeks. Never landed."

"Why did she do it?"

"You obviously don't know your Freud. Jesus said no man knows what the hour of the day is."

"Aren't writers, liars?"

"Great writers are desperate. Everyone is desperate. But writers prepare for death. Can you possibly see Hemingway going out any other way? We all want out."

Twenty one steps. Winding staircase. My father's mother's 400 square foot apartment. Honest. Humble. Sweet. Religious. Sensitive. Seven Day Adventist. One summer I stayed with her. Walked long walks. Taught me butterflies and birds. At night, read. The only person that ever read to me. Her arm was the softest pillow. Lost in exotic, I were. Chipmunk Willie. The Little Red Hen. Joe Joe The Monkey. Dostoevsky couldn't touch them. In the end, she died horrible. Alzheimer's. Her love was incredible."

NS

Journal Entry 29 – **LET'S DREAM IN THE MOONLIGHT**

November 10, 1982

Fourth joint.

Leaving the dogs behind.

Different hike to proposed site.

Climb steep. Hit ridge. Wooded. Dense. Naked. Laurel. Rhododendron.

Mountaintop Point.

Fifth joint.

"A lot like The Triangle."

"Shhh. Thought I heard someone."

Motionless.

Whiff. Smoke.

Distance. Somebody chopping.

Motion. Dark Star. Easy.

Sneaking.

Crouched. Leathery green.

Laying flat. Peek.

Below. Bench. Kid. Skinny. Red headed. Suspenders. Barefoot. Machete. An oak crashes. A black man. Torn pants. Barefooted. No shirt. An ivory bill undulates.

An hour.

Seventh joint.

Trees fall.

Sun shafts bench.

Hoeing.

Seeding.

They pause.

Our faces drop.

The kid says something.

A grouse flushes.

We look. Then look again.

The two disappeared.

Whisper.

"They were close."

"I don't like it."

"Did you recognize them?"

"No."

"That black man never quit watching."

"The kid liked him."

"What should we do?"

"Let 'em have the site."

"Yeah."

"I grew up at the end of Aopehh's Bridge. As a boy the pigeons attracted me. I'd climb over the bank, walk up the tracks, lean a board against a telephone pole, climb up the pole, and in between the wires make a grab to a catwalk, pulling myself up. Once there, I'd catwalk out to the concrete pillars some 50 feet high and shimmy up a steel brace, checking on nests. At nights, I carried a flashlight, blinding the pigeons, sometimes catching one. One night, on my tenth birthday, I caught a lost racing homer. Had on an address band along with its racing band. Charles Heitzman, Jeffersontown, Kentucky. His great champion. Forced down, weakened and lost due to a storm. I returned the racer. Was rewarded with babies. Changed me forever.

When I was fifty three years old I was asked to come to a friend's beautiful estate in Cincinnati, Ohio to train his racing homers for the biggest race in Ohio. A 400 mile race for pigeons under a year old. For 17 days I lived in my friend's main racing loft. Turned the birds into "steel." Importantly, had them fall intensely in love with their home. On race day, 669 racing homers were released at dawn on the first Saturday in November. In a tremendous storm with strong headwinds. All day the storm persisted. By evening, my friend's invited dignified guests departed, disappointed in having not seen a racer wing home. I sat by the loft next to a lit landing board looking into the

145

black sky, nursing a whiskey. Everyone called the race secretary officially reporting no returns, except us. I wouldn't allow it. I could feel something in the heavens. My friend said that I was drunk. Told me to give it up. Come on in. Impossible. An hour later, I remained, gazing upward. Rain kept hitting my face. There was a ghostly patch of grey, a lighter colored cloud, mysteriously stuffed in between the blackness. Then, a dot. So very high. Nearly imperceptible. Falling fast. Aimed perfect. Wings folded. A checker hen. Diving down. Landing less than a foot from my face. Wings drooping, she moved toward the loft's opening. Then stopped. Turning her head, she looked at me, smiled. Then, walked through the trap, officially clocking. I dropped my drink, yelled for my friend. All across his lawn he kept calling me a liar. Upset with my joking. When he opened the door, she was at the feeder. Nobody will believe this, he said. You're the only person that could have gotten a bird. That night fanciers came. She was the only one having returned. I named her, All Alone."

NS

Journal Entry 30-- **THE VERY THOUGHT OF YOU**

November 14, 1982

The price of admission to The National
Racing Pigeon Show in White Plains, New York---
-your mind.

6:30 PM. Friday. LaGuardia Airport.
Picked up Big I and Jim. St. Louis competition.
My van holds us and all our birds. I've not slept
for thirty six hours.

Big I looks like Hell. Pigeon allergies. "I
told them to be careful handling my birds. Then,
some airport guy flips them. No telling what they
look like. I prep all year for this show. Then, a
flip job."

"Remind me to send that man some
money."

My van is laden in white pigeon bloom.
Two days of pigeon accumulation. The fine dust
makes Big I cough as his lazy blue eyes turn
red.

Also in my van are Bob and Ten Percent. I
picked them up coming through Springfield,
Ohio. Bob has on his pink 'Van Dell' jacket.
Stacks of brass latched cherry crates, divided
inside by individual stalls bedded in dried sugar
cane, stack from the floor to the ceiling. Pigeon
heads poke from every opening.

Long Island Bridges. Window is down.
Unusually warm for this time of year. Big I stops
coughing.

"Three times each. Who's gonna win number four?"

"I'm sure they haven't forgotten my boycott."

Manhattan. A billion lights.

Driving to White Plains we park. Unload crates. Coop entries in individual wire exhibition cages stacked in neat rows in the basement of the Westchester County Center Building. Each bird, cleaned, feathers, feet. Each bird, talcumed. Every bird, fed, watered, counseled.

It was 4:30 AM before Big I and I stopped pigeon talk and slept. At 6:30 we rose to leave The Holiday Inn and re-enter the cool show hall. Every bird being re-inspected. Trimming and splicing frayed and broken feathers. Coloring toenails. Re-watering. Capsules of cod-liver oil. Swapping lies with hoary New Yorkers. The show hall fills with smoke and brag. Outside, The Statue of Liberty is being shut down. Corrosion. The arm holding the torch is weak. John Lennon gave one million to help repairs. The cold ocean laughs.

The National Judges sit behind tables working the birds. Inspecting. Eliminating. The judging slowly winds down. Tomorrow, BEST IN SHOW will be announced. Big I and I have six birds each going into the finals.

At the hotel's bar. Sitting with two girls. Black haired. Dark eyed. Irish. Slick dancers pulsating to the strobes.

"Have you ever been in the clubs?"

"No."

"Check them out. A lot of costume. You can do a line. Nobody cares. The old Mafia is dead."

"Writers do the hardest lines."

"That what you do, a writer?"

"No, I raise wildflowers and pigeons."

"When I was a sophomore in college I gave some
of my swim team mates three young pigeons.
The birds were un-banded. Born at a bad time. I
had no space for them. And didn't want to kill
them. My swim friends were going home to
Florida for Christmas. I asked if they'd let the
birds go about fifty miles away. Maybe the poor
things would find a place to survive. About three
days later, around noon, in a heavy snow, I
noticed one of the birds sitting on my little cage
beside my wife's house. I let it in. Three weeks
passed before I saw my swim friends again. In
the dressing room one of them asked if I had
gotten any of the birds back. I told them, the
youngest one. The guys became quiet. Had
trouble believing me. Oh I got him, alright. I was
then informed they had forgot to let the birds go
in Kentucky. They actually were released in
Florida. I was dumbfounded. The pigeon was
only 85 days old, had never been trained. Flew
nearly 500 miles through the mountains and

snow in a day and a half. The following year, I bred ten full siblings to the bird. Totally dominated The Lexington, Kentucky Racing Pigeon Club. I sent one baby to The Twin City Gold Band Futurity in Minneapolis. My swim team pooled $400. The bird won, setting a new a record. We split $4,000. From then on among my swim team mates I was, Birdie."

NS

Journal Entry 31---**OUR LOVE IS HERE TO STAY**

November 25, 1982

Thanksgiving. Chicago.

I've been invited to judge a pigeon show. And go pheasant hunting. Four days, fully paid.

South side of Chicago.

I'm waiting at Denny's to meet the Rob Gajeweski, the show's unemployed organizer. Amish surround. Beards. Thick glasses.

Finally, Rob's head gestured at a glass door. A human praying mantis. Six three. One hundred and thirty pounds. Jabberwocky. Sandy hair under a green beret. Rob made the habit of beating fanciers out of money. Cold checks. Confusion. Promises. He catered to me because I was partial to the Europeans view of showing Racing Homers. And because Douglas McClary, the noted English showman and writer, was my friend. Rob's small loft was McClary's blood. Following his pickup we drove toward the glow of Chicago's northern lights stopping at a frame house crunched in between other humble images.

A few hours of sleep. Rob tapped my foot. Breakfast. Seventy five year old mom. Cataracts. Broke a dish. Chipped a teacup. Life was a nick.

"Did you see Brando in *ONE EYED JACK*?"

"I think so. What about it?"

"There's a scene where he is talking to Ben Johnson. Guess what he uses for a toothpick while talking?"

"You got me?"

"A pigeon feather."

Outside. Bad cold. Three inches of snow fell. Rob fetched Babe. Boney English pointer. My over-under Browning went behind his seat with his double barrel Stevens.

On the road. Headed to Chicago's best game preserve. Rob handed me a forged hunting license. Showed I was an in-state resident, Richard Gajeweski.

"We're brothers."

Arriving. Dark. Hope we hunt Area 13. It's booked. We settle for a long wait until 11:00 to hunt Area 4. Giant fireplace. Mounted teal, deer, hunting pictures. A chart listing the numbers of different wildlife killed in each area. Among us, unemployed steel mill workers.

10:45. Safety and rules lecture.

"Two pheasants, either sex, per person, the limit."

In the field. Forty hunters with dogs await launch. Loud OK. Dogs scatter. Labs. Setters. Pointers. Sniff. Wag. Whistles. Shouting. Arms waving. Clapping. Polish and Hungarian hunters.

Fifteen minutes pass. Hunter approaches dog on point. Rob beats him. Shoots. Kills sitting pheasant.

Saucy expletives.

The next bird, flushed, landing in a tree. Distinct silhouette. Rob shoots on the run. Misses. Second blast, puff of feathers. Babe calms down. An hour later, ten pheasants. Back at the truck, unloading.

"Let's go back and get the limit."

Going back.

Babe on point. Old man and woman approach. Tin soldiers. Shotguns sideways to the ground. Goofy lab at their side.

"My dog is on point. Is this your all's bird?"

The couple acknowledge. Flanking Babe. Preparing to shoot. I flush. Bird comes up. Couple blast. I hit the ground. I'm never considered. Only the death of that colorful target flying untouched into the distance. I give the couple their only bird.

Back at Rob's truck. Some baby face with double barrel. Clean. No stick tights.

"You guys have any luck?"

"A couple."

"Mind if I look?"

Rob opens truck door. Two cock birds on the floor.

"Nice birds. Would you fold the seat over?"

I sat on the tailgate talking to Babe.

Baby Face lifts out birds one by one. Unzips jacket. Uniform and badge. "I thought you said, a couple?"

"I did. We got a couple each. The others belong to friends."

"How many friends have you got?"

"Five."

Baby Face pauses. Rob looks at me. Baby Face points at a raked out area in the gravel. "Some woman's accident."

"We met her. And her husband. Uh, Richard, why don't you go. Get John and our buddies so the game warden won't have to wait."

"OK. They were over by those trees on the creek.".

Luck.

A father and son. Hadn't seen a bird. My plight explained. Help agreed.

Back at Ray's truck. New faces act. Lifelong friends. Pick up four nicest pheasants. Baby Face inspects licenses.

"I thought you went after John. This man is, Floyd. His son, Tom."

"John is still out. Uh, Richard, go get John."

"OK."

"No. You guys stay right here. I'll get John."

Game Warden walks off.

"Did he get your license plate?"

"No."

"Throw them birds in the truck."

Streaming down the highway.

Me and Old Fitz. 86 proof.

"It was a miracle homing pigeons came home to Aopehh. More the miracle, its people."

NS

Journal Entry 32 – **GLOOMY SUNDAY**

November 27, 1982

Chicago.

Rob's eyes held every fancier's fascination. Intoxication. Alone with a pigeon. Backyard garage loft. Chicken wire. Bent nails. Swirls of feathers. Rob shut out the world. An occasional coo. Flutter of wings. No one asks questions.

"Did you ever see *DAY OF THE JACKAL?*"

"No."

"About a plot to shoot de Gaulle. At one point the assassin gives the law the slip. Know what the detective in charge does?"

"No."

"Goes inside his pigeon loft."

"When dad had his fruit stand he'd get me ride down to Macon, Georgia with him in his truck. We'd go out into the peach orchards and melon fields. The black pickers would load and I would count. Everyone trusted a small boy. Once headed home I'd tell dad the real count. Always much more. He'd smile. I'd feel wonderful."

NS

Journal Entry 33 –**EASY LIVING**

November 29, 1982

Sensi, Dark Star, Rollanotherone and I stream through the night. Ten gauger. A Who concert. Lexington.

Twelve hours ago I finished judging in front of 200 Polish fanciers. Rob didn't win BEST IN SHOW. When it came time to pay for my gas home, he stole money out of a cigar box.

The Who once accompanied The Beatles. Their drummer OD'd. This band brought on Cincinnati's death stampede. Townsend quotes Conrad.

Nearing Rupp Arena. BEHIND BLUE EYES. Triangle Park's lit water fountain spouts. Horn blowing lunacy.

Joe Bologna's Pizza Parlor. Beer. Leave.

Entrance. Law. Searched. Nothing.

Good seats.

Who's last tour. Twenty five thousand. Sold out.

Townsend. Tall. Slender. Burr. Glass-eyed. Gyrating. Three hours. *A PRETTY GIRL IS LIKE A MELODY.*

The light show. Luminous explosion. Lights in faces.

One human joint.

159

"When I applied for a teaching position at Mariemont High School in Ohio, I had to cross a picket line composed of striking teachers. Once I got to see the superintendent I found myself sitting across from a man behind a mahogany desk in a blue pin stripe suit. An American flag went from the ceiling to his plush carpeted floor. I sat straight. He looked at me. Ink pen tapping. Said I was the first person he'd ever interviewed that was wearing blue jeans. I explained, they were my best. Found them canoeing down The Rockcastle River. Fit me perfect. He wanted to know why I wore them. Because they are comfortable, I said. He went on to tell me that a teacher gains respect by what they wear. I believe people earn respect by what is in their heart. A monkey can wear a suit but it is still a monkey, was my response. He declared we were diametrically opposed in viewpoints. That I would not work out. I went back to the van. Told Mike about the interview. The strikers stopped us. Asked if I got a job. I reached in my cooler, pulled out a Budweiser, popped it. No, I told them. Why not, they asked. They're desperate. They'll hire anyone. I know, I said. My swim coach sent me up here. Told me all about it. Highly recommended me. Also getting a beer, Mike informed the strikers, Can't you see, this is the writer, No Sweat. He's over qualified to be some teacher. And we drove off."

NS

160

Journal Entry 34 – **THE MAN I LOVE**

December 2, 1982.

Black Hole's.

"You watch movies. I read. That's the difference between us. The difference in the generation. We might get out of this century. But not the next."

"Guess New York will get it. Is the bomb necessary?"

"Who can say what is necessary. Nothing is as it seems. Freud said the voice of intellect is soft but never rests until heard. Women are lucky. Their worries are over a new car, a washed dish, dresses. Duty is clear."

Stepping out into the moonlight there was a circular formation of clouds around the moon.

Black Hole stared. In his dark eyes were mirrors reflecting the cream yellows. "It's either a lunar halo. Or God I pray, someone in a holding pattern."

"When I discovered petroglyphs in Aopehh I contacted the most renowned experts in the field, Costigan and Riley. They drove in from Louisville and spent all day making molds and photographing. Two months later, they informed me that the markings were Viking. Translation, HAVE BEEN HERE LONG TIME. COUNTRY DESOLATE.

      Nothing has changed."

NS

Journal Entry 35 – **THE SAME OLD STORY**

December 7, 1982

Aopehh.

Sweet Lick Knob.

Eighty five degrees.

"The only thing up here is grass."

"This mountain is so obvious."

"That's the beauty."

"The search planes land over there. At the Coalwash."

"Lips has a painting of Sweet Lick Knob hanging in his office."

"How could you think such a thing?"

"Jack London said he felt as though he should've, by birthright, never been allowed to think the thoughts he had."

"I was sixteen before I accidentally learned that dad had killed a man. And that mom's family had been instrumental in keeping him from going to prison. Years later, likewise, my wife played an important role in getting his child molestation, involving my sister's daughter, case dropped."

NS

Journal Entry 36 – **ON THE SUNNY SIDE OF THE STREET**

December 13, 1982

Main Street Aopehh. UK is beating Illinois. Eastern is beating East Tennessee. Two televisions blare through my parents home. Wide Eyes was taken to the field stone house so that True would give her dancing lessons. Wide

Eyes also takes lessons from Barbra Ann,
Lexington's Belle.

"Mom, where's True?"

"Gone. I haven't seen her for two weeks."

Last year, True told mom she was going to
town to get toothpaste. Three months later, she
returned offering no explanations. True was still
fat. The hump in her nose got fixed when the
plastic surgeons rearranged her beaten face.
Her Neanderthal live-in caught her living in with
his buddy. Smashed her face beyond
recognition. Nearly killed her. But that was last
year.

There'd been many years before.

True had Gulf Stream blue eyes, straight
brown hair and dark skin. But she was fat, loud
and full of brass. She'd gotten a giant eagle
tattoo that cheapened everyone near her. A
tattoo with some lover's name printed under it.
It could have been anybody.

It was only because of mom that True had
the tiny dance school. When mother was sober
she'd drive into Aopehh bringing the little girls
back to the house. She had stolen money from
dad converting the basement. Plywood floors,
mats, wall mirrors, stereo, costumes and
posters.

The liquor store money dad had stolen over the years moved my parents and sister out of our tiny apartment over the theatre and pool room to a showy Main Street spot next to The Christian Church. It was my father's Graceland.

The house meant everything to dad.

Far more than mere family.

My parents had paid for True to attend Eastern Kentucky University. Bought her clothes. Paid for her to stay on campus with her car. I had helped fill out her schedule knowing which professors were easy.

A month later True OD'd. One night she ran her car into Eastern Kentucky University's Daniel Boone statue standing in the middle of campus. Her wasted companion collapsed on the sidewalk. She made it to her dorm, falling down a flight of stairs. Remaining there until Security arrived.

While being ambulanced from hospital to hospital Security searched True's room. Bent spoons, surgical tubing, syringes, un-prescribed pills, cocaine and a suitcase of marijuana were confiscated.

True was given two choices.

Quit or be kicked out.

Applying the second semester to Western Kentucky University, True drove a silver MG. Bowling Green was nearly two hundred miles away. Every other week she would fly home on dad's un-rung bootleg cash.

True never attended a class. In two months she had two separate hit and run charges. $20,000 in law suits. And $10,000 in bad checks. When the grades came out, straight Fs. The phone bills, wrecked car and flights of unexplained disappearances took its toll.

Mother was an alcoholic. Married to dad, she had no choice. She had reached the stage where truth was rare. The youngest child in her affluent family; A family once owning farms, hotels, theatres, groceries, airplanes and a creditable known last name.

Mom's mom was the last of sixteen children. The hunch backed woman wouldn't allow anyone to say the word, lie. Such was, country, she informed. In time, because of mom's two brother's liquor and laziness, mom's family faced bankruptcy. Mom's oldest brother, the politician, fled to Florida. The other claimed he was an artist.

Before the rise and fall, mom had gone through a strange period. Mom's father told me more about it than anyone. He and I were close. I believe he felt sorry for me. He loved me more than anyone. Was kind and gentle. So patient and understanding. I felt safe being near him.

When mom was between nine and twelve years old she never spoke a word. Was wheel-chaired to public school. Just sat and stared. When I asked mom, she said it was typhoid. That her hair fell out.

At times I felt like mom and I were a falconer and her falcon. She would keep me starved for so much, especially affection. Upon release I would soar. I had soared out of high school into anthropology. My head swelled with thoughts. But my wings grew heavy. I fell to the earth to be back next to my falconer. We both suffered the same physical and emotional wrath of dad.

Dad hated mother's mother. And she hated him. He was all that her sons weren't. Robert Mitchum handsome. Personable. Able to steal more than he spent. Mom's mom had offered her a new car at age fourteen if she would not marry dad. For twenty years I dwelled with them. A day never passed that he didn't curse mom's family. Always vowed he'd someday buy and sell them. Now, that that prophecy was in some ways true the hate among dad and mother's family was intense. Everybody smiled. But no longer were there family get-togethers that I so cherished as a child. My cousins treated me horrible because I didn't have their last name.

Father maintained mom's family had cheated her out of what was hers. In the early 1950's to the early 1960's, large amounts of

168

easy money had been given to mom's brothers. But never mom. Mom's family never really accepted True or I as family. Our last names were differed. Mother had not been given property or money. But most of all she had never been given time or love. Her proud mother was one of those southern women incapable.

Mother stood there in the modern kitchen. Black and white tiled floor gleamed. She could not offer any more on True. The house meant everything.

More than love.

"On my first 500 mile race with The Lexington,
Kentucky Racing Pigeon Club none of the 235
entries made it home on the day they were
released from Pensacola, Florida. Before
daylight the next morning I climbed up on top of
the Irvine Theatre. At dawn, a silver bar yearling
cock broke the sky flying steady out of the west
from Richmond. Less than a minute behind him
was his brother, the same bird that had hatched
with him in their nest. One by one some minute
apart all ten of my entries winged home. That
evening I took my racing clock to Lexington to
learn the results of the race. The club members
stared. All were older. Lifelong veterans of the
sport. Had been racing many years before me. I
lived 23 miles farther from the release point than
anyone. No other birds had homed. And none
returned the third day. Instinct and love
combined is a wonderful force."

NS

Journal Entry 37 – **WHO WANTS LOVE?**

516 Poplar

Aopehh, Kentucky

December 15, 1982

Dear Joe,

Thank you for the Christmas card. I taped it on my doorway. Most the cards are fanciers.

I got off to an early breeding season. Leaving the loft lights on 24 hours a day. Light stimulates sex, not temperature.

I'm trimming rump feathers. Increasing protein. Giving more space ratio. Rationing feed. Conducing fertility.

I'm concentrating on pale blue bars. Mating blues to blues. Recessive to recessive. Which becomes dominant. Despite rhetoric, blue bars are the color most desired. Particularly pale blue bars, which are more recessive yet. And most difficult to breed. My recent article, *COLOR ME BLUE* was rejected for publication. Not surprising. Truth rubs.

I'm basically line breeding. Lining genes. To some extent, slight cloning. Developing and maintaining a family is a living art. A subtle and changing art that slightly evolves with each passing generation. A reflection of the artist.

It was good seeing you at The National. Don't take it serious. Supposing that one pigeon is more perfect than another for any number of reasons is all human. I remember being a boy. Happier with the birds than now. Striving to be the best killed innocence.

And more.

Merry Christmas.

No Sweat

"No wonder willows weep, they look like giant
marijuana plants."

NS

Journal Entry 38 –**THINGS ARE LOOKING UP**

December 22, 1982

It was on my left as I drove up Cow Creek.

Night.

The radio pushed Black Sabbath.

Eighty MPH.

Two mountains over was Aopehh's three-story star. It was somehow supposed to be The Star Of Bethlehem. Metal rods and light bulbs. It beamed from a mountain known as, The Rockhouse. That pointy thing appeared heavenly suspended. Had to be facing off and aimed at Richmond, Kentucky because it was wet over there and that was where all the sin surely was. Astronauts could see it. NDN, while president of the JCs cooked up the idea for the thing. The JCs needed money. Media blitz. NDN was also in charge of WMARI, Aopehh's radio station. Buckets of donations came out of every wretched hollow donating to the thing's creation. Aopehh got a warm feeling looking at it. The JC's cleared nicely. Way more than enough. Nobody said nothing. And the money kept coming in. Just like the saints when they go marching.

Such info was tight.

I only heard it after some potent Triangle and Turkey got passed around.

This new thing, a giant crucifix with multi colored Christmas lights, faced Cow Creek.

The star wasn't enough.

Parking, Rex and Ruff wagged. Dark Star's porch light came on. I stepped up the winding stone stairway that he and I had spent a month in making. Coming into the wavy, low ceiling kitchen, Dark Star rocked back and forth in his black wicker rocker next to a pot-belly stove.

174

Rollanotherone sat at a table rolling a joint. Red agates lined the windows. Purple and white African violets intermingled. A sassafras root as big as a man's waist sat on top the refrigerator. Between the images set a block of government cheese.

"Have you checked out the cross?"

"You can see it from our kitchen window."

"I spoke to Mrx today. He's in trouble. Two charges. One to five for growing. The other, five to ten for manufacture. Mrx figures, two years. Wishes he'd never sued Shy."

"He sued Shy!"

"Yeah. And you know what buddies he and Ibold are. You get Ibold against you, you're in trouble. Destroy you in court."

"Mrx says he isn't going to implicate anyone else. Got word he's dead if he rats."

"The law will want to know who else is involved. A million dollars was going somewhere."

"It's all suppose to come out in January. Gonna be a hot winter."

The dogs barked. The guitars arrived. Rollanotherone stood by their Christmas tree, spider-webbed in angel hair. New faces appeared. Two 350 watt speakers aimed back at the cross. All the lights went off. Only a candle remained. Pounding sounds shook the floor.

"WILD THANG! YOU MAKE MY HEART SANG! YOU MAKE MY EVERYTHANG!"

"My mother was the most beautiful woman in
the world and I was blind."

NS

Journal Entry 39 – **I HEAR MUSIC**

December 25, 1982

Santa had on his t-shirt during this
seventy degree record warm Christmas. He sat
with Sensi watching Wide Eyes tear at packages.
Santa sat quiet blinking his eyes, absorbing
tears, smiling, trying not to destroy the moment.

Wide Eyes had gotten a Smurf sleeping bag, television, aquarium, rock tumbler, art-deco set, auto harp, dolls, games, books, candy and clothes. With each gift she had hugged Sensi, kissing, smiling in excitement.

Wide Eyes was thrilled knowing Santa had consumed her cookies and milk. Our home lingered with his fresh absence. A cherish able linger where we tried to cling to something we could not keep.

Wide Eyes was a day before her fourth birthday. At a time where she cried at the death of a flower, the thought of growing old, hunting a grouse, a doll being mistreated, or a melting snowman.

As the day moved I caught a sparrow in my pigeon loft. It had been eating my expensive mixtures of feed. Wide Eyes carefully watched. "What should I do with him?" I asked her. "Should I kill him?"

"Let him go, daddy. So he can fly and sing."

I handed the bird into her moist hands. The sparrow's heart was nearly bursting. Wide Eyes released the bird. Her face glowed.

As we returned to the loft I noted a baby racing homer having died during the night. Wide Eyes' attention concentrated on the lifeless figure, stiff and saurian with skin and forming pinfeathers. Sorrow was in her brilliant eyes.

"We will bury the baby," I said. As we finished patting the ground I looked to see a tear.

"Daddy, will the baby pigeon ever live again? If we dig it up later, will it be alive?"

"No. Death is forever. When we buried this baby we can never again expect to see it. Everything alive eventually dies. Let's be happy. You and I are alive. Your mother and I love you. We will always love you. You have given us life. You are my angel. Be happy you live in Aopehh. There's many places worse. Sweetheart, we have a lot more pigeons. Death is a part of having them. I am happy you are sad over the bird. Be afraid, it's alright. Oh Wide Eyes, you are precious."

That afternoon we drove two miles to my parents modern house on Main Street. The Cadillac and Lincoln were parked in the driveway. Knocking at the side door I found it unlocked. The house was empty. Then I saw mother. She was lying on the fake leopard couch next to the paneled wall and slate bar. Raising her bloated body upright she wiped mucous from her mouth trying to make a sentence. Her botched platinum-blond hair and un-focusing gray eyes then sunk back into the mohair. I looked for dad and True. Both were gone. The rooms were so familiarly quiet. That same quiet from my childhood. The house had that same stench of alcoholism.

A smell of no love.

Coming back to mom I stood close at her side. A slight smile appeared over her face. Her little boy was near. The house was grey. All the drapes were pulled. I felt of gloom. I sensed death. Emptiness entered into my heart. Oh mom, you dear fool. You hurt wretch. You kindred spirit. I would tell you I love you. Say it a million times. But I cannot. I couldn't cry. I could only ache.

"Daddy," asked Wide Eyes, entering the door. "Are we going in?"

"No, baby. Your grandmother isn't well."

Sensi stood looking from the door.

We left.

There had been nothing of Christmas at that house. One set of elk antlers had tiny colored lights taped to them. All the other antlers were bare. There was no tree. Nothing. Just mom on that couch.

Several hours had passed when the phone rang.

"No Sweat, have you seen your mother the past two weeks?"

"I saw her a few hours ago."

"She's been falling down drunk all week. She's driving me crazy. Between her and True, I'm going broke. I'm going to have to sell my house. True hasn't been around in over a month. She's out doped up with some goddamn piece of shit. I can't give a bunch of bastards a couple a hundred a day to baby sit a drunk and a whore. It wouldn't do any good anyway. She's a goddamn fool. You wouldn't believe. I know you know. But you only know half of it. I've nailed our bedroom door shut so she wouldn't sneak off from me in the night to get a drink. I've tied her leg to mine at night. It doesn't do any good. She's got pills and booze hid all over the fucking house. She hides vodka in Scope bottles. She's got bottles hid in hutches, dried flower arrangements, under the sink, in the bathroom, in True's closet. Last time she was here, True found a quart of vodka in her dance chest, empty. Empty bottles are in every spot you can imagine. She takes valiums and unicons by the handfuls. You just don't know. The goddamn drunk is going to fall from the steps or OD. I'll get blamed for murder sure as Hell. She says she's gonna get in AA. Well whoopee. Fuck. Everything is great. Fuck. I wish she'd just go back on that religious kick. Get back with that goddamn family of hers. They don't give a shit about her. Never have. I drug her ass over to her mother's. You know what that damn old woman said? She said, 'There ain't nothing wrong with her.' I want you to come here. I want to show you how goddamn much your mom has drunk since Tuesday. I don't know how many pills. She drank two cases of my imported Liebfraumilch.

181

She drank two cases of warm Budweiser. Come out here. You won't believe it. How many years do you think she's been drunk? Do you remember when you were thirteen years old and kept marking 'X's' each day on the calendar your mom was drunk? What did you mark? Eighty-nine of ninety days. Well, she'd been a drunk many years before you started noticing. I've done everything to get her to stop but she won't. We'll go to bed cold sober and two hours later I'll hear something. And she'll be stone dead drunk. I'll look at her and say, 'You're drunk.' And she'll say she's not had a drop. She swears she doesn't drink. I've grabbed her hand while it was full of pills and she'll swear there are no pills. That I am making it all up. Last month I sat a half gallon of Fitzgerald on the bar and said 'Hell! Drink to your goddamn heart's content!' Are you gonna come out?"

"We are fixing to eat dinner. Then we'll stop by. Sensi made a prune cake. We'll bring you some dinner. I wanted you all to eat dinner with us, but..."

Later, we returned to a house as dark inside as it was out. When I first knocked no one came. But just as we were leaving dad opened the door.

A small light over the stove of the spacious chrome kitchen reflected a quiet man looking out toward the glass doors facing across Main Street to the gaily lit brick home of my grandmother. Without turning on the lights I knew mother rested on that couch. Tonight, her 'Robert Mitchum' was by himself. It was the last place on earth where he wanted to be.

Merry Christmas.

Turning on the light, the coyote's face on the wall rug glared in anger. The moose stared at the elk. Dad entered his den where mom lay.

"What would you do with that? What am I going to do? How would you like to go to bed with her?"

It was then that my sister appeared wearing one of dad's deer hide vests and jeans. She kissed everyone. "I'm OK. I haven't been shooting up." Her arms were bruised and her hands swollen. She was a youthful degree from mom. We all knew it.

Dad put his large palms to his forehead. "My God!" he said. Then he stared at me in disgust. "Can you believe this? Am I the only sane son of a bitch in the world?"

True rolled back her eyes, exhaling cigarette smoke. "I've heard all your shit before," she said, walking to the door. "I ain't listening to it tonight." She left for the driveway. A car waited. A car always waited.

"Hook, my high school principal, proclaimed Jiggs Stokes the smartest person ever to graduate from Aopehh. Our IQ barometer. An absolute genius. Now, top man at something big and complicated. Hook told my scared class of '69 that it took Jiggs more than two full hours to take his terrifying history final. That we'd be lucky to do it in less than five. Everyone studied for months. If you flunked, you had to suffer another year in school.

I finished the exam in under 20 minutes.

Never missed a question.

Perfect.

Sensi had remembered all the questions from the year before when she took it. Wrote them down and gave them to me. They were the only ones I studied. I looked them over one day before the test.

I banked on Hook being lazy.

When I rose to turn in my paper my class paused, looking up.

They felt sorry for me.

Defeat.

Another year in prison.

Might as well be drawn and quartered.

Hook smiled. Did his silent whistle routine. Tapped his foot.

That smile slowly turned downward. The whistle stopped. So did the tapping as he flipped through my test, reviewing my answers.

When I walked out the door there was yet one more smile.

Mine."

NS

Journal Entry 40 – **MEAN TO ME**

December 31, 1982

Dark Star's place.

Thirty spiny lobsters thawed. Half gallon of Rhine. Buttery prune cake. Bowl of crunchy coleslaw. Double fisted Idaho potatoes. Cream cheese and red-orange jalapeño pepper jelly on sesame rye.

Kitchen lamp reflects two hippies. Sweet smell. Wooden bowl. A glistening cola lies beckoning. Rollanotherone frets over homemade bread and melted butter.

"Pig out!"

Custer and Mary smile.

"Where did you get the lobsters?"

"Caught them."

"Where?"

"Palm Beach."

"Hard to get?"

"Can be."

"You just wade out and get them?"

"No. Gotta dive."

"Snorkel?"

"Sometimes."

"Deep?"

"Usually."

"You ever been around sharks?"

"About every dive."

"Any close calls?"

"Yeah.The worst was when dad, Sensi and I were off South Bimini. I speared a black grouper. Fifty pounder. Got him with a pole gun I had special made at Rockwell. Usually, I hit 'em behind the gill. But this one I got in the head. I couldn't get the spear to push through or pull out. Blood went everywhere. The grouper kept thumping. Making distress noises. Dad and Sensi were low on air. We were at 90 foot. Dad took my bag of fish and we surfaced. The grouper jerked the whole way. On the surface it was pouring rain. Our boat was anchored about 500 yards away. We had to swim against a strong current not making much headway. About two hundred yards out from the boat dad handed me the bag of fish. Then came a shark behind me. About eight foot. He disappeared. Then came two more. Five footers. In the next few minutes there was over a dozen. One tried to take my grouper. I poked him. Dad and Sensi were screaming for me to drop everything. I didn't. The rain had them panicked. When fresh water mixes in salt water it makes it blurry. Messes up the surface. One second you see a blur. The next, sharks. We were about fifty yards from the boat when dad started shouting for help. The guy on the boat stood watching. The sharks kept getting braver. I was knocking them off every ten seconds. They stopped coming at the grouper and began coming in on us. That's when we made it to the boat. Dad was exhausted. Sensi was in shock. The rain was pouring in our faces. The captain said the anchor was hung. And that we didn't have anything to worry about. The only sharks around there were black tips. After the rain quit the water smoothed out. The captain sliced us some conch and squeezed lime. Then, fixed us a drink."

The dogs started barking. Others were coming.

On the front porch pistols were shot into the sky.

Echoes disappeared up the hollow

I held Sensi

"Mother hadn't been dead a month until dad had a young Canadian whore living with him. She had laid in bed with him at my parents' home long before mom had died. There had been many just like her over the years. Mom knew everything. I managed to get the Canadian whore to leave by calling her a hedgehog to her face. Actually, I was being nice. I could have called her many other things. A couple of years later another woman charmed and married dad. This was her third marriage. She was no green hand in understanding what happens to property when you marry someone in Kentucky. She had been married to an attorney. She was 21 years younger than dad. She couldn't help but see and know that dad was losing his mind. Sensi and I certainly knew it. So did my sister. Dad couldn't remember anything. He was 78 years old. He couldn't finish a sentence. He didn't know people's names. He was nothing of his old self. He was that perfect target for someone wanting to rob a bank without a gun. Someone that taught Sunday School. This woman made certain that there would be no pre-nup. Told my dad that she was rich and didn't need his money. But then she would not marry him if there was a pre-nup. She should have been in politics. Right off after the marriage, she made my father concrete over mom's, my sister's and my name near the door of dad's house. The house that I had helped build. She didn't know that. She didn't care. A year later, I learned from my sister that she had sold everything of mother's in a yard sale. I'd heard nothing. I got nothing. Not even spit. In a very short while she managed to get herself in control of all of dad's assets, which, for the first time in his life, were rapidly dwindling. One December she sent me a Christmas card. I looked at Sensi. What brass. It brought back my remembrance of when Butch Cassidy and Sundance robbed a bank and then sent that bank a photo of themselves dressed in finery, thanking them. I knew how that bank felt. Only worse."

NS

Journal Entry 41 –THEY SAY

January 1, 1983

Mom and dad's. Their New Year's Day Brunch. Aopehh's finer drunks. Mom's about as happy as she can be. Burgoo. Elk burgers. Jumbo shrimp. Lobster tails. Wig Wam coleslaw. Cooked apples. Liquor. Televisions blare football. Wagers. Dark Star, Rollanotherone, Doc,

Blackwidow, Sensi and I sit at a sunken fireplace away from the others.

"You ought to see our place since the fire," laughed Doc. "If I'd've known the insurance was gonna pay like it did, I'd've torched it a long time ago."

"We've got new carpet, two color TVs, a video, two telephones and a waterbed with silk sheets," grinned Blackwidow, winking.

"When the Fire Department was ransacking they stole all our marijuana. Even the roaches."

"They got my jewelry."

"Told us to get out. They hung around. Made certain no looters would hit."

"Doc's dad came in today. Came upstairs and shouted, WHEN ARE YOU GOING TO GET A JOB! Doc said, I'M GONNA MARRY ME A DOCTOR LIKE YOU! THEN, I AIN'T NEVER GONNA DO ANYTHING EXCEPT PLAY THE HORSES AND STAY IN PALM BEACH!"

"What did he say to that?"

"Nothing. Just grumbled."

True said Blackwidow pressured Doc into marriage. Greg Alman supposedly had proposed to her about the same time. She was going to

191

wed him. But then Doc finally gave in after a week of shooting up.

Down from Booneville, Swallowtail and Slowtalk set up their electric piano. Doc walked two houses over returning with one of his Gibsons.

"Are you still illustrating?" laughed Swallowtail.

I had been Swallowtail's campaign manager in his bid for Aopehh's District Judge. His marijuana reputation lost the election. Lips, his opponent, was arrogant, vengeful and had his way with boys. Campaign slogans, DO YOU WANT A MAN FOR A BIG JOB OR A BLOW JOB were Doc's creations. One night Sensi and I spotted Lips dressed in black atop a ladder against a telephone pole ripping down our Swallowtail signs. Tailing us, he threw his pick up lights on bright. Tried to wreck us. The sheriff, bootleggers and lawyers were in his pocket. I never stopped. He packed a pistol. The next morning my phone rang. It was Swallowtail. Relaying that someone had ruined our campaign covered wagon on the Richmond Road. In it, had been a brass bed holding a sign. YOU CAN GET ON THE WAGON WITH SWALLOWTAIL OR IN THE BED WITH LIPS. White paint everywhere. A rubber glove remained. I cut out four of the fingers, left the middle one, mailed it back to Lips.

"You won't believe what's happened on Buck Creek. Two growers caught two guys ripping them off. The guys got loose. Now, the growers are facing kidnapping charges. Want me to represent them."

By now dad's Fitzgerald 86 proof voice dominated.

After everyone would leave he'd smack mom, yank out her hair and curse her family.

Certain as night.

And darker still.

"When I entered college Viet Nam was still going.
At Eastern Kentucky University the men were
required to take two years of ROTC. I was kicked
out of ROTC class the first three times I came.
Long hair. When we had our President Day's
Parade I took off my ROTC jacket, put on a black
armband and laid on the ground. One ROTC
student stepped on my chest. Another, my face.
After the parade, I along with about ten others,
had my name reported to some big wheel at
EKU. My swim coach, Don Combs, managed to
keep me from being expelled. I had to do ROTC's
laundry every day the rest of the semester in
order to earn a D minus."

NS

Journal Entry 42 – **AM I BLUE?**

January 8, 1983

"Doc came by last night. Wanted to go with us."

Oak door. Brass latch. Knock.

Doc's father appears. A walrus with a glass eye.

"Doc told us to fetch him. Going grouse hunting."

"He's asleep."

"He told us to get him."

"He ain't got any!"

The door shuts.

Back in the jeep.

"What was he talking about?"

"Who knows. He's lost it."

"Wasn't he almost sixty when he had Doc?"

Stopping at store. Bologna sandwiches put inside hunting jackets.

"Should we call him?"

"Go ahead."

Phone.

"Blackwidow, it's No Sweat. We were just there. Walrus stopped us. Wouldn't let us in. Is Doc up?"

"He said he doesn't have any money. He can't find his mother."

"What does he need money for?"

"Hunting license and marijuana."

"Forget the license."

"He's not well. Know what I mean? Better go without him. Come back later. It's complicated."

Back in the jeep.

"What did you find out?"

"It's complicated. That's the word Blackwidow used."

"I wish I had his complications."

"Blackwidow said he needed money and couldn't find his mom."

"Wouldn't that be something? Wake up. Mom gives you a thousand. Then go back to bed. If I had his money I'd live in the Rockies. Hunt every day."

"Doc has been on heroin since High School."

"Custer said it was like having an orgasm in your stomach."

"That's one side of it."

Parking. Cornfield. Creek. Annie jumps out. Wags tail up Long Branch. Over-unders receive shells. Upstream. Walnuts. Annie's snout. Grassy edges. Scarlet and junco flash. Algid freshness.

Dark forest. White pines. Magic. Emerald branches. Thousands of soft. Blue giants. Fairy. Needled floor. Stillness. Exotic. Boone smells. Owl calm.

"Ever read Robinson Jeffers?"

"No."

"He says life is a double bladed axe. One side, flesh. The other, spirit. The handle, truth. He believes seeking the truth is better than good work. Better than survival. Holier than innocence. Higher than love. If I do write, I'd like to keep him close."

"This place sure has the trees."

"Could pay off the property with them."

"You'd be cutting your own throat. Kentucky walnut is the most beautiful in the world. Best grain and color. We get the purple. If you find a curly walnut you're talking twenty five thousand for one tree."

Suddenly, a grouse flushed.

Firing.

"I got him!"

"You fired, too?"

Walking. Ejecting shell. Loading. Annie, wagging.

Next to the creek lay breast feathers intermingled in the golden grass. A few feet over lay the grouse, gasping. I picked up the warm bird. Red, brown, beige, black and gold camouflage. Cardinal top knot. Red phase. Cheeky face. Large passages for hearing. A large pupil compared to a pigeon. Iris, dark vermillion.

"This is this year's bird. Clean legs. No snowshoes."

Continuing hunt. Open area. Rotting log cabin. Leaning guns. Sitting. Sandwiches. Six gravestones. Scattered plastic milk jugs.

Dark Star walks to a cedar.

"Come here!"

"What is it?"

"Not sure."

At the base of the tree, plastic. Two rocks weighted. Beside, a Clorox jug.

"What's that?

"Fertilizer. This is somebody's scene."

Moving. Searching.

"Come here! A marijuana plant! Taped and tied. Had buds."

"Whoever did this stripped the branches."

"Probably too hard to pack stalks."

Spreading out we found some fifty stalks around six feet tall. Long dead. The plastic at the base held moisture and stopped weeds.

We left.

Night was near.

It was always near.

"For four years I swam distance for the best team in Kentucky. Forty hours a week for Eastern Kentucky University's coach Don Combs. I was then the only collegiate athlete from Aopehh. My coach's father's name was, Earle; an exceptionally handsome man that batted on the NY Yankees baseball team; Murder's Row with Lou Gehrig and Babe Ruth. I didn't like that name, Earle. But around him, it was just fine."

NS

Journal Entry 43 – **TRAVELIN' ALL ALONE**

January 14, 1983

"Meet me and Mrx on River Drive at Qucikdraw's. And bring a joint."

I was soon sitting in the backseat of Swalowtail's cramped Chevy Citation. Swallowtail and Mrx sat up front.

"We got Mrx's trial put off until the end of February."

"Good. Stretch it out."

"They're going to hang me any way it goes."

Swallowtail handed me two blue folders. On the edge of one it read, CLIENT: MRX--- ADVERSE PARTY: COMMONWEALTH OF KENTUCKY VS. On the inside of the folder was: TYPE OF CASE: CULTIVATION OF MARIJUANA. The other folder read: CLENT: TRIDENT, ZIP AND LOCK—ADVERSE PARTY: AOPEHH CRIMINAL CASE. On the inside was: TYPE OF CASE: ROBBERY, KIDNAPPING, MARIJUANA, UNLAWFUL IMPRISONMENT.

"No Sweat, I need your help on these two cases. I'll pay you. Get us a good jury."

Inside the folder, on the first page was a list of names selected to be jurors for the upcoming Aopehhean Circuit Court. Some would be selected to be on The Grand Jury.

"What are you smiling about?"

"This list."

Mrx. was in trouble. We recently learned he'd been up or murder, grand larceny and moonshining. But then, nobody's perfect. The State Boys had found a million dollars worth of marijuana growing on his property.

"We sure don't want this person," I remarked. "He's the superintendent's puppet on the School Board. Helped get Dark Star fired over the marijuana belt buckle. This woman here, her son is Aopehh's new dentist. Society's classic coward. And you better make certain this woman doesn't get on. She's the new doctor's wife. Hates herself. And bad wants company. You sure don't want this woman. Her son is a lawyer in Richmond. They're that uppity brand of Catholics. I went to school with her daughter. The flag bearers of good. She came up to me on Election Day. Appalled I campaigned for Swallowtail. Come on now. Sweetcakes. She's Ibold's ex. They're supposedly divorced. Like this list was supposedly selected at random. He bought her a three carat diamond at Christmas. Gave her a house, a car, a farm. How do you think she'd perform?"

"Looks bad, doesn't it?"

"Well, the bottom line is that mom has been drawn. If she gets on, we may have a

202

chance toward a hung jury. Mom couldn't convict anyone. Life is jail enough."

Swallowtail beamed.

Ibold had long known my family. Particularly mom. He loved her. He always spoke low with a cigar in the corner of his mouth . No one ever understood him. A farmer with barrel-sized pumpkins, sugar cured hams and fortified blackberry wine. In court, he did all the wrong things just right. A master of badgering and implying. Toyed with tempers. Thrived on divorces. Cold and crude. A cat in heat. He'd let loose with his shrill voice, hold the queer volume, tapering down until running out of breath. No one could hear what he was saying when in the midst of his confab. Let alone, object.

"Did you bring me a joint?"

"Can a pigeon fly 700 miles on the day?"

Once home I began to study every juror. I wanted to void the old ones. But they were Mrx's peers. Some, I didn't know. I began making calls.

One juror was married to a young railroader. Most of the young railroaders smoked marijuana. Another juror was a conservative hippy that worked at the greenhouse. He looked OK. Another of the younger jurors had recently caught his wife sleeping with his best friend.

They smoked. My eyes could not leave mom's name. The one person that Ibold and Swallowtail would take for granted.

Quitting the juror profiles, I stopped late into the night.

The next morning I found myself immersed in the two cases. Police reports. Testimonials. Newspaper Stories. Notes.

I was surprised that the foreman of the Grand Jury that indicted Mrx was the biggest of all Aopehh's marijuana growers. Back in the summer he'd lost his crop for the first time in eight years. Twice the size of Mrx's.

On the second count against Mrx, the Grand Jury foreman was one of my neighbors. True's lover. Broke in my house. Stole everything while I was in Florida.

In both instances, twelve out of twelve had voted to indict Mrx. I set the case aside. Began studying the Tridents. They'd lived on Buck Creek for ten years. Snuck in from Dayton, Ohio. Inherited farms. Kept to themselves. Believed they were pioneers. No one had ever heard of them. Now, everyone did. Reading between the lines it was obvious that the two boys claiming to have been kidnapped and tortured were liars.

THE CITIZEN'S BLADDER front-paged two lambs agate hunting. Out of the dark a marijuana fiend brandished a weapon. He was joined by another wild weed man with a Cerberus that was set upon their handcuffed and gagged bodies. Miraculous escape. They found refuge at the domain of Goose. Goose controlled all the marijuana sold on the backside of Barnes Mountain.

I called Agateman.

"Did you hear about the agate hunters being attacked by wild men?"

"One of them might know agate. The other doesn't. They've never brought me any to cut. They weren't agate hunting."

"I was checking my pigeon records. I always put down the type of weather every day and I noted something. Those boys say they were hunting on December twenty-seventh. My records show that it rained hard all day on the twenty-sixth. They couldn't have hunted in muddy water."

"I've seen the Trident's property. Gate and fence. Big KEEP OUT sign. Those boys knew what they were doing. One got caught stealing a guitar out of some preacher's house. The other broke into the church and stole the sound system."

"Which church did they rob?"

"First Somethin' Or Another in Sugar Hollow."

Next, I phoned a woman kin to Goose.

"I'm working for Swallowtail on that case. Those kidnappings on Buck Creek. Can you tell me much about Goose?"

"Honey, there ain't nothing he won't do."

"I heard that Goose put those boys up to stealing the Trident's marijuana."

"Neither one of them or their parents have ever worked a day in their life. One just got out of jail. Some girl is suing him. Over a baby."

The next afternoon, Sunday, Swallowtail called.

"You been working on the cases?"

"That's all I've been doing."

"The Tridents are supposed to be in my office at four o'clock. Try to come up about three. Tell us what you know. Bring a joint. Oh yeah, have you heard the news? A bulletin just flashed. A body has been found in Aopehh. They're connecting this murder with the three murdered in Harrodsburg and Lexington. All over marijuana."

An hour later, I was at Swallowtail's hillside house. He wasn't there. But Slowtalk was. Vanning on to Swallowtail's Booneville Law

Office we knocked on a locked glass door. Swallowtail let us in. The office was a dark rectangle chute of six square paneled rooms. Slowtalk went to the front room. Tiny TV and coffee maker. I was ushered into the next room with Swallowtail shutting the door behind me. Already seated were two guys. Both, short brown hair, clean faces and beseeching expressions.

"Guess you two are the buzz," I said. They were about five five. A hundred and twenty pounds.

"Zip, Lock, meet No Sweat. He's the person I've been telling you about. Races pigeons. Sends them out with miniature cameras and gathers information. No Sweat, these boys and I go way back to my hippy days. One time at their place we had an apple butter feast. Terrible. Black stuff off the kettle got mixed in. But we ate it."

"Did either of those boys have packs or any hammer like tools when you found them?"

"No."

"Where did you first spot them?"

"Walking along the ridge. Through a telephone line clearing. Carrying garbage cans full of our marijuana. I got around on them. Fired my pistol in the air, twice. Told them to march back. They asked, was I going to kill them. I said, it wasn't my decision. When we got to my brother's I shot twice into the ground. Let him know we were coming."

"They weren't agate hunting. Those cliffs are limestone. Agate comes from shale."

"I marched them back to where they stole my marijuana. Handcuffed them to a tree. They begged for their lives. I said I wasn't going to kill them. But they wouldn't shut up. Kept crying. I ripped my shirt and gagged them."

"What about the dog?"

"One of them fell. Got bit on his leg. I bandaged it. My dog was on a leash."

"Doberman or German Shepherd?"

"Rottweiler."

"Is that like a pit bull?"

"They eat pit bulls."

"What happened next?"

"I went to my house. Made some calls to the law."

"The law?"

"I tried to call one attorney. Couldn't get him. Got another. He'll swear to it. I also called the jail. "

"They say you robbed them."

"They begged us not to kill them. Swore if we let them go they'd give us anything. Never say a word. I got their billfolds. Wanted to know who they were."

"How did they get loose?"

"Those were cheap cuffs. When they got free they went on and stole our marijuana again."

"Brave, weren't they?"

"Next thing we knew, the law was down on us with search warrants."

"You are being sued for one hundred thousand dollars for damages. All they want is money. We've got a good case. You were just defending your property. No Sweat can blow the agate story."

"Will we have to serve any time?"

"If you don't, it'll be a miracle. Whatever happens, they've still got you on marijuana. Over five pounds."

"My brother isn't like me. I can do time. He can't."

"Mom remains the key in all this."

"One Thanksgiving at my uncle's my mother's mother came into the far back bedroom where dad was whipping me with his belt. She took it. Told the drunk, she better never see him whip me again. He left, slamming the door. Later, after she left, I got it worse than ever."

NS

Journal Entry 44 –I CAN'T GET STARTED

January 24, 1983

Back yard. Hammering a geode. Black Hole's voice comes down the hill. "Come up for some tea." Twenty degrees. Gray. My finger

bleeds. Chip of agate. Entering Black Hole's.
"Bleeding pretty bad?"

My hands are cold. I didn't feel it. Takes a
fool to hammer agate." Iodine and band-aid.
"Saw where Reagan went to a black high school.
Told them to hang tight."

"Captain Ronnie."

"Our governor is fried chicken and Miss
America. Our president, an actor. We get what
we deserve."

"I'm once more that segment of the
population that's gainfully employed. They called
me back to work at The Unemployment Office."

"Welcome to nine to five."

"Do you believe God is dead?"

"No. Just stoned."

"CS Lewis says God is dead. Died from
laughing. Do you believe that death is the end?"

"Yes."

"Frost said he had a lover's quarrel with
the world. On his tombstone he had put, if God
will forgive me for all the little lies I told him, I'll
forgive him for the big lie he told me. Have you
been happy. Happy three straight days?"

"I don't know. What is happiness? No."

"Women have no souls. What comes from them? A child. Women kill themselves. Or you. Sometimes both. Look at Audry."

"I read where Meyer Lansky died. The Feds were at his funeral taking photos of everybody's license plates."

"I enjoyed Meyer and Paul. We had many meals together. Fine people. Very moral. Paul, Meyer's son, graduated with me. We roomed together. I stay in contact with him. He was West Point's handball champ. His brother, Wolf, is the mayor of Hollywood, Florida. Meyer died down around there. Paul is a teacher out west."

"I'm working on the kidnapping case for Swallowtail. The Tridents scared those boys pretty bad. Gave them two choices. Dig a deep grave or be buzzard food."

"Man loves sin. The missiles are coming. Sure as night and day. Man is trying to be more than he is."

Black Hole began crying.

"Them that go to church, need to."

NS

Journal Entry 45 – **ROMANCE IN THE DARK**

January 28, 1983

"Better come get me pretty soon if we're to make it on time," spoke Swallowtail. He was calling on Friday afternoon from Aopehh's cedar paneled restaurant, The Cedar Village.

Sensi was sick. Virus. Slowtalk sat in her black Salvation Army coat as we headed to Swallowtail. We stopped, Sensi vomited.

"Hope the law didn't see you."

Back during the election Slowtalk had grown dizzy, throwing up. I took her from the courthouse to the hospital. When Doc's mom found out she was Swallowtail's wife brows lifted. Tongues wagged, Swallowtail's loose wife OD'd.

Actually, she'd eaten bad sausage.

There was a period during the election when Aopehheans were being rumored by the opposition that Swallowtail wasn't married to Slowtalk. That the photo in The Citizen's Bladder showing Swallowtail, Slowtalk and their three children was fiction. The children had been rented.

Near the end of the election we announced a live hour long Swallowtail Show on the local radio. Aopehheans would be allowed to phone-in to WMAR, speaking directly to him. We were to air immediately after a morning of religious zeal. A few days before Swallowtail was to be at WMAR we got word---sabotage. Knowing Lips, it figured. Lips had twenty of his cronies ready to tie up the lines asking loaded questions.

My next door neighbor, NDN, was one of those skinny electronic junkies. A communication guru. Had free television. The gas and electric bills were comical. Long distance calls got flushed in a black box. A Catholic by trade. He eyed Sensi and was good to Annie. NDN had built WMAR. Put in twenty years as Manager. Left with a sour taste when beat out of gaining ownership. Retreated to The Coalwash to fix gadgets. The employees at WMAR continued to revere his presence. Mom's brother, Aopehh's County Judge, said, if you want to know a man's politics, go to his neighbor. He was right. NDN was for Swallowtail. Swallowtail in some strange way represented freedom from the tyranny of the mountains.

Came daybreak that Sunday our counter offensive was surmounted. NDN and I arrived at WMAR as it went on air, praying and saluting the flag. NDN gave orders as though he had never left. WMAR's employees moved enthusiastically. We gained control to a sound-proof room. A long table sat off to one side. There were chairs, a phone and microphones. NDN told me to stay in the room. If anybody knocked I wasn't to let them in. He began packing in a telephone switchboard, tape recorders, phones and ear phones. Made direct link-ups with other WMAR rooms.

NDN and I saw Lips as the tyrannical king and we the peasantry. The whole curse had grown from a black seed planted by Kentucky lawyers. Prior the 1982 election, misdemeanors were handled by County Judges. A County

Judge could be anyone. But the lawyers ganged up wanting all the action. Next thing Kentucky knew, only lawyers could be elected to render justice. It all happened so fast that we went to bed one night and when we woke up Lips was running Aopehh.

NDN got a notebook. I began writing questions. He continued hooking up equipment. Every fifteen minutes he announced the time. Finishing thirty questions, I handed the notebook to him. He scanned the words. "Beautiful," he said. Then we started calling friends.

"Hello, Doc."

"Yeah."

"I ain't got time to explain. Write this down. Word for word. Then, call this number back. WMAR. Act like you are calling in on a live program and actually asking Swallowtail your question. Be sincere. Here is what I want you to say: 'Hello, Swallowtail, did you go to Law School? Lips says you never graduated.'"

"OK."

When Doc called back NDN received the call. Then, on cue, Doc performed the script while NDN recorded onto a reel to reel recorder.

Next, I phoned Rollanotherone with a different question. "Swallowtail, those are sure fine children I saw in the newspaper. Are they really yours? That Lips told me they weren't."

Then Sensi. "I phoned in to tell you how sorry I felt for you when I saw what someone did to your fine wagon and sign out on the Richmond Road. That was just awful. The Lord knows who did it."

The calls and recording continued. Finally, I called myself. "Mr. Swallowtail, I'm calling out here from my old farm on Sand Hill. I know you are a Christian and a pepper farmer. I just want to let you know that we farmers and Christians are behind you."

Time had been inching. We finished none too soon. NDN played back each question in order as I neatly re-wrote them word for word. When Swallowtail and Slowtalk arrived, they wanted to know had we proposed any strategy to counter Lips. Worry was on their faces.

"Swallowtail, these are your 'live questions' you'll be getting in about twenty minutes."

"This reads like No Sweat," spoke Swallowtail, scanning.

"No Sweat and I will take care of everything. Go in the main room. Sit down. Accept calls. Leave everything to us."

After a brief introduction, Swallowtail and Slowtalk were taking 'live calls.' Meanwhile, off in our room, NDN and I were taking the actual live calls. He orchestrated Swallowtail's program keeping Lip's henchmen at bay.

"Ma'am, will you please tell me the question and I will relay it to Mr. Swallowtail."

"I want to ask Swallowtail what year was it when he got caught growing marijuana?"

"Is it true Swallowtail got a thirteen year old girl drunk, then raped her?"

"I hear Swallowtail owes money all over the state. Does he write cold checks? Has he ever taken a bankruptcy?"

"Please hold the line ma'am, there are several callers ahead of you."

Though we had barely lost the election we tried not to show it. When I picked up Swallowtail standing near the street in front of The Cedar Village he slid open my van's door handing me a book. *GUNNING FOR JUSTICE* by Gary Spencer. "Got a joint?" he asked.

Arriving at Morehead I remembered competing there. Four firsts. The 500, 1,000, mile and the last relay. 'EEL OF THE MEET.' "I hope Skaggs doesn't get out on the stage and thank the Lord and Kentucky for everything."

"If you were twenty-eight years old and getting Grammies, you'd thank the Lord, too."

When Ricky took the stage he announced, "I'm glad to see the governor ain't here. I'm glad Francis J. Mills, who called me 'Rocky Scruggs,' ain't here as well."

From out of the dark a voice shouted. "RICKY HONEY, WE IN KENTUCKY KNOW WHO IS NUMBER ONE! KENTUCKY LOVES YOU!"

"The mayor gave me the key to the town! I've tried every lock I can find! It didn't open any of them!" said Ricky.

A girl behind me screamed. "THAT KEY WILL FIT MY LOCK!"

"When I asked my grandfather what he thought about my cousin getting married he said, *well, when you mix nothing with nothing you get nothing.*"
　　　NS

"My great great grandfather was with John Hunt Morgan. Gave Morgan all of his fine thoroughbreds. Some of the best in the confederacy. At the end of the war he hid in cornfields. Never surrendered. As a writer I like to believe I am a lot like him."

NS

Journal Entry 46---**BLUE MOON**

February 7, 1983

"True and Blue offered Wilma one hundred dollars if she would tell them where we hid our marijuana."

"True and Tim, her last lover, use to break in dad's liquor store. Dad knew it. They'd rip off a thousand dollars, a case of whiskey, whatever. The next day, True would act surprised. Blue won't last. Nothing lasts with True."

"Wilma said, Blue was in love with True. Talking marriage."

"In love with True? He's in love with dad's money. True lets everyone know she is from a rich family. Blue thinks he's struck gold. When he finds out she's been with every biker in ten states he'll dump her. Dad says his mother gave his brother everything. And him, nothing. Says the same thing about mom and her family. Over and over."

"Wilma didn't tell them anything. Blue left the hundred on the table. Told her to take it when her memory was working. She made him take it back. He left mad. I can't believe your sister would rob you."

"I wish it were just money."

"Red skies. Red whiskey. Redheaded women.
What else is there."
NS

Journal Entry 47---**I DON'T WANT TO SEE
TOMORROW**

February 12, 1983

Morning. Knock. Badwhite.

"We going agate hunting?"

"Come in. Be ready in a minute."

"Where we heading?"

"South Fork."

"How do you get there?"

"Go across the Wagersville Bridge. Stay straight until we hit a sign pointing to McKee and Sand Gap. Eight miles past that."

"Think we'll have any luck?"

"If we just find part of a geode in this particular creek, it'll be worth the effort. Agateman has mineral rights to most of the good red areas. Not this one. Won't be anyone there with this snow on."

A half hour. Vanning. Hard snowing. Roads covering.

"Let's call this adventure off."

"You joking?"

"No. Do you know where you are at?"

"No. Never have."

A mile later.

"We'll freeze to death."

"Walking will warm us. Let's stop and talk to Rose. He'll know what's best."

Going over a mountain. Parking. Shack. Smoke. Chimney. Curtain moves. Porch. Four growls.

Five minutes.

Rose opens door. Crisp winter air gives way to inner hickory fire.

Yellow vinyl couch. Rose pokes stove. Flames. Two lilac curtains drape doorways. Cedar framed portraits. Jesus. Massacred girl.

Rose. Scabrous. Bristling countenance. Burr. Slatey nails. Blue-white bare feet. Oil stained blue shirt and pants. Factory. Stretched back. Toes toward heat. Rat terrier, lap.

Rose's wife. Gray. Something faded. Shirtwaist. "Honey, wharn't you the one whut was up in here a while back with another-n and his wife?"

"Yeah. Dark Star and Rollanotherone."

"She's a good hearted thang, ain't she? You'll have to be shor and bring her back."

"She's the best I ever set a bucket under."

Rose began checking his pockets. Five knives.

"Elk antler?"

"Elk horn."

"Rose can look at any knife and make one just like it."

"I was offered fifty dollars for that lock back."

"How long does it take to make one?"

Dirty socks. Boots laced. "Three days."

Young beagle.

Terrier issues threats. Rose puts hand over dog's mouth.

"Hit's been reurn't ever since hit's been full grow-d. Hit ain't got no sense. Petted too much. Hit won't let no dog near him."

"Do you know a Johnson that lives up here?"

"He's out on the ridge. A good boy since he got religion."

"He comes to prayer meetin's every Tuesday."

"Seen Agateman?"

"No, I hain't. He come up here and got all I had. Bet I give him five hundred pounds of red. Said he was gonna ship it out west and we'd split. I hain't seen nary cent. Hit's goin' on a year now."

"Nobody has to drop a bomb on America to defeat her. Just let out one big hog call. There'd be nobody left."

NS

Journal Entry 48- **UNFORGETTABLE**

February 18, 1983

The gray wanes. Spring hides beneath the leaves. Sensi is teaching. Wide Eyes stares at Sesame Street.

I'm in bed with books and family photos. This one of Wide Eyes in white lace at Christmas. An embroidered rose on her collar. Innocence stares openingly. Resplendent blue eyes. Is everything alright? Inside that face is my mother's father. My ruby of man. He had tried with mom. Quiet. His theatre was mine. Free run. When I threw snowballs from the balcony, put honey in seats, set bats loose, ran across the stage--he always forgave. Tolerated everybody. Kept the families whole.

Now gone.

My mother's mother said an angel stood at the foot of the bed all night waiting for him on the morning he died.

I can almost believe it.

Mom held his hand as his life disappeared.

Slid his watch off. Gave it to me.

A cheap Timex.

Priceless.

If Sensi or Wide Eyes should go.

I'm so blessed.

"When I was twenty one years old I ran in a three way race for Mayor of Ravenna, Kentucky. Finished second. The other two tied for first."

NS

Journal Entry 49---**JUST ONE OF THOSE THINGS**

February 19, 1983

Dark Star and I. Shale creek. Hunting agate.

"Rollanotherone is paranoid about this year. Blames losing the baby on last year's scene."

"Gotta be a place. Forget The Triangle."

"And Sweet Lick."

"I know a spot on the other end of the county. Not a hard walk. Near the river."

"If we stay low, we might get by."

Purple hepatica. Lime cliffs. Bracket fungi. Rattlesnake plant. Wintermint.

Two soft miles.

Inside an earthy cabin. Boards. Gone existence. Broken furniture. Mason jars. Crockery. Blue and white speckled pans. Rat chewed army jacket. Piece of boot. Walls, faded newspaper. Out back. Rabbit fur. Rusted Prince Albert can. Fresh hole.

A half hour.

Crossing railroad tracks.

Beyond sycamores, Kentucky River.

Knoll. Cedars.

Stretched out, moss.

Opening. Briars and yellow grass. Below, cane breaks.

Dark Star kicks dirt. Black. Limestone bits.

Two creeks and the river.

Jeepable.

"I realized while working at a heat plant that I was only working at the little one getting ready for the big one down below."

NS

"Americans use more water than anybody. But the kind of filth Americans possess is quite repellant to water."

NS

Journal Entry 50---**THE FOOLISH THINGS**

February 25, 1983

Dark-suited Swallowtail came through my door. Shook off snow. Took off his jacket and tie. Laid them across my cannonball bed. Stretched out beside them. "I'm beat," he said, staring at the cracked plaster ceiling. Raising up, he unbuttoned his vest. "Got any smoke?"

"What about wine?"

"No thanks. I'm on a diet."

"Dope diet."

"I don't smoke that much."

"Just every time you see me. Want a killer?"

"No. Too much wastes me."

"Life's a waste. What's the difference?"

The phone rang. Mrx. Was Swallowtail and I coming.

Half way through the joint Swallowtail was laughing. "No Sweat, this is choker."

"Purple Triangle. Want to see Doc's latest?"

Reviewing sketches.

"See that cross on the distant mountain. Look at the daisies sunning by the trailer. All those treelike bushes are sinsemilla. See the KSP on the hats. Look at that State Boy on top of the trailer holding up HI MOM. Check out channel 18's news squad. That's Cecil B. Demille sitting in his chair with the megaphone."

Sensi appeared. Struggled through the door with a double armload of groceries.

"I need to borrow your hubby for a while. Do you mind?"

"Only if you bring him back."

THC'd to the max. Swallowtail and I floated up frozen Cow Creek. Turned off onto a snow covered gravel road going up a hollow toward Cambell's Branch. Stopping. A pack of dogs surrounded my van.

In Mrx's Hollow were hay balers, weed cutters, ploughs, backhoes, bulldozers, tractors, nearly a dozen vehicles, two barns, corn cribs, hogs, cattle and chickens. On a hillside near some pines and cedars was his burned trailer. Off to our right were fenced Dobermans. In a bowl of muddy beans, we were. Surrounded by mountains.

Mrx came out wearing overalls. "Y'all get out and get in my truck. It's four wheel drive."

We sat waiting for Mrx's truck to warm up. Swallowtail questioned. Curious because of the bankruptcy he'd recently filed for him.

"Mrx, who owns that new van?"

"It's not new. Almost a year old."

"Yeah."

"It ain't been started all winter."

"Who owns the tractor in the barn?"

"That's like the van. Belongs to one of my kids."

"Who owns the tractor in your yard?"

"One of the kids."

"Who owns this truck?"

"Belongs to a friend in Indiana."

"Mrx, whose bus is that?"

"Some religious organization. I forget."

As we trucked up Mrx's hollow Swallowtail looked at me. "Mrx, whose goldmine is on your farm?" Mrx. remained silent. We parked at the trailer.

"So this is the eastern seaboard center for all marijuana traffic?"

"See that piece of plastic and broken crate? That's the famous greenhouse."

"The jury should see this. The TV and newspaper left you thinking this was a much larger."

Mrx presented me with his newly written lease made out to J.W.Smith. A point by point counter on every issue raised by The Kentucky State Police. The electric bill showed that J.W. Smith paid Mrx. Then Mrx paid the utility company. J.W. Smith was to grow peppers. Also a paragraph stating that Mrx would not allow alcoholic beverages or any disturbances.

"Mrx, this says, if I happen to get caught growing marijuana, I confess."

"Ibold sings his songs. We may not like his tunes. But they're his tunes. We have to acknowledge them."

"We should go a verbal lease route. Nothing concrete. Tell the court you agreed to pay the electric as long as J.W. Smith didn't exceed some rate."

"I've gotta go with what I have. My wife really believes I had the land leased. If she learns different it would break her heart."

"Mrx, are you from Aopehh?"

236

"My wife was born in the house we live in. I was born three miles straight back. Up on Furnace Road, where they found that body."

"Let's forget that."

"If an old hollow log was filled with hundred dollar bills and Ibold knew where he could find that hollow log, this case might go differently."

"The Judge is up for re-election. With as much attention as is on this case, he'll have to do right."

"Better swear in Mrx's wife and preacher."

"I don't want to hide behind religion."

"Pick up this week's CITIZEN BLADDER. On the front page you'll see who is running for Circuit Judge. Go to the middle. A hundred churches paid for the ad."

"It won't matter. Aopehh is Aopehh."

"Marijuana shortens life. That's its popularity."

NS

Journal Entry 51---**I'LL LOOK AROUNG**

February 28, 1983

MRx's home. Swallowtail and I sit at a cramped kitchen counter. Mrx is frying country ham. The fat sizzles. Mrs. Mrx reaches in a deep freezer pulling out a loaf of her carrot pumpkin cake. Two pot bellies blaze. We chew sapporific meat. Swallowtail and the Mrxs had weathered a day in Aopehh's court. The evidence against them was crushing.

"You did great today. Except near the end. You hesitated too long when asked the name of the person that was leasing your property."

"I wish they'd catch that Smith man," spoke Mrs. Mrx. Her ice blue eyes were upset. Mrx. knew we had the decency to reinforce his lie.

"Tomorrow, you better call Mrs. Mrx. The jury will think twice before they crucify an old man with a loving wife."

"Ibold will break her down. Have her crying."

"If they put me in prison I am not lifting a hand to work."

"At the worst you'll serve three months. The judge will probate."

"If mom hadn't got kicked off the jury it would all be different. Ibold doesn't leave anything to chance. He knows I campaigned for you. Gave me two cases of JW Dant to hand out on your behalf. He hates Lips. Lips rumored Ibold had sex with his stepdaughter. That came close to getting Lips done."

Swallowtail walked into the living room. Above a couch were photos of children and grandchildren. Violets addressed the window. A piano sat in the corner. Beside it, leaned a guitar.

Everyone sat on the couch as Swallowtail sat opposite in a willow limb chair playing the guitar in the dim light. Outside, the afternoon sun was melting the snow. "Several years ago, " spoke Swallowtail. "My grandmother wrote me a letter. She's dead now. She begged that I cut my hair, shave my beard and straighten up so that I might someday go to heaven. She said, there'd be no hippies in heaven. I loved her. Loved her letter so much that I sat down and wrote this next song. It's called, **THERE'LL BE NO HIPPIES IN HEAVEN.**"

The room was suddenly haunting.   A ballad. Swallowtail's story after dying. Meeting his grandmother in heaven. Beside her was Abe Lincoln with his beard. On the other side was George Washington, a revolutionist that grew marijuana. Behind her was long haired Jesus. Swallowtail ended with , *WHEN THE ROLL IS CALLED UP YONDER I'LL BE THERE.*

240

"You come in and out of this world alone. But as long as you are an outlaw you'll always have company."
NS

Journal Entry 52---**GOOD MORNING HEARTACHE**

March 1, 1983

Aopehh's Halls Of Justice.

"If you don't convict this man our marijuana laws are worthless," spoke Ibold.

Five minutes later.

Jury foreman clears feminine voice. "We the jury find Mrx guilty on both counts and recommend maximum sentencing."

Twenty years. Twenty thousand dollars.

Evening. Black Hole's.

"They didn't actually prove anything. No mercy."

"Plato said, every man wants justice for his fellow man and mercy for himself. Don't you understand? The guilt lies in the jury. Not Mrx. F. Lee Bailey couldn't have saved him."

"Mrs. Mrx said they were treated as evil. The jury owned black hearts."

"When you are in the business you must accept the business. I'm afraid Aopehheans. like Liddy, think that when Nietzsche said there was only one sin---cowardice---they think it's holding your hand over a candle. Nietzsche was speaking of moral cowardice. Something

Aophheans prefer not to discuss. That's the issue here. Not a clandestine underworld. Three and four syllable words like guerilla or marijuana frighten. Do you believe marijuana is bad for a person?"

"Bad? Probably. Our government proclaims it'll make you grow tits and cause you to lose all memory."

"Doesn't your generation smoke to feel surrender? God isn't laaaid back. Ignorance is ig nor ing. Aopehheans choose to be ignorant. In this nation it is against the law to die. Stress is just another word for hate. How do stress deaths compare to marijuana deaths? After love-- physical sex--man is always a little sad. He knows he's ruined Eden."

"Swallowtail said they gave Mrx five years for marijuana and fifteen years for lying."

"Swallowtail's problem isn't a marijuana tattoo. But morality."

"No wonder the Sioux believed they were humans and we, white creatures."

"You're starting to sound like Tevis. He hated this place. You can't imagine. No Sweat, it's ok to feel bad. Particularly here. Go ahead and feel bad. We were never meant to feel anything else. Read the Bible."

"I spent over four straight years initially writing *THESE PRECIOUS DAYS*. When I wasn't writing, I was. Found myself in another existence. A private one. Refuge. How many hours a week? How many hours are in a week? I taught myself not to talk about my other existence. Afraid it would bore. I was crazy. Alone with no rules. Much was written while I sat in my van waiting for my daughter to get out of school. Sometimes I parked in the Richmond cemetery. Sometimes, in a large parking lot in the middle of town. One morning while writing I found myself surrounded by police. Local and State. Three cruisers. Blue lights. An officer approached me. Wanted my license. What was I doing? At first he never believed that I was writing. Three of them searched my van. Saw notes. Ink pens. Wadded paper. Notebook after notebook. Words. They had trouble accepting I was a writer. The bank had been watching me for the past month. Had seen me parking. Figured I was casing. The police let me go. Ordered to quit writing. At least, there."

NS

Journal Entry 53 – **THAT'S LIFE I GUESS**

March 10, 1983

Black Hole's.

"Just finished some real fiction."

"What?"

"A thick green book put out by the Ninety-Third Congress. Five hundred pages of fine print. Interviews. Graphs. Photos. Recipes. Called, MARIJUANA--HASHISH EPIDEMIC AND ITS IMPACT ON UNITED STATES CONGRESS."

"Why would you read something like that? You should already know what it will say."

"Some West Point--SAC General with law and medical degrees put on the investigation."

"He's got his hell, we've got ours."

"You've heard, turn on, tune in, drop out?"

"Leary."

"Leary is in this report. He says we should turn on to our sense organs, tune in to the earth's natural energy and totally drop out of man's social games. Detach ourselves from artifacts and symbols. Quit school. The present education methods are neurologically crippling and antagonistic to our cellular wisdom."

"Did you read about Leary being a West Pointer?"

"No."

"Put in three years."

"Wasn't he the assistant professor of psychology at Harvard?"

"Yes. Spends time in Switzerland. Plays games."

"Leary says each person must establish harmony with their nervous system. A person should go to the woods carrying an unopened tin can, a candle and a cut piece of fruit exposing its seeds. You are to sit down leaving one foot with its shoe on and the other bare. As you smoke marijuana you observe the three objects. And meditate on the fact that your body is over two billion years old. Society hates drugs because it gives them visions of beauty and love."

"If society wants to blame its problems on marijuana, that's fine. They're afraid with good reason."

"Establishment experts claim Marijuana stops sperm production, causes birth defects, hormone imbalance, inhibits puberty and causes abnormal muscle movements. Shrinks claim marijuana users suffer psychotic schizophrenia, become apathetic to the point of indolence, have reduced interest in socializing, lose contact with reality and suffer hallucinations and paranoia."

"What do the experts say about alcohol?"

"Marijuana has cumulative properties. Tolerance does not occur with marijuana. The more one smokes the less it takes to get stoned. Marijuana is one to two percent THC. Good hash, fifteen percent. The active ingredient in THC is Delta-9. If you and Delt-9 ever meet, you're hell bound."

"Matthew told Jesus he could not eat some kind of animal because it had six toes and wasn't circumcised Jesus looked Matthew in the eye and told him, it's not what goes into a man's mouth but what comes out of it."

"The report mentioned Coleridge, De Quincy and Huxley. Opium eaters. Termed them, fictional writers of the radical left."

"Far more people have died for their dope than their God. All governments have their murderers. America tries to create sensationalism because it's a non-sensational country. The only thing we want is pussy in our face and four steel belted radials."

"Have you ever made out a will?"

"I haven't got anything to leave. Wills are designed to give lawyers money. I've never seen such a nation needing senseless litigation. It's a reflection on society. Plato said, a nation of lawyers is a nation soon dead."

"Do you dislike Swallowtail because he's an optimist? Or because he is Aopehhean?"

"Because he's like every lawyer---cheap. Where did you get that Congressional Report?"

"From NDN. He interviewed Gatewood Galbraith on WMAR. Galbraith was running for Agriculture Commissioner. A UK Lawyer. About forty. Wears dark frame glasses. NDN had him on WMAR when he was the president of The Kentucky Marijuana Feasibility Council. Galbraith explained why he advocated legalization. And how he'd love to see Kentucky marijuana bases. The switchboard lit up. The first caller was Jim Harris. He lives in the project next door to The Singing Brower Family. They're supposed to be blind. Sell brooms. But they know the difference in a one and a twenty. Jim always called to complain about the sidewalks. The only other time was when the Cincinnati Reds played out on the west coast and the game went past ten o'clock. That was his bedtime. If that happened, he'd call at the beginning of the national anthem sign on asking for the score. Anyways, he was upset that NDN allowed such a hoodlum on air. Told NDN he hoped Galbraith went back to Frankfort and wrecked. One lady called asking Galbraith had he ever smoked marijuana. He said that he and some friends once rented a sailboat off Key West and went out past the legal boundaries of the United States' jurisdiction. They smoked all day. Loved every moment. After the Galbraith interview WMAR lost most of its sponsors. One preacher, Harold Driver, demanded equal time. When Driver came on air he brought in The Congressional Report. After he quoted some paragraphs he left it for NDN. NDN gave it to me."

"When Darwin joined a pigeon club he learned a little about pigeons. And a lot about people."

NS

Journal Entry 54 –**I WISH I HAD YOU**

516 Poplar

Aopehh, Kentucky

March 15, 1983

Bill:

This mild winter is allowing a great breeding season. I'm concentrating on powder blues. The color owns mystery. The whiter the blue and the wider the bars requires careful gene manipulation. Powder blues are recessive in color and pattern. The lighter the blue, the more recessive. As in art, there should be no alliance to a standard. Our pigeons should be expressions of one's heart. All that IS a racing homer. Balance, class, expression, style, type. An artist works out of love. Neither seeks or needs explanations. These fads with degrees of stance, stages of molt, tightness of vent, mean nothing. They're as absurd as if someone handed you a standard for what is perfect love. Our sport is blind. Those in power and those coveted are lack vision. We continue to grow more political. Sentiment hinders success .Inevitably, showing racing homers is doomed.

I was upset today to find my best blue bar young cock floating face-down in the bath pan. My first time in twenty eight years with racing pigeons I had a bird drown. At first, because his feathers were saturated turning him from powder blue to grey, I didn't realize he was my best bird. He must've taken a bath with a full crop. Possibly, another bird bathed at the same time.

"Big I" has started a fan club under the guise, S.H.O.W., Show Homing Organization Of The World. The Europeans can't help but smile. Such ignorance. In truth, this organization is limited to a handful mindless fanciers located in the eastern U.S. Give them time, they'll turn on him."

I hate hearing that The Midwest Classic Show may come to an end. I wasn't aware so many of the members worked in the same factory. Will sure miss the dandelion wine.

Some showmen deny color. Claim to be color blind. Such lie. Is it not color that first grabs one's eye? Contrasts. Uniformity. Richness. Vigor. Beauty. And this be denied? Why then are the birds divided into colors?

It's enough to have me back racing. The innocence with racing is far more compelling.

No Sweat

"When my mother's brothers got through stealing all mom's inheritance they gave me the large painting of her father that once was the centerpiece in my grandparent's home. Even in death they couldn't look him in the eye."

NS

Journal Entry 55 – **SAY IT WITH A KISS**

March 21, 1983

"His father ran a poolroom. Never knew his mom. Raised hogs in Nashville. When his house was burning, ran in and saved a bag of marijuana."

Sensi poured more rum.

Willie at Rupp.

Van rolls.

Heart of Lexington. Hyatt. Parked bus. Mural. Mounted Indian looking downward. Bus sign: **ON THE ROAD AGAIN**.

Parked.

Shivering trench coats pass booklets. First page, The Emerald City, Never-Never Land, creativity and imagination. Next page. Sketch. Sandaled, sleek girl smoking water pipe. Stuff about turbulent 60's, mind altering drugs and the concept of alternate reality. IF WE ACCEPT THIS THEORY THAT REALITY IS ONLY WHAT WE PERCEIVE IT TO BE THEN THERE IS NO LONGER ANY NEED FOR FANTASY. Page ten: LORD, I PRAY THAT THE PERSON READING THIS WOULD RECEIVE IT WITH AN OPEN HEART AND CONSIDER THE REALITY OF YOUR DEATH AND RESURRECTION.

The booklet was printed in Key West.

Black beans and yellow rice. Sensi. Blue bikini. Fresh fat limes. Rum. Boats. Snappers. Groupers. Conch. Lobster. Hush Gulf stream. Dolphins. Blue heavens. Hush Hush. Coconut palms. Clear water. Turtle tracks.

A gust of Kentucky air smacked my face.

Reality.

No introduction. 8:00 PM.

Willie.

Lone Star flag drapes. *WHISKEY RIVER.*
20,000. Lee's beard. Long greasy hair flipped
back. Baggy jeans. Black T-shirt. White, flabby
arms. Worn, maroon track shoes. Red
bandanna. Patriotic guitar strap.

Bobbie. Willie's sister. Hair to the floor.
Bangs keys. Hawk feathers Stetson. Claws Baby
Grand. Silver stars shine from her boots.

Willie nurses Budweiser. Sits atop
amplifier.

*GOOD HEARTED WOMAN IN LOVE WITH A
GOOD TIMIN' MAN.*

Marijuana lingers.

Flood lights stream down. *BLOODY MARY
MORNING.*

Girl lays rose on stage. Security nabs.

*ANGEL FLYIN' TOO CLOSE TO THE
GROUND.*

10:30. LUCKENBACK, TEXAS.

Fat figure with SIR PIZZA on back gyrates
massive rear in my seated face.

WHISKEY Unforgettable *RIVER* again.
American flag unfurls. Willie bows. Throws

bandanna into crowd. Man hands a fifth of Jack Daniels. Willie chugs.

Outside. Temperature dropping. Light snow.

Trench coats continue.

"When my mother and sister came to my home
see my new born daughter just back from the
hospital my sister stole $600 out of my billfold.
All the money I had. A month's work. I never got
a penny back."
NS

Journal Entry 56 – FOOLIN' MYSELF

March 23, 1983

Dropping Wide Eyes off to school, Dark
Star and I vanned toward Lexington's Bluegrass
Airport to pick up a racing pigeon. A beautiful

silver English import. An introduction to my breeding program.

"I got a call late last night. Eddie. He's a dispatcher at The State Police Post in Richmond. Asked, was I clean. Said, better be. Something heavy going down in Aopehh. Rollanotherone stayed scared all night."

"There's always something going down in Aopehh."

"Wonder what the cruisers and TV crews were doing in Aopehh this morning?"

"Probably Lips. He got busted stealing a tractor."

Stopping mid way on Clay's Ferry Bridge. Back up on I-75. Dark Star rolls a joint on my cooler between the front seats. A tiger striped seed rolls on the floor. "Gotta be cool this year. Stay low. Be clean."

"How's our marijuana coming?"

"I've contacted six people. None are interested. There's a big scene in Marion county. Prime tops going cheap. Some grower got by with more than a ton. Aopehh's buyers are going to him. There's one guy that might buy everything in two weeks. Would five thousand be enough?"

"Plenty."

"This guy says Aopehh is too hot. He's been going to Tennessee."

"I'm calling our new site, Delta-9."

"Would hate to get captured there. Only one road in and out. "

"Gotta go camo. One work the tiller. One stay lookout."

"Need us a misty morn."

"Have everything ready. Tools. Fertilizers. Gas. Seed. Packed lunches. Move quick."

"We need more than one patch. April is the best month. Last year we made too many trips. Something like, ten."

"There'll be wild plants come up at The Triangle . There's room for another patch up our grouse hollow."

"I'd just like to raise enough one year so that we could turn honest."

"Build a greenhouse. Start an orchard."

"I want out of Aopehh."

"Five hundred pounds of sens. That would make us honest."

Nearing the Keeneland Race Track we pulled into the airport. Quarantine had gone well. The crated bird was thick with bloom, relaxed and in good condition.

"Let's take the old road back to Richmond."

"Did you see where Nixon kept secret agents on Lennon? Called him a national threat."

"The Maryland bunch say they've never seen dirt as sweet as Kentucky's"

"Last night I read about hemp seed in THE PIGEON. Levi said it made the birds happy. HIGH TIMES is advertising Afghan and Moscow seeds for five dollars each."

"Sure hope we can pull off Delta."

"We will. Our luck will turn."

On our way back we drove under The Clay's Ferry Bridge, crossing a smaller bridge. Part ways up the next mountain there was a panorama of sky, mountains and river valley. We parked. THC heightened our senses. The March breeze caressed our reddened eyes. "This place is old to me," I said. "I've been here before."

After picking up Wide Eyes I let Dark Star out at the head of his hollow. Traveling back I met Rollanotherone. She was at the gate in their jeep waving her arms. Her sausage face was flushed. Beads of sweat varnished her forehead. "No Sweat! Go back to the house! Right now! Take all the marijuana! Get rid of it!"

Rollanotherone's mouth had flapped quicker than she could think. "What?" I asked.

"Tell Dark Star that phone call we got from Eddie was nothing to laugh about. The State Boys have arrested sixty people all over Aopehh! They're to arrest another sixty! They couldn't get some. True and Blue were the first ones they got. Busted them before daylight."

"What do you want me to do with the marijuana?"

"I don't care Throw it in a ditch! Dump it in a creek! Just make certain it's off our property!"

Backing up I went back to Dark Star's muddy front porch. Tails wagged.

"What is it?"

"Rollanotherone has commanded something be done."

"Where did you see her?"

"She all but hit me head on in the driveway. Said the law dogs ain't finished making a big bust. Ordered that all our marijuana be dumped. Acted like the law was headed here any minute."

"It would be stupid for us to move anything, right now."

"I'm just reporting Rollanotherone's ranting. She'll be hot if she comes in here and sees us burning a joint, drinking Kool-Aid and doing nothing."

"I'll call Eddie. He'll know if the heat is close." (Calling).
"Hello. What's happening? Yeah. Is all cool on the eastern front? Thanks. All's well. Twenty troopers arrested sixty Aopehheans. Trafficking. Got True for preludes'"

"I'll call NDN. (Calling). "What are you hearing? All the arrests have been made."

Rollanotherone stormed in. Dark Star and I were rocking near the stove. Triangle spearmint loitered the air. Dark Star's cob pipe lay on a table. "It's OK," he said. "We've checked the situation."

"How do you know?"

"Made some calls."

"Alright. Be fools! You two deserve to go to jail! After they put you in don't say I didn't tell you to get rid of it. They're probably headed here right now."

At five PM we turned on WMAR. Sixty arrested. True, preludin. Blue, preludin, amphetamines and marijuana. At the same time Lexington's local TV channels began coverage of the story. Footage of Aopehheans being brought to jail and fingerprinted. One hog-jawed trooper claimed over a million dollars in marijuana.

Dad had been gone from Aopehh all day. Supposedly a car sale. You never knew. That evening he returned to his car lot, drunk. His special mean drunk. Drunk beyond blues and jazz. Whistling drunk. That same whistling drunk he came home one night after I had driven home from a swim meet. He found me studying for an exam in anthropological theory. Hit me in the face. "I'll show you what the Goddamn fuck college is good for," he said, ripping up my book. I never responded. I knew better. I was an old veteran of his whistling drunk. I learned as a child that it was always best to pretend to be asleep when he came home whistling. I could hear that whistle through the hallway that lead down the stairs to the door that led up the steps to our apartment. That whistle gave me precious warning time to disappear. The last six years that I stayed with him, I slept in a sleeping bag on the floor of our back pine--made porch. It was the best place to go unnoticed. When True's news filtered down mother got wind. She'd been sober enough to cook but the news sent her back to the couch. Her glazed gray eyes turning familiarly Fitzgerald inward.

Sensi, Wide Eyes and I found dad alone in his car lot office. His face was pink. The garbage was full of Budweiser cans. He sat alone, Budweiser in hand. "I'm tired of being a goddamn father," he said. "I can't believe I've worked so fucking hard to wind up with an alcoholic and drug addict. True has ruined my reputation. She's destroying my business. Your goddamn drunk mother will want me to help. Fuck." Another Budweiser was crushed and thrown, missing the garbage. "I've given everything to my children and this is what I get. When are they going to start buying me things?"

All was quiet in dad's modern Main Street house. Caddies and Lincolns rested. Deer heads stared. A stretched coyote rug owned a snarl. Popping another beer, he stood by his slate bar. "I haven't sold a car in three weeks. I'm going to lose my house and everything. Drugs are different than alcohol. And by God I dare any son of a bitch to tell me different!"

Mother laid passed out on the couch.

Around eight PM the phone rang. It was True calling from jail. She asked dad would he go her bond.

"You've made your bed with that scum! Now sleep in it! Get your own goddamn whoring, fat, marijuana ass out!" Dad slammed the phone down. "True said her bond was five thousand. I ain't getting her ass out. Not this time."

Dropping off Sensi and Wide Eyes, I went to visit Doc. Half the Aopehheans arrested were his buddies. Having a late supper with his mom was Aopehh's District Attorney. Upstairs, he and Blackwidow were laid back watching TV. They had just got back from being three weeks at The Colonnades. Neither had a tan. The stay cost Doc's mom twelve thousand dollars.

"Doc, who is the undercover?"

"Two guys and some girl."

"What do they drive?"

"A silver Camero. One drives a brown blazer. Deputy Walkers went into the poolroom this morning with a bunch of warrants. Johnnie Isaacs came up to him joking. Asked if any were for him. Walkers laughed, said, yeah, three."

"They captured True and Blue. There goes the dance school. Do you think Blue would put a narc onto Dark Star? He had some Alaskan buyer wanting to pay top dollar. Dark Star never sold him anything. It's had me worried."

"Nah. Did you see my new dirt bike?"

"When did you get it?"

"Today. Mom thought it would keep me out of mischief."

Back home. Black Hole called. Wanted to know if True was still in.

"Yeah. Dad's drunk. Mom's passed out."

"Are you going to get her?"

"Dad doesn't want her out."

"Being in jail doesn't help. Only makes a person worse."

"I'll call him."

Hanging up and dialing.

"Dad, you should get Tue out. Whatever she is, she's your daughter. No one will think less of you for helping her. It doesn't matter what she's done. Or how many times."

"I'm not going to. If I get her out, she won't come home. She'll just shoot up. And find more trash to shack with."

"Do what you will. You always do. If she were my daughter, I'd be there."

Watching the eleven o'clock news. Same stories repeated. Only, this time, another story. About a decapitated body found at two PM under The Clay's Ferry Bridge. At the exact spot where Dark Star and I had parked. I remembered. When we had pulled in there was a black limo caddy pulling away.

I went to sleep hoping we would not be implicated.

The next morning True called.

"Lips let me out on my own recognizance. Everybody's families came to help them. Not mine."

"What happened?"

"Bullet and another State Boy knocked on our door at 5 AM. The moment I unlocked the door they pushed it open."

"They have a warrant?"

"No."

"Your being the only girl out of sixty arrested upset dad."

"Bullet followed me into my bedroom and watched me dress. Then, handcuffed me. Put the cuffs on Blue so tight it sprained his wrist. They flipped the bed, pulled t every drawer, turned over the couch. Went through my pocketbook, everything."

"They find anything?"

"One joint. And some diet pills. Two weeks ago I was washing dishes when some guy came. A friend of Blue's Collet. Collet had this guy with him that drove a silver Camero."

"What did he look like?"

"About six one. Two hundred or thirty pounds. Long black hair and beard. Was drinking moonshine. Blue let them in. Collet bought some diet pills and they were gone. I was washing dishes the whole time."

True had been ruffed up, illegally searched. Spent a night in jail. And now faced, god only knew. A day later back at her dance school, one to five dangled in her twitching face. The long sleeve leotard hid needle marks. But not swollen hands and red eyes. She was teaching ballet and jazz. Frail ponytails cart wheeled, flittered and pirouetted. She pranced in their midst to *MY DADDY IS TAKING ME OUT*. They watched in the mirrors.

"When I went to get my sister out of jail in Florida she stood by the bars shouting for me to go to Hell. I was already there."

NS

Journal Entry 57 – **SPREADIN' RHYTHM AROUND**

April 6, 1983

Swain dawn. Budding aroma. Subtle Spring. Brooding warblers. Half ton pigeon droppings. Dr. Pepper. Seed-filled Ritz can. Birds en rapport. Chickadee bandit. Velvet coos. Tapping.

Land cruiser. Camo Dark Star. Tiller. Hoes. 10-10-10. Ale-8s. Delta-9. Swisher Sweets. Jasper guerillas. Trespassing. Low range. Logs block. Incline. Clearing. Railroad. Crossing tacks. Styx. Tires paw. Binding angles. Desperation. Rail sliding .Shale obliquity.

Distant train. Tepid sweat. Train closing. Dark Star strong-arms. Last gasp. *Coup de grâce.* OVER! Blur sanction.

Vae victis aura.

Vibrations. Spellbound. Slight smile. Caboose dissolves.

Tillers chew. Fertile black. Nitrogen air. Mother earth. Vigil slips. Delta-9 evolves. V shaped. Near cedars. Fifty thousand seed. Thousand Triangles. Scatter.

Loading. Sweat drenches. Cotton-mouthed. Bending. Sweet stream. Face. Head. Submerges. Numbing. Withdrawn. Black Baptism. Reborn. Alive.

Racing shades. Five blisters. Burst sting. Last hill. Fretting. Slick treads. Hit her at a run! Wheels spin. Bury. Backing down. Pigeon sacks fill ruts. Air released.Twelve pounds. Stick pokes valve. Face absorbs musty air.

"If we don't make it this time, we're caught."

Straddling. Whining. Victory! Sack evidence gathered.

Swisher Sweets. Boughs slap. Scratch. Bouncing. Mired window. Mired faces.

Reductio ad absurdity.

"Harry Dean Stanton was born in Aopehh. A marvelous actor like all Aopehheans. Could've easily gotten his crazy check and government cheese. The MD that delivered him all but raised me. She delivered most of Aopehh. Including Sensi and me. What a devoted soul she was. Special. A combination of humility and intelligence. Oh, the secrets of Aopehh she owned. Amen. She was my neighbor and Godmother. On the day Mr. Stanton was born she said that he was the hairiest baby she'd ever seen. That's how he got his name."

NS

Journal Entry 58 – **I'M GONNA LOCK MY HEART**

April 16, 1983

Vert redbuds. Cream blossoms. Scarlet catchfly. Comely lady slippers. Hairy spiderwort. Rays intertwining. Shadows in midday forest.

Camouflaged. Moving. Triangle. Soulful woods.

God winks. Thousands of marijuana plants peep.

Transplanting. Spacing.

Reverie.

There's a third party out there. The Triangle is gesture.

Below our ridge lays the remains of Mrx's massacre. When leaves turn, choppers will come.

Back in the jeep. Another patch agreed.

Jeeping. Country store. Swishers. Bologna. RC's.

Up river. Kentucky bottom. Cryptic soil.

Images fleet. Railroad tracks. Four novice guerillas. Weekend warriors. Camouflaged. Balancing rifles. Never spot us.

Down faces. Whisper. Step light. Plant.

Miles further. Abandon cabin. Insulating newspaper near chimney. Yellowed *Courier Journal.* April 7, 1930. **GANDI'S WORKERS ARE SHOT**.

River's edge. Weeds. Sycamores chatter. Barking squirrels. Dense sumac hide our narrow strip. We'll come back. Throw down purple.

Afternoon. Wide Eyes cannot take dancing. True is back in jail. Failed to show in court. Given 90 days. Additional charges. Wires have melted. Too much acid.

Nine PM. Aopehh's dungeon. Call.

"Are you sober?"

"Sober? I was never drunk. Who is this? No Sweat?"

"What do you need?"

"No Sweat, please don't tell Wide Eyes I'm in jail."

"She already knows. We saw dad. You can imagine."

"I'm so ashamed."

"It's the breaks. You and I. World without love."

"I'm getting asked all sorts of questions. What should I tell the police?"

"North is south."

"Dad hated his father. He did all he could to make certain I hated mine. He failed."

NS

Journal Entry 59 – **I'LL BE SEEING YOU**

April 25, 1983

Camouflage. Three film canisters of seed. 10-10-10. Hoes. Machetes. Es #1. An American flag pin rests on pocket flap of my army shirt.

"Guess you heard about True?"

"No?"

"Went into convulsions."

"Yeah. They took her to the hospital. She's OK."

"Where's she at?"

Back in jail."

Mom lay swollen drunk on the fake leopard mohair couch in dad's modern Main Street house. She'd stolen two thousand dollars from him, lying when caught. And lying about stealing whiskey from the next door neighbor's kitchen. She'd given the money to True. Hoped it would help. The cash went straight for pills. True's reason for convulsions. When dad got it all straight in his head he slapped and backhanded mom's face. Busted her lip. Pulled out hands of her hair. Cursed. Threatened divorce. Bloody lips swelled. Glazed eyes reddened above black. Mother rarely moved. Vodka played Russian Roulette. The trophy house was again still. Dad stayed away from home. Claimed he lived in a car. At nights, in Richmond and Lexington bars, he sang blues to young drunks. Strangers. Old Fitz 86 and water filled his scarred knuckles. The same scars he got when killing a hitchhiker. Once a week he kicked in mom's locked door, cursed, smacked, hit, smashed furniture. Then, returned to his whores and holes.

Some things you can't outrun.

Blisters. River bottom. Soft. Marvelous. Rootless. One side, river. The other, redbuds and dogwoods.

"Looks like a HIGH TIMES centerfold."

Finished.

Heading back to jeep. Salem's discovered.

"Fresh."

"Too fresh."

"Maybe the Buckeye that owns this land?"

"Rollanotherone is pregnant again. Two months."

"Christmas baby?"

"Yeah."

"Wide Eyes was born on December twenty-sixth. We have it on June twenty-sixth."

"Mom asked, why do you write about death? It
bothered her. Why don't you write about
something else? She asked me the night before I
met Marsha Norman."
NS

Journal Entry 60 – **GUILTY**

April 27, 1983

Lucid. Blithe. Leaves stretch. Clover. Pigeons ruffle plumage.

Up steep Sixth Street. White wooden houses eave to eave. Black Hole's domain. Rusty gutters. Cracked foundation. Black screen porch.

A wren saluted. Bees worked.

"No one knows truth. It horrifies," spoke Black Hole, fetching two Ale 8-1s. "Even when they hit the bread lines, people will always have their six packs or Ale-8s stashed. Or their radial tires. This nation doesn't know hunger. Hunger is a western concept. A toy. The only starvation is abstention of wisdom. Bellies may protrude in the midst of ribs. But the hunger is all western. Nature runs the show. She has her checks and balances. Mountains dissolve. If a group of deer are left on an island they don't need western ideology. Keats said that death was life's high mead. Malthus and Darwin approached with slide rules. Nature laughs."

Annie was sniffing out a snake. "Leave that snake alone," I said. "Get over here."

"Do you think there will ever be peace on earth? Dogs are like humans. They don't know whether to bark or bite. Their curiosity is aroused and they're scared of their own ignorance. The snake is giving Annie the most precious of gifts."

"What's that?"

"Death."

"Time is the greatest gift."

"Time is slow death. Sensi says she's gonna get you to apply for teaching again."

"I'd never get hired."

"I'm qualified to teach at Columbia. But not at Aopehh's High School. Kentucky ranks last in education. Who cares. Just as long as we've got a good basketball team. Education is completing a term paper entitled, *WHAT THE S.E.C. MEANS TO ME.* Man has a soul. Despite all evidence to the contrary. Aopehh is a poor place in a desperate time. The backwater of society. The sludge. You'll not find a soul here. All we can do is pretend and chant hymns. Wait out our time. If you can show me any real beauty you'll be another Faulkner."

"Don't forget Jesse Stuart."

Laughter.

"Dark Star was in our office carrying Dante."

"I told him you'd get him an extension on his unemployment. And to slide you a few bucks."

"That's the typical mentality of your generation. Has it ever occurred --- qualifications."

"With Captain Ronnie? Are you joking?"

If you'll observe what Aopehheans call love you'll see hate. Hate is all America has. Our only real surplus."

"I hate Aopehh."

"That's normal, for here. Freud is out because he offered no solutions. Truth is horror. There is only tragedy. The church excommunicated Copernicus and Luther. Lenny Bruce said that when he was interested in the truth he was interested in the truth. And that's the worst kind of truth to be interested in."

"Thoreau would've seen beauty in Aopehh."

"Thoreau's soul was cities. Not some frog pond. He said that any man more right than all his neighbors makes a majority of one. Ask any ghetto black what that means. Not an Aopehhean. In Aopehh, sex takes the place of truth. Incest. Jesus never said he was going to tell the truth. He said HE was the truth. You know what happened to him."

"Not really. I'm tired of Jesus. I'm Jesused out. How many have to keep on dying in his name? "

"Freud saw the unconscious as nasty. He said that fear and repression are cultural necessities. The practice of honoring women is a myth homosexuals don't recognize. Women are humans, not possessions. The church and military are run on homosexual libido. Goethe said that man needs another man. That he'd create a second man for himself if none existed. Homosexuals suffer self hate. America puts them in jail, mental wards or on comic strips."

Walking inside the old porch to his kitchen Black Hole began boiling water. A Spartan existence.

Such a lonely and brave soul.

The distant bedroom oozed in jazz. Tea in hand, I went to his dim bedroom and began rocking. On a mantle at the foot of his West Point blanketed bed was a photo of his father. A spectacled, small man. A silver beaver pendant draped the picture. "They say your dad was the best scoutmaster there ever was."

"He always told me he was nothing."

"The opposite of my dad. Once a month every Sunday he'd call his mother and curse her out. He hates the family he came from. The family he married. And the family he made."

"No Sweat, be grateful your father is who he is. Look at what he's given you. A fertile heart."

"Did you go listen to your friend, Tevis?"

"Yes. He quoted Keats. Did a lot of cursing. The UK professors were like groupies. Signed autographs. Tevis has handled alcohol better than I thought he would. A doctor went with me. He said that he thought Tevis was a man of means. Now, he wasn't sure."

Laughter.

"I reckon we'll try to leave on May twenty-fifth. Thirteen weeks on Singer Island. Money is going to be a problem. But I can't take a summer here."

"That summer day that Will Lang's daughter, Luisa Lang, called me at the at The Colonnades Beach Hotel's swimming pool I did as she asked and walked across the street to her apartment. She wanted me to read what I had finished of her father's novel. She asked me if I had enough of his notes to finish the work. As I read to her I thought she passed out from being drunk. I left her alone and went back to my apartment to put up the manuscript as I had so far done and then went back down to the beach where I saw Jeff Schmidt, a lifeguard and diving friend of mine that was working on duty. He asked if I had heard the news about Luisa being found dead. I rushed back across the street and found the police there having already blocked off her room with caution tape. I had no idea that she had taken pills before I came to her apartment. I had no idea that as I read to her she lay there dying in front of me. On our first meeting she had told me that the first time she ever got drunk was with Ernest Hemingway. That he had gotten her drunk when she was a little girl by giving her several glasses of wine. The same kind of Burgundy she was serving. She told me that she never lied about anything except her drinking. When her mother flew down to have her cremated she gave me some of the letters that Ernest Hemingway had written to her father. I sold these to Joseph Madellena in California for almost nothing because he told me he wasn't sure if EH had written them. That was one of the biggest lies ever. I took the money that I got from the letters and was able to go in partners with my lifelong friend, Larry Lynch, on buying a boat that we hoped would now allow us to scuba dive off the outer reefs of Florida and the Bahamas. Shortly after, Larry was killed in a motorcycle accident and his wife gave me the other half of the boat which I had named after my mother. Mom had showed up at the dock one day where I had the boat, singing Happy Birthday to me as she brought the license to the boat. I boated her up the Kentucky River. As we sat in the flybridge she talked about the old days when I was a boy and how she and I would come down to the river and play. A week later, she dropped dead of a heart attack. I could never sell that boat. Some things have no price."

NS

Journal Entry 61---**COMES LOVE**

May 1, 1983

I never figured on Sensi. A class ahead. Nice.

I was always ashamed to bring friends to my home. Our apartment was dirty. Mom could be down. Dad sold fruit on the street. Now he hustled whiskey.

One evening a football player asked me to fetch Sensi. He didn't have transportation. She was giggly. A child. Girl. Freckled. Long red hair. A dream.

Two days later at the water fountain my shoulder was tapped.

"When are you going to take me out?"

"Tonight."

Picking her up at her small house I felt better. She wasn't rich.

Her minis were very. Continuously chattered in a chilling voice. We kissed.

That first year she was tease and insecurity. One night I wrecked a $50 Comet. A tractor pulled us out. Her ribs were broken. She wouldn't tell her parents.

Her dad was silent. A railroad engineer. Smoked cigar stubs, read the paper. Watched me out of the corner of his eye.

Her mom tolerated me. I wasn't a good catch.

Sensi was special. Her parents objected to her taking dance or cheerleading. They drove old Fords.

She had her own bedroom. A canopy bed. Dolls everywhere. Kept a picture of me.

Her two young brothers constantly fought. One was hygienic. The other, red-headed, freckled, country.

I wrote love letters. One word sentences. Only she and I knew what they meant. She loved them.

In caves she helped dig Indians. Became the race secretary of Lexington's Racing Pigeon Club. Knew every wildflower. Owned respect.

Some said we looked like brother and sister. She was valedictorian. Had also been her graded school's valedictorian. Won all academic honors.

On Saturdays she worked for ninety cents an hour for ten hours on Saturdays at The Five And Dime. Spending money.

Working in a light bulb factory that first summer she earned enough to go to college. Her parents wouldn't allow her to accept a five thousand dollar academic scholarship to Transylvania.

She was pre-Med. 4.0. Worked as a secretary for the Biology Department. Saturdays, at The Five And Dime. Sundays we went to her family's Methodist Church in the country. Vocal amens.

By my side in all things. She encouraged college. No one in either of our families had ever gone. She taught me.

The boisterous swim coach had a place in his heart for me. Gave me a chance. She came to every meet. Boring things. I swam distance.

College was her cake. Brilliant memory. Entire Biology notebooks, word for word, precisely regurgitated. Her parents told her no medical school. Too much money. She cried. Her junior year she gave up being a doctor.

When she became a senior she wanted us to marry. I was scared.

We stood. Her in a purple velvet mini. In Eastern Kentucky University's 's Chapel. Only three there. Two brothers and a girlfriend.

For twenty years she's been the most precious part of my life. Has coped with my darkness.

If her sweet love failed.

She's steel. My partner. Haunting.

What strength I own.

I never figured on her.

"I went hunting with Jack. Just he and I. The
original godfather of Kentucky red agate. I snuck
off from him playing a trick. Along the creek I
made grouse tracks in the snow. Each larger
and larger. The last track must have been a foot
in length. Rose tracked them. Looked at me.
Never said a word. A glorious day. Found a
gorgeous red agate One minute after I let him
out he went into his garage. Got his shotgun.
Blew his head off."

NS

Journal Entry 62 – **SOLITUDE**

May 12, 1983

Against the cold van window I rest my head.

Rain drops stream connecting down.

A grackle disappears in gray.

Alone.

Out of step.

Waiting.

Cursed. Blessed. Vanquished.

Tears match raindrops.

She's teaching.

She's learning.

I'm waiting.

Starlings fuss on the ball field

Next to an empty beer can.

Winds move city trees.

Traffic. Power lines.

Construction.

Work.

Schools are about out.

Education at end.

Never thought I'd lose.

Come on sun.

Come on death.

I'm worn out

Waiting.

"All my life I had studied early mankind. When I wound up working at the heat plant I sure never knew that I would be working with them."

NS

Journal Entry 63 – **DID I REMEMBER?**

May 17, 1983

Five beers deep in the heart

Of lush lime, olive and Kelly woods.

Emerging shadows dally, trace.

Jarring jeep rattles ruts.

Doves coo queer three beat mourns.

Sanctuary.

Crooked Creek.

"I found him over there. Part of his hand still up to his face."

"He was scared to look."

Wildflowers. Scarlet.

"And he lived back in here?"

"Lived good."

"Take me to his place."

"His German wife, Heidi, still there?"

"Good lookin'?"

"Alright."

"Big tits?"

"No."

"Long hair?"

"Yeah. Blonde."

"Blue eyes?"

"Brown."

"This road was like this that day."

Gear down.

Cool shale creek.

"Up there's the place."

Faded, two-story, barn-chalet.

Cluttered porch. Open doors.

"Hello? Anybody home?"

Cozy couch. Walls full of books.

Stairway. Plants. Agate.

"Hello? Anybody home?"

Silence.

A gentle place.

"And Bob lived here?"

"Yeah. Bob was OK."

Bob was a Yankee.

Three times across the chest.

Once up close---shotgun

In the face.

"He's buried over there."

Dirt.

Death wish.

Anyone home?

"The State Boys said, mafia."

"I heard, Heidi."

"The State Boys, probably."

"Maybe them two off Pea Ridge."

Six beers deep.

"Stop. I've gotta piss."

Aopehh.

"Everyone said I should be dead. They looked at my crushed van. Saw where half of me went through the windshield. My wife's brother said Jesus saved me. Mom and dad said to get up and shake it off. The surgeons said I had to have a major neck operation. If not, would be paralyzed. Instead, I asked to go through an intense physical therapy program. Was OK'd for a week. Until my insurance company got the first bill and stopped the $500 a day expenses. While there, I was tested by a young psychiatrist lady from New York. About five hundred yes and no questions. Three days later we met alone. She said I lied on the test. That I'd gone radically off the scale in respect for authority. And it was impossible that I had had a happy childhood.
  ---I never lied."
                NS

Journal Entry 64 –**IT'S SO EASY TO BLAME
                THE WEATHER**

May 18, 1983

"How were the Kinks?"

"Loud. LOLA collapsed Rupp.

"They do *ALL DAY AND ALL OF THE NIGHT?*"

"Yeah. A fight broke out near the stage."

"Much marijuana?"

"Tons."

"I spoke to Swallowtail, yesterday. The Tridents paid fifteen thousand to get all charges dropped."

"What a rip."

"We need to check our scenes."

"All this rain. They should be doing something."

"Delta at daybreak?"

"Bring a sprayer. Could be a blue mold year."

"Did you hear about the jail?"

"No."

"The State Fire Marshall closed it. Roundbelly, Dillion and Possum got mad."

296

"What's happened?"

"Roundbelly commandeered a blue Church Of God bus. Backed it up to the jail. Had posters, AOPEHHEAN PRISONERS WITHOUT A JAIL taped to the sides. Took fifty prisoners on the bus down in front of the capital."

"In Frankfort?"

"Yeah. They paraded all day. Guess where they went for supper?"

"Church?"

"No. MacDonald's. It's no longer you deserve a break today. It's you deserve a break out. They piled into MacDonald's. Roundbelly was first in line. After Big Macs and fries they got hot fudge Sundays. Roundbelly ate four Big Macs and drank three shakes. All on TV."

"Celebrities."

"Somewhere out there, there is a blue church bus full of Aopehhean marijuana prisoners. Prisoners with no jail. Only stopping for Big Macs. And sometimes, an order of fries."

297

"I was handcuffed and taken to the Pattie A. Clay Hospital. The Saturday night third shift doctor sewed 37 crude stitches into my eyebrow as his assistant preached to me about Jesus. Then, I was re-cuffed and taken to The Richmond, Kentucky jail. Stripped and searched. Given a paper-like gown that went to my knees, open down the back. Also, a pair of sandals four sizes too large. Then placed alone in a frigid concrete room, five feet square. Its door was solid steel. The only thing was a small, lidless, stainless steel commode. I laid on the bare floor, curled, trying to get warm, fighting pain, a headache and a light that never went off. I took some of the bandages that had been put on my head from the wound and re-wrapped them across my face to help stay warmer. After three days I was brought out and told that I was being charged with attempted murder. Then, returned back to the room."

NS

Journal Entry 65 – **YOU BETTER GO NOW**

May 19, 1983

Ten PM. Five blisters goad. Tub fog rises. I'm face level with water. Outstretched hands. Filthy. The long day's black glistens. TALES OF BRAVE ULYSSEUS carves the air. "How his naked ears were tortured by the sirens sweetly singing...carving deep blue ripples in the tissues of your mind...tiny purple fishes run laughing through your fingers."

THE COURIER JOURNAL lays. Front page. **DRUG CASE IS CLOSED UNDER STRANGE CIRCUMSTANCES**. Sitting wine down. Rhine spills across the headlines.

Back porch. Clump of muddy camouflage lays over old boots. Outside, rain trickles. Musty. Washing tracks. Breathing life. My pigeons are roosting. Each in their spot. Heads tucked. Some sitting on their belly. Some shifting weight on one leg.

At daybreak, Dark Star and I appeared at Delta-9.

"My wildest fantasy!"

"Can't see the weed for the weed!"

"We best get to work."

"What do you guess? Six? Seven thousand?"

"They're so hearty."

"Nobody could spot this. Or believe it."

"We got caught here, our ass is grass."

"Our grass will be grass."

"Can you see the law trying to count all this?"

"They can only count to twenty four. That's why they made that law."

"Seven thousand three footers."

"How does this compare to Mrx's field?"
"Much better."

"We should transplant as many as possible. More space. More buds."

"I can't see the marijuana for the marijuana."

"Be careful stepping. Those are thousand dollar bills."

"I'll dig. You transplant. Love to see two thousand virgins."

Twelve straight hours. Sweat. Cramps. Blisters. Most the plants were still bunched. In fresh cleared ground I dug five hundred spaced holes. In each, went three plants. Delta-9. Now, a "V" along a cedar hillside. Such calm.

Everywhere, the smell of mint. Glorious Guerilla Garden. Secret stage. No audience invited. Ancient saw-tooth plant. Morality. Religion. Life. Death. Ignorance. Wisdom. Laughter. Tragedy. All entwined. Friend or foe. Place and time dictated.

Reaching for the newspaper. Wet. **DRUG CASE CLOSED UNDER STRANGE CIRCUMSTANCES**. Lips was playing his fiddle. Dark melodies. This time, some Courier Journal staffer, Dunlopper, was scratching. Truth was trying to whisper. Some Buckeye got nailed by the law dogs. At first the dogs thought he was stuck. That thought vanished when the Buckeye staggered. Inside his stolen Mercedes was a leather brief case with a pound of sinsemilla, eight ounces of coke, a book, *HOW TO CULTIVATE MARIJUANA*, unidentified pills, drug paraphernalia, prescription drugs in improper containers, chemistry books, a ledger listing names, fifty thousand cash and references to foreign and Lexington connections. The Buckeye had laughed. He was the former Kentucky governor's nephew. Soon thereafter the Buckeye's charges were all unexplainably dismissed. Compliments of Lips. Lips had received a phone call from Mad Rita, Lexington's socialite charity belle. Nobody said a word. But the matters got restirred when the FBI searched a Lexington businessman's home, Mr. Sholom Aleichim. Aleichim was close with Kentucky's governor. In the midst of the investigation the Buckeye's name kept surfacing. Lips refused to discuss the case.

"Most of my cousins are in prison. The ones not are lawyers or preachers."

NS

Journal Entry 53 – **IF DREAMS COME TRUE**

May 26, 1983

Friday afternoon. 101 degrees. Overcast. Swarms of people. Pavement. Swelter. Sweating. Crying. Artificial. Parents scold. Frustration. Tepid impatience. Coca Cola. Ice cream. Babies lugged. Strolled. Dante. Wheelchairs. Castle. Pirates Of The Caribbean. Space Mountain.

Haunted Mansion. Utopia. Never-Never Land. Magic Kingdom. Valhalla.

Heartattackville.

Since daybreak, Sensi, Wide Eyes and I have been in Disneyworld. Arrived after vanning nine hundred miles nonstop. Our annual pilgrimage. Fifteen bucks a head. Six straight years for this ritual. Wide Eyes' fourth. Swallowtail's penniless daughter's first. A corpulent Cuban strumpet moderately clad in buffoonery breaks line.

Get use to it.

This scorpious maze had to be envisioned on LSD.

Man jumped out of his monkey suit, alright. Watch things climbed.

Liter. Subterranean mole men radar.

Walt ain't dead. His brain, Elvis' and Kennedy's are in an aquarium.

For another fifteen bucks we could probably see them.

Lilywhites baste. Turn lobstery. Hooray for cancer! Three caterwauls for the liquid filled bubbles sprouting on skin! Ain't this fun! Check wallets.

Magic ain't cheap.

Gaping hillbillies trudge. Gawk. God, I'm hungry. Wish I had me a Big Mac. And a new T-shirt.

Land of the fat. America! I'd sing to Thee if my mouth wasn't fulla your tasteless pork chop! Relish on blouse. Mustard on pants. Barbecue on chin. Belch. Head to the next ride.

Fidel's tribe are gorgeous, when young. Slick. Lean. Olive. Gleaming smiles. Attentative eyes.

We got in the rat trap by monorail.

Culture captives.

Wide Eyes gazes at me. "Oh Daddy, I've found heaven."

Ratworld's staff moonlights making toothpaste commercials. Everybody is a virgin. Where's Haley Mills?

At two o'clock we sat down on a street corner waiting for the three o'clock CHARACTER PARADE.

Imagine, Aopehh having a character parade.

As the nearing minutes ticked down individuals grow into shoving crowds. At two thirty a patella stabs my lumbar. At ten till some warthog squashes in beside me. Two hundred and ninety pounds vs. one hundred and forty.

If the Spartans could hold Thermopylae I can hold this spot.

Maybe.

Her hair is curly bronze. Pock marked face. Light mustache.

Across the crowd-lined street the masses jockey for positions. One child has his head hung in between guard rails. Once freed, whipped. An elderly lady gets her foot crushed by a roving wheelchair.

Is there a doctor in the house.

Suddenly, Wide Eyes screams in agony. Her one dollar popsicle is stuck to her tongue.

Yanking.

Blood gushes.

The drums begin.

Brass crashes the heavens.

Oompah.

Ah, the parade.

The only wish I have on any star is to disembark. Cut and run.

Finding refuge in Ratworld's City Hall, Sensi tries to acquire a room in The Polynesian Village. I sit on the outside steps. Thousands of faces. Thousands of Ratworld T-shirts. Five American flags top surrounding buildings. Blue, yellow, orange balloons escape grips. Goodbye cash.

Heaven must be tired of those balloons.

"No Sweat! We've got a room!"

There is a God. "How much?"

"One hundred and forty dollars."

"Plus tax." Thank you, Jesus.

Later.

Being bumped and jarred on the Indy 500.

Riding the skyway. A brilliant black grackle grackles. Fans boattail. Below, white stains.

My sentiments, too.

Aboard tiny boats being funneled into cool darkness. Spanish galleons fire cannons. Pirates rape ports. Prisoners bargain escape. Captains drink rum while playing with stolen jewels. Shipmates chase wenches.

Am I back in Aopehh?

Epcot.

Day's end, The girls and I watch a 3-D movie. *JOURNEY INTO IMAGINATION*. Four children, black, yellow and white run across an open field.

For a moment I was a butterfly, a seagull, the cosmos. One with all things living and dead.

Then it was over.

We step outside.

Plastic flowers.

"One trip to The National Pigeon Show in New
York I stopped and picked up Francis Barnum
at his home in Ohio. He'd been with Farah
Fawcett the past two weeks, sculpting her for a
company that was modeling dolls. Tough job.
The State Boys pulled us over in New Jersey. A
Kentucky van. Made me take out all my pigeons.
Stacked them on the side of the interstate. Each
crate searched. One trooper put a handful of
dried sugar cane that I was using for liter in a
bag. Sent off for analysis."

NS

Journal Entry 67 – I CRIED FOR YOU

Colonnades Beach Hotel
Room 4150
Palm Beach Shores
Singer Island, Fla. 33403

June 12, 1983

Dear Black Hole,

If Aopehh becomes too much you are
welcome to reside in my loft. The birds
understand. Wonderful shrinks.

Honest. A law here allows only one car
load of Kentuckians at a time. Smart island.

The weatherman says it's hailing in
Kentucky. Ain't that the truth.

There's a fat farm within the hotel. Too
many chocolate truffles. Women desiring outer
perfection. The need an inner fat farm much
more.

Wide Eyes splashed a drop of water on one
of the inductees at the corner of the pool. The
bathing cap and shades invoked management.
Wide Eyes has been using tanks since age two.
Scares the hell out of observers. Just in the pool.
Snorkels the inlet. Jumps off the pump house.

Sensi and I saw our first rainbow around
the sun. Palm Beach ordered it. Probably, Rose.

I've made fourteen dives thus far. The pace will pick up in the next two months. Shark stories saturate the area's media. More sharks here than any spot on earth. Most of them, Jewish.

Spent a full day on an old PT boat with a retired Cuban Navy Officer. Just him and me. And a quart of rum. He was bad lonely. Showed me photos of his dead wife. Spilled his entire life. Made me dive for his wife's pearls he once accidentally dropped. Never found them. Did have a black six foot cuda stare me down.

Give Annie a scratch behind her ear.

No Sweat

"For several summers Sensi and I roomed next door to John D. MacArthur at The Colonnades Beach Hotel on Singer Island. John always gave us any key to his hotel because I'd bring him down a country ham and a gallon of moonshine. There were several mornings when he would join us at our table for breakfast. And in time he would take food from our table and pitch it to his nearby pet ducks. One day he stole a slice of tomato out of my sandwich. I wasn't so concerned about him taking that tomato as I was his taking the tomato I was married to."

NS

"On the day I set a record at Irvine Graded School for getting four paddling on the same day I shared that fourth with my best friend, Stevie Blanton. We walked back into the classroom all but smiling. Important to save face. If Stevie hadn't committed suicide he might've made a good writer."

NS

Journal Entry 68 – **A FINE ROMANCE**

June 25, 1983

"Bye. Take care."

Swallowtail's daughter got on the plane.

"I can't believe Swallowtail never sent you a dime for her care."

"Honey, he's a lawyer."

"He still owes you five hundred dollars."

"He owes everybody. That's why he's moved to Wickliffe."

Leaving Ft. Lauderdale's airport we drove to Carol and Charlie's. Carol had taught school with Sensi. "Kentucky is in today's paper," she said, opening her door. The headlines read: **WILL DRUG PROBE BLOW THE LID OFF LEXINGTON**. The New York Times followed. LEXINGTON, KY.---**COCAINE FOUND IN THE HOME OF GOVERNOR'S CLOSE ASSOCIATE**. A federal grand jury was looking into illegal prostitution, gambling, cocaine and marijuana trafficking---among Kentucky horsemen, socialites and politicians. Lots of no comments.

I set the paper down.

"What's it say?" asked Sensi.

"The FBI raided Sholom Aleichim's house. Found a bunch of stuff connecting the governor. Sholom flew to Europe. Can't be located. They also nabbed the president of Matonia Race Track. He's head of Thrifty Spend Farm. The former head of New York's FBI, whom Governor Sanders named to head Kentucky's Justice Department, was fired. He helped Kentucky's Transportation Secretary tape a conversation with a man who thought his twenty-two thousand dollar political contribution secured State Road contracts. He's the man who initiated The Kentucky State Police Special Investigation Unit. They did the corruption inquiry."

"And?"

"There ain't no more ands. Everything has been abolished."

"What about Mad Rita?"

"They won't touch her. Wouldn't be any more contributions."

"Any mention of Lips?"

"Andy Divine, the sheriff in THE MAN WHO
SHOT LIBERTY VALANCE, and I, flew the same
racing pigeons. They were the Sion strain that
originated in France. We got our birds from
Charles Heitzman, Jeffersontown, Kentucky, the
man that imported them and was both of our
friends. Andy had a cat trying to get his birds
and he caught the cat and tied a stick of
dynamite to it and let the cat go after lighting
the fuse. The cat ran straight underneath his loft
and exploded, blowing up his loft and all his
racing pigeons."

NS

Journal Entry 69 – **BACK IN YOUR OWN
BACKYARD**

June 28, 1983

Sensi and I sat on a grassy bank fishing with grasshoppers. Pitts Lake. Pines and oaks. One blue heron. We were laughing. Going to live forever. She spoke about my writing. We stepped to the water's edge. Mixed in the grass was spearmint. A grouse and her chicks froze. A hawk circled high. A red-topped woodpecker undulated. Coming to shade. An icy spring. We waded out to our waist. Dropped lines. Caught fish with scarlet eyes and painted blue streaks. Bare feet in blue clay. Gnats near ears. Dragonflies warred.

Then we heard something. Not a yellow jacket. Not June bug. A quick hum. A hummingbird. Zipping. Unique grace. Appeared and disappeared without a care. In front of us was a sycamore. Lime leaves surrounded by pale. Twenty feet up the hummer disappeared. Along one of the lower branches was a silver nest. Reflecting greens sat carefully eyeing.

I climbed. The hummer flew. Two babies. Big as nothing. All eyes. Spongy nest. Lichens. I held still. Then, a buzz. Little by little the buzz grew braver. Hovering. Finally, inches above her babies. Poking needle tongue into their beaks. Releasing sweet wildness.

I woke up.

"Dark Star was rushed to the hospital. Intestines twisted. I got there as soon as I could. Pale. Death's door was upon him. I gave him my best red agate. My heart placed it in his weak hand. All gesture of hope I owned. The last round up. He'd never found a red agate. Hunted hard. But never a smell. I knew he was going to die. At best, just a few hours away. At least he would go knowing he had finally gotten a Kentucky red agate. The next day he was sitting up all but ready to go caving. The agate rested on his tray. Damn, I thought. Now that you've survived, do you think you could give my agate back?"

NS

Journal Entry 70 – **EASY TO LOVE**

Colonnades Beach Hotel
Room 4150
Palm Beach Shores
Singer Island, Florida 33403

July 4th, 1983

Dark Star,

It's been a few hours since I read your
letter re disappearance of Delta 9. I was
beginning to feel almost at ease. Aopehh, a
distant dream. Tonight I feel like I am right
there. Gutted. She wields her dull axe. Death is
my only out. How am I to walk a gentle path
when this world murders? How can I pretense
sanity in fiction?

Mom lays drunk. Dad says that True is in
a Rehabilitation Institute in Corbin. Thirty days
in lieu of jail. Likely, she'll be in less than a
week. Dad fixed it with Shy. Mom and dad will
pick her up on their way down. When we left
home she was on bond facing seven charges.
Dad said she then disappeared. The clinic was
robbed. Next thing, she was calling from the
Richmond jail on new drug charges. Dad said to
hell with her and left her in jail. A few days later
he saw ambulances scream by the car lot
headed for Miller's Creek. True and Blue had
somehow finagled out of jail and wrecked on the
Miller's Creek straight stretch. Flipped a pick

up. When the law got through they went from the hospital back to jail on more charges. Blue headed for the pen. But shy fixed True.

Sensi's mom sent us this week's CITIZEN'S BLADDER. On the front page are two cows standing in a pond. There's also a story about two jumping off the bridge. One broke his neck.

I cannot know my place in this madness.

I remain frightened.

No Sweat

"Paul Sion was the greatest racing pigeon flier in France. Mons Stassart in Belgium. Charles Heitzman, Jeffersontown, Ky., the owner of Heitzman Bakeries in Jeffersontown, Kentucky, bought their best. He became the best racing pigeon man in our nation. Was so longer than anyone. Brought dash to our beloved sport. Elegant lofts. Detailed records. Fliers from all over the world came to see him. Suited celebrities. I met the legend at his home as a small boy. For some reason he took to me. Gave me baby racers that he charged others thousands of dollars. Taught me genetics. Gave me that love you have to have in order to be successful. One day about every month my grandfather took me to his home. Always better than any Christmas. When I became old enough to drive I would go with my wife to his estate. He loved my wife. All that red hair, freckles and such an innocent and grand smile. Powerful racing teams of his fliers twisted and whistled through the poplars on his estate. More than enough to lift loneliness. Heitzman was a grandfather of special order. In the end I watched The Master wilt. Our sport wilted with him. Racers were released over his grave."

NS

Journal Entry 71 – **UNTIL THE REAL THING COMES ALONE**

Colonnades Beach Hotel
Room 4150
Palm Beach Shores
Singer Island, Fla. 33403

July 16, 1983

Dear Clyde,

You asked about my birds. I've paid a lad to care for them in my absence. He owned the calm of a good loft manager. I pray he doesn't fall in love over the summer. I returned one year to such a predicament. The birds were a disaster.

Fanciers fall into this sport out of need. A love denied. These feathered serpents fulfill that lack. Whatever love is gained from this madness is narcissistic. As is the nature of all love.

This is the underlying reason why a showman feels hurt upon losing a class.

No Sweat

"In a remote tidal cave in the central area of Eleuthera, an outer island in the Bahamas, I discovered 19 Arawak burials. The exploration was filmed by a marine biology school. The Arawaks were those Indians living on the island when Columbus landed on it. At that time Columbus called the island, Cigatoo; It was the second island he discovered on his first of four voyages to the New World. These 19 Arawaks were the most ever discovered buried in one place throughout all of the Bahamas. I had never before seen such cranial deformation."

NS

Journal Entry 72 – **OUR LOVE IS DIFFERENT**

JULY 18, 1983

"High tide is six," I said.

Bo and Angel smiled. "Meat run," replied Bo. His gleam matched his gun. It was already five. Still hot outside. Some kind of brawling Sheriff's Convention was going on with The Colonnades. Nobody gets drunk like the law.

"Your yacht ready?" I asked. Bo's little bass boat was in the parking lot.

"She's ready. You're sure they'll be on the point?"

"Have I ever steered you wrong?"

Laughter.

"Ain't it five hundred bucks a snook if we get caught?" asked Angel, lifting a fifth of Lord Calvert to her lips.

"Yeah. And they'll take all our gear, boat and car. And give us time. I'd hate to look over at a bunch of rapist, murderers and bank robbers and tell them that I was in for shootin' snook."

Larceny flowed in Bo's and Angel's tanned Jacksonville veins. Long hairs. Movie Star handsome. Outlaws. Long-time friends for a week or two every summer. Bo was deadly with an arbelette. Angel, a Baptist minister's swamp cat daughter, deadlier with Lord Calvert. "God bless the Marine Patrol," she said, inhaling nefarious smoke. Her leopard tan-through bikini was all but a footnote.

Heading for a boat ramp some half mile distant we stopped at a liquor store fetching a quart of Lord Calvert. Angel put the bottle in a cooler. I'd told dad our plans to hit the south wall at high tide. If he wanted to be our bagman to be at the pipeline near the mouth of the inlet. When we neared the spot he was there.

"When I was getting certified my instructor said to select dive partners cautiously," said Angel, searching the cooler for a cold one. "He said, 'A fool on land--a fool in the water.'"

Going just outside the south inlet wall we pitched anchor. It was almost six but the inlet tide always ran just a little later. Having prepped our gear going out Bo and I wasted no time going over with cocked *arbelettes*.

The water was warm, calm. Hundred foot visibility. We swam side by side, Angel and dad lagging. We were soon forty feet deep in The Palm Beach Inlet. Spear guns were against the law. Shooting snook only added insult to injury.

Spotting two lobsters we shot quickly. Thump-thump. Twist-twist. Dad's bag. A little deeper, a circling group of silver shadows milled head on, combing the granite rocks searching for croakers.

We weighed into the largest concentration with no directness. The first two were shot at the same moment. Perfect hits, middle of the body just behind the gills. The snook became wary, yet fish-indifferent, dispersing into smaller groups, targets in a shooting gallery. Dad and Angel snorkeled along the surface close to the shadows of the inlet wall. Surface watchdogs for the Marine Patrol and The Sheriff's boats.

As dad's duffel began to fill he grew nervous. "We've got enough!" he said. But Bo and I had gone snook blind. Underwater buffalo hunters.

We left. When we returned we had seven more snook dangling in the lines of our *arbelettes*. Our guns and bags could hold no more. Bo's air was zero.

A converted trawler, some sort of official dive boat with all manner of flags and antennas, had pulled close during our dive. Dad and Angel had not spotted it because of the wall.

I still had air, though little. The snook were handed to me. Bo, Angel and dad climbed in the boat. I remained. Faint drifts of olive colored blood oozed from the bag. The snook on the guns pulled and jerked. Finally, Bo's hull came over. When I broke the surface a hand pushed my head back under. I was sucking air and HAD to come up. "Keep down," whispered Bo. "A boat is scoping." I got a breath and dove down hiding the bag under a rock. Pulling the boat next to the wall afforded the opportunity to pile in the kill. Bo and dad strained. Dive gear was laid over everything. I handed Bo the two guns with the seven snook. He laid flippers over them. I slid out of my tank. It was pulled in and laid over the bag as I climbed in. The motor was shifted from neutral and we headed back to the middle of the inlet.

"Let me out at the pipeline," said dad, afraid. "A fine is one thing, time another." Slowing, he jumped into the water with our regulators. Pilot regulators. Scuba Pro's finest. At least the law wouldn't get them.

Nineteen snook were in the boat. Directly ahead was a small, pine-tree island. I'm gonna stop there for a minute," spoke Bo. On the other side of the island was a Coast Guard Station.

Pulling into a sandy cove Bo cut the motor. As we hit shore a Coast Guard boat appeared. Angel's ripe curves captured their attention. They went on. Bo and I began untangling fish. He was Gregory Peck in DUEL IN THE SUN. While rearranging we looked up from our shady spot. The speedy, white-with-blue-stripe Sheriff's boat was aimed dead at us. We dropped everything. Angel stepped away. Prison was coming. Angel tiptoed and arched. Dropped her top and waved. Enticement at its finest. The boat slowed. Then made in a giant fishtail. Sun glassed badges smiled.

"God, he's pulling away."

"Angel, Lord Calvert!"

"We might as well have a load of smack. Wouldn't be no worse."

"Here you go, No Sweat, chug it down. Get you a bump."

"Jacksonville bumps. Kentucky pulls."

"Quit hoggin' The Lord."

"We need a chaser."

"Here's ya a beer."

"FOOLS ON LAND FOOLS IN THE WATER!"

Laughter.

More pulls and bumps.

"DON'T BE A-FEARED, NO SWEAT! THE LORD IS ON OUR SIDE!"

Outlaw fine. Full tide. Pink consumed the heavens. No law nowhere. Them dogs. Slinging the Lord into the pines we got back in the boat, popped more chasers, slitting the water back to the ramp.

As the Sheriffs of Florida orgied on one end of The Colonnades we filleted on the other. Not a fish under twenty pounds.

"Meat run."

"Winter meat."

It began to grow dark as we piled the fish. Angel turned on Bo's lights. We laughed, drank and listened to *'DREAM DREAM DREAM BABY, HOW LONG MUST I DREAM.'* Dad thought he was a guard at Fort Knox while we butchered in the bathroom in his apartment. Every door that could be locked was locked. No calls taken.

Mom's iron skillet worked overtime. Fresh fried snook. Nectar of the Gods. I can't recall her happier. Dad downed a fifth of Old Fitzgerald while singing Ella Fitzgerald's *'IT'S TOO DARN HOT.'* Amongst the grease everything was Fitzgerald. Dad never knew that Angel dumped a handful of microdots on one fillet he consumed.

Just as well.

Everything was Fitzgerald.

My sister and her new boyfriend had just arrived from the same dope dry out reform center. This boyfriend's name was, Chops.

Chops pushed three hundred and fifty pounds. A bronze haired Elvis with a monstrous black panther tattoo. He popped annibuse pills every five minutes. "They help my cravin's," he informed. He was somewhat more delightful than my sister's normal loves. Hadn't introduced himself by putting a knife in my ribs. This one had most of his teeth and didn't smell. Laid back. A human lude. Loved cathead biscuits and his memaw's sorghum. I felt almost sorry for the blubbery thing, smacking his lips, dreaming of fresh fried snook and getting in with our family. He thought we were regular people.

Around two in the morning we all sat in the dark, feeling the ocean breeze, listening to dad tell his jail stories. Mother was in the apartment passed out. An empty quart of cheap vodka sat upright in the cupboard above the refrigerator.

At three AM, Bo, Sensi and I retired to my apartment.

"No Sweat, I can't figure you out. You talk like an atheist. But you're the best friend I've ever had... I wish my father were still alive."

"Died in a car wreck, didn't he?"

"He burned alive. Was pinned."

Silence.

"Get me up tomorrow."

"It is tomorrow."

"Well, get me up day after tomorrow."

At seven my eyes opened. A radio blared on the patio. My sister and Chops were Bear

Jamboree dancing to *'DREAM DREAM DREAM BABY, HOW LONG MUST I DREAM.*

"Bo's uncle bought a 20 acre island 40 miles off the coast of Belize in the 1960's for $15,000. Built some huts. Turned it into The Turneffe Island Dive Lodge. After Bo's father was killed he offered Bo a job, guiding and bartending. Bo worked there for ten years. Then his uncle was offered 5 million for the island, deciding to sell. Broke Bo's heart. On the last day on the island Bo got drunk with some natives. One of them took Bo up on his bet of a hundred dollars. Bo proclaimed that his dog could swim out and fetch a stick, bringing it back quicker than any of them. Once Bo threw the stick, GO was sounded. Neck and neck the dog and the native swam. At the last second the native grabbed the stick, swimming in, asking Bo for the hundred dollars. Bo judged the race unfair. His dog had no hands. The race would have to be done again. This time, you could only take the stick by biting and holding it in your mouth. The native agreed, doubling the bet. Bo threw the stick farther out. Again, the native and the dog were neck and neck. Both simultaneously biting into the stick. At such time there ensued a tug of war. Both submerged. Seconds passed. Then, Bo's dog, stick in mouth,. surfaced, swimming proudly in front of his exhausted foe. Won two hundred dollars."

NS

Journal Entry 73 – **MOANIN' LOW**

July 20, 1983 4 AM

Steady breeze. Hope the waves aren't big. Starry night. Black ocean. Dad and I are headed north off Singer Island. Bo and Angel follow, pulling their boat. EVERY BREATH YOU TAKE radios. A1A. No traffic. Seven filled tanks and dive gear fill my van. It's opening day of Florida's Two Day Sportsman Lobster Season. Lobster hunters are granted two days to hunt lobsters before commercial lobster trap men blanket the ocean with their crate-traps. High tide will be around 7:30. We'll need visibility and calm.

An hour later.

Driving through Salerno. Turning off. Gate. Sprit Park.

Boat in water. Loaded. Moving. Heading out. Stuart Inlet. Meanest inlet in Florida. Five foot swells at mouth. No biggie for here. Dive boats race by. Bo's boat nearly flips. Dad blows BC.

Outside inlet's fuming jaws. Calm. Star's fade to awake. Blues. I'm turned backwards at bow. Dad, middle. Bo and Angel, stern. Half mile out. Coast, Jupiter Island. Peck's Reef. Shallow. Six to forty feet.

Forty to fifty boats fly dive flags. Mark reef's outline. Best spots. Divers bob. Divers splash.

Tossed. Sea mist. Tanks clang. Backpacks adjusted. Spit Soap. Masks. New head threaded, Bo's shaft.

"Stop. I'll check."

"Need gun?"

"No."

Jumping.

Snorkeling.

Water isn't cold. Don't need jacket. Getting breath. Going down. Images shape. Nice ledge. Good hiding. Lobster. Need air. Looking up. Flipping. Going.

Surface.

"Drop anchor. Looks good."

Dad hands anchor. Thirty foot. Breath. Going down. Pressure. Swallowing. Ears pop. Pressure gone. Swallowing. Feel fine. Anchor hooked. Should hold. Looking up. Boat's hull.

Tight. Air. Surfacing. Breathing. Climbing. Boat. Tanks clang. Miss toes.

"Good here. Not much current. Thirty foot visibility."

"No Sweat, what's that riffle over there?"

"Just a tiger. Let me know when you see a white. I have trouble getting them in headlocks."

"Are you serious?"

"Know why the pigeon fell off the Irvine Bridge?"

"No?"

"He was dead."

"No Sweat, tell Angel about scuba. She didn't complete her training."

"Tell her what?"

"About breathing. If her ears start hurting, what to do."

"Angel, stick the regulator in your mouth and breathe. Don't take the thing out unless a great white bites you in half. Then it won't matter. If your ears start hurting, you've gone too deep. Come up to where the pain stops. Pinch your nose and blow all the way to the bottom. Blow hard until you feel your ears pop and don't hurt. You'll be OK. It's not but a mile deep here. Don't worry. One way or the other we are going back from where we came. The porpoise once lived in the ocean, then came out, lived on land, saw what was here, went back. They say his brain is like ours. Ha." Connecting dad's regulator to his tank. 3,000 PSI. Adjusting his weights. Lead squares pinch fat. Mask covers balding forehead. Mesh dive bag rolled. Gloves. Orange BC.

"Will you hook up Angel?"

"I don't like BCs, weights, or snorkels. The less, the better. If you're gonna dive, buy your own equipment."

Dad leans backwards. Roll-falls. Rocks boat. Clumsy standing in flippers with a tank on your back.

"Bo, lower your tank or it'll beat your neck to death."

Jumping.

There's dad. Looking at his gauges. Regulators noise breathing.

Hog snapper. Curious. Rooster comb. Easy target. White flesh. Delicious. Changing color. Red.

Shot. Bagged.

Combing reef. Dad and I. Bo and Angel. Angel seems alright. Big lobster. Don't get excited. Don't waste air. Bubbles. Five pounder. Deep hole. Block hole with gun. Budging. Slow. Come on. Shallow crack. Cornered. Grabbing. Hold firm. Ol' boy, you're had. Pulling out. Jerking. Flipping. Inspecting. Legs bury, clasp. Eggs. Spongy orange. Underneath tail. Against law. Twist. Strong. Pull. Tail from body. Tail, twenty bucks. Don't get this in restaurants. Dad frowns. Puts in bag.

Urchins. Touch. Black dot you. Swell. Numb. Cuda. Popping jaws. Heard lobster. Distress. Rubbing antenna. Come on. Closer. Headshot. Come on. Bluff. Cuda fades. Might as well shoot every lobster. Mask leaking. Too loose. Thumb and finger against top, pressing. Breath through mouth. Blow through nose. Water forced out. Leak quits. Salt air burns eyes. Blink. Another lobster. Shallow hole. Grab base antenna. Don't ease grip. Another female. Twist. Pull. Front half crawls back. Dead and don't know it. Bluehead and damsel munch insides. Forty pounder once caught here. Could be another. Getting colder. Darker.

Back in boat. Fish and lobster tails. Hide. Middle compartment. Against law, just tails. Especially, eggs.

"Bo, let's move south. Get closer in."

Moving.

Stopping.

Snorkeling. Checking. Looks good.

New tanks. Angel staying. Blue eyes tan.

Five pound mutton hit going down.
Shark. Ten footer. Strong. Bull? Where-d he go?
Dad didn't see. Hands like jaws. Dad, watch my
hands. Opening. Shutting. Shark's mouth. One's
near. Dad understands. Bo is eyes. Watching
flanks. Sharks love blind sides. Ankles. Legs.
Reef no good. Gauge check. 1,600 pounds.
Where's boat? Pointing. Dad. Bo. Stay here. I'll
go up. Locate boat. Return. OK. They
understand.

Surfacing. There's boat. Guessed right.
Current stronger.

Going back. Dad. Boat's that way. Where's
Bo? Wish he'd stay close. Don't need the worry.
Air getting low. Sucking regulator. Dad
surfacing. I stay. Maybe one more lobster. Air
getting tough. Get anchor on way up. There it is.
No rope? Boat must be mile gone.

Surface. Wish I had a BC and snorkel.
Anchor heavy. There's dad. Where did the dive
boats come from? "Dad! " Anchor, spear gun
hard. Dad better get here. I'll drop anchor. "Dad,
blow your BC some more."

Dad bobs. Nervous. Speaks. "I lost a
flipper."

"How?"

"Came off when I was blowing my BC. Couldn't go back."

Least thing, dad panics.

Voice from dive boat. "Buddy! You've got a spear gun!"

"Yeah. Ain't no crime, here."

"You better not let THE MAN catch you with it! He's right over there!"

"Where?"

In a yellow boat. Checking everyone."

"You ain't seen a little boat with a little gal in a little bikini drift by, have ya?"

"Yeah. She was trying to start her motor."

"Never mind. I see her. Thanks."

Angel. "What happened?"

"Here's your anchor. Wore me out. Let's get out of here. THE MAN is close. Keep this bag low. Hide everything."

One hundred yards away. Bo unloads dive bag's tails. Angel handles motor. Eighteen tails in the live well, middle seat. One legal lobster remains in the mesh dive bag with the fish. Lays plain in sight next to dad. I stretch. Lay back at the bow. Look at dad, Bo and Angel. They're end-of-the-day diver tired. Gummy feeling. Bo's black hair, rich. Angel's, sun golden. Dad's, grizzled.

Sheriff. Twin engine. White cigar. Blue-green stripes. Big star. Pulling alongside. Looking us over. I lay back. Heart pounding.

"Any luck?"

Bo. Nonchalant. "Na."

THE MAN looking. "Take it easy." Revs motors. Leaves.

"Bo, Gregory Peck's got nothing on you."

"Whew wee," sighs dad.

Angel smiles. "Did you catch the glare off his pistol?"

"I've got to have a cold Byuur!" Dad explores cooler. Beer spews.

Journeying. Anchored boats. Dad has white towel over his shoulders. Fast drying. White sailor's hat folded over forehead.

Half hour. Heading toward inlet.

"Bo, I see a boat. He's bearing down on us. It's THE MAN." Horror image growing. "Bo, it's THE MAN." Five minutes. "HE"s dead on us." Leaning back. Innocence. Yawning. Pretense seasick. THE MAN is going to nail us. Why didn't I dump those lobsters? Wish I'd never broken the law. Wish I'd never seen a lobster.

Stopping.

Nightmare.

Yellow boat. Two uniforms. Sunglasses. Marine Patrol. Badges. Black stripes. I'm sick. Arms over face. Perform. Academy Award. Hold steady.

"Are you all having any luck!"

Bo. "Na."

Truer words were impossible.

Angel's hair shakes, no.

They'll shave that head in the pen.

"Uh uh," I utter.

Dad sits hunched over. Face down.

Our boats, side by side. Their boat is six feet longer on each end and a yard higher. THE MAN leans, holding our boat. HIS hand, inches from eighteen tails.

"Uh. We got a lobster," speaks Bo. The perfect gentleman.

"You don't mind if I have a look?"

Bo hands dive bag. Lobster and fish are inside. THE MAN takes the lobster out. Inspects. "This one lobster isn't going to be much for four people."

Laughter. "Ha ha."

Dad remains downward. No laugh.

"Ah, I seen a shark," I stutter. The definitive epitome of God's singular dumb diver from Kentucky. Coming--To--See--Jesus--- Scared.

"You did! Was it a big one!"

THE MAN loves the fear in my face.

"Uh huh," I respond.

THE MAN makes noises. Thumps, Theme song to *JAWS*. Laughs. No Marine Patrolman fears death. HE is Tarzan.

I up my fear. Eyes agog. Slight head twitch.

Dad is motionless.

"We figured you all had the limit. Were turning in early."

"Has anybody had any luck?" I ask.

"No. One boat had four divers. They got four lobsters. That's the most we've seen."

"There's none out here."

"That seems to be the story. Well, you all take it easy. Don't let the sharks get you!"

"Will do," speaks Bo.

"Roger," adds Angel.

Dad stays down.

Five minutes pass.

Brokeoutofprison jubilee.

Dad's popping another. What actors. Brando. James Dean.

"Well, dad, how did you like the way me and Bo handled 'em! Did-ja ever see two finer citizens!"

Laughter. Genuine.

Empties sky fly, landing in white furrow.

"Fools on land, fools in the water!"

Laughter.

Angel bumps THE LORD. "Are ya ready for another meat run! Bo and me wanna get back in time for one more!"

"Chalk me off sick!" hollers dad, beer sailing.

Angel fires fat J. Eight gauger.

The inlet is bumpy.

Not as bumpy as LORD CALVERT.

Boat at ramp.

Loaded.

The Police radio, *EVERY BREATH YOU TAKE.*

Mood.

Indigo.

"When I was first cast into Richmond's jail to pay my DUI debt to society I was somewhat apprehensive regarding my fellow inmates. Immediately I sought a corner top bunk. Flipping the channels on the TV my cell mates finally stopped to watch *COOL HAND LUKE.* Harry Dean Stanton was in the movie."

NS

Journal Entry 74 – **HAVING MYSELF A TIME**

July 22, 1983

Five AM. Pecking on Bo's window. Sleepy face appears.

"Meat run!"

Six AM. The mouth of Palm Beach Inlet. Calm. Alone. South wall.

Busting snook.

Bagwoman, Angel. Green drifts of blood surround her.

Seventeen snook.

"Let's get out of here."

Dad's not in his apartment. We dump the snook in his bathtub. He's down at the pipeline looking for us.

Last day of The Sheriff's Convention. Empty fifths. Whores filtering back to the mainland.

Dad's back. Nervous. Ranting. The Marine Patrol and Sheriff are over on the south wall. He bolts the apartment door. Pulls drapes. Locks us in the bathroom. No maid service today. Slimy fish all over creation.

Laughter.

Dad raises hell. Paces. Hasn't had his morning beer.

Blood pools. Hands ooze in fish mucous. Strings of guts. Fillets pile. Skeletal carcasses with eyes agog plop into sacks. Yellow rolls of eggs laid in the faucet. Giant scales clog drains.

344

Slit. Slicing. Knives feel down backs. Over ribs.
Through belly. Mmm. Thick, white meat.

Inlet warriors taking scalps.

"You boys are gonna run out of luck."

"I'll just tell them were from Kentucky.
They'll understand."

"If you act guilty you are guilty."

Dad sharpens knives.

Noon.

Thirty four fillets lay stacked on a long
towel. Layers of divine eating. Each fillet enough
for four people. You can't buy snook. A sport
fish. Against the law.

"Why dad, shame. Me and Bo ain't law
violators. Heck no. Why, there's twenty-four
hours in a day. We hardly ever break the law
much more than thirty or forty minutes on any
given day. If you'll stop and think, that adds up
in our favor. Me and Bo are actually, basically,
law abiding citizens twenty-three hours or so out
of twenty-four every day."

Dad unlocked the door. Hands us two
beers. Pops his. "You're right, son. I don't know
why I never saw it like that. One thing more. You
two are aimin' on dividin' with me for usin' my
bathroom, ain't ya?"

345

Outside, True and Chops sat on the patio listening to The Eagles. *TAKE IT TO THE LIMIT ONE MORE TIME.* Both inhaling their mid-day hoagies and smoking marijuana while rubbing oil over their blubber and tattoos. They seemed happy being away from the institute.

Even mom was up and about. Adding more Crisco to the skillet. Waiting for her bite of fresh snook. And rolls of eggs

"By the way, men and women have
the same number of ribs."
NS

Journal Entry 75 – **NIGHT AND DAY**

July 23, 1983

Up late. Near morning. Dropped acid with
Bo and Angel. An electric staircase plays under
my eyelids. Neon. Overlapping staircases in
black.

Goodbye kindred spirits.

Six AM. I'm on BYE Y'ALL, a thirty six cruiser. Our captain is a capricious Swiss with partially burned off tattoos on each forearm. It's his twelfth boat. We're headed out to the open sea. Crossing The Gulf stream to The Bahamas. Going to fish nights and dive days. We put up fifty dollars each to cover the gas.

Dad, Sensi and I are making are making our fifth trip to the Islands. Sensi and I are fearful. We left Wide Eyes with two girls, True, Chops and mom. We're only to be gone two days and one night. We got the trip because we knew someone that knew someone. There's a total of six of us besides the captain and his lean first mate, Charlie. The whole bunch are green about fishing and diving. They are soft spoken Floridians. We're full of hope to have a good catch. Pay for the trip. And then some.

Three hundred gallons of gas. Plenty enough to get to the West End. Going out Palm Beach Inlet. "See that wall," I point to sun glassed Charlie. "There's plenty snook on its point. But not as many as there was a month ago." The Gulf Stream is a black velvet blue. A blue that mesmerizes your soul. Is clear in your hands.

I lay inside staring out the back door. On a table are printed napkins. **A MAN'S PLACE IS ON HIS BOAT.** The sky is pale. Lighter blue than my best pigeon. Looking ahead, it's easy to understand why people thought the world was flat. Looking back, Palm Beach and Singer

Island begin to disappear. There is constant movement in the boat. Three sleek women in bikinis adorn the bow. Blithe bodies supplicating sun. Dad is getting drunk. Vodka and beer. In the islands there would be rum.

"I was in jail once," announced dad. "Three months in Iran. Locked up with SS officers. Got me down in a Bazaar, selling bed sheets. I got a hundred dollars each for them. Any white material brought money. I'd wrap a sheet around my waist, put on a loose shirt, suck in my gut and steal them off the ship. I managed to get out and back on my ship after serving as a waiter on another ship for Iranian students."

Around noon frigate birds began diving. Close by bonitos broke the surface. There was land in the distance. Grassy Key. Just south, West End. The captain was silver. His hair. His presence. He'd been around money.

"How long have you been over from Switzerland?"

"Twinteee years."

"Switzerland beautiful?"

"Vereee beauuutiful."

"The Alps?"

"The Alps."

"Don't we need IDs to get into the Islands?"

"Sheet on dee customms. Waste of time. Dis shotgun my customms. Do you see dat key? Dat is Grass Keey. Dat's mareewanna Island. All mafia."

Docking, we flew the Bahamas flag; It said we had been checked out and OK'd by Bahamian customs. Heat. No breeze. Docked boats. Thin black children in torn clothes cleaned discarded bonita and cuda. Land felt good. I remained at the ruins of The Jack Tarr Hotel as the girls got an old Cadillac taxi to take them to fetch rum. When they returned they told me about some chages-eyed native having been asleep on his counter. Six liters of dark Mt.Gay at four dollars each.

Afternoon. We're headed to a tiny island, Memory Rock. The barnacled white hull of BYE Y'ALL zig zags between the shallows. Boils of sand erupt from her inboards. Charlie pours the captain another vodka.

"There's been a dozen shark attacks in the Islands this summer. Two were killed. One got it when being trolled behind a boat looking for a dive site."

The talk rang bells. Five years ago, dad, Sensi and I had surfaced in a storm. On that day we knocked sharks off for an hour before making it back to the boat.

As the day wore on I wondered about our captain. He'd been steady vodka all day. Had emptied a quart and was on another. Always a glass in hand.

At seven o'clock, six miles northeast of Memory Rock, we dropped anchor. There was still enough light for a dive. Dad, Sensi and I geared up. Jumping over we got our bearings. Dad motioned to the surface. He didn't see a ledge, thought we shouldn't make the dive. He was always scared. I could see in Sensi's eyes that she didn't want to make the dive either. Both were remembering the sharks. I continued descending. They followed. Mike, snorkeled above. Whatever happened, we were on our own. At ninety feet I shot a hogfish. Dad was shooting another hog when I saw a big lobster under brain coral. What had appeared as a flat bottom from near the surface was actually a coral jungle harboring grouper after grouper. By the time dad shot another fish, a strawberry grouper, and I a Nassau, two hogs and two more lobsters, our gauges read 500 pounds.

At the surface the captain asked if I would go back and free the anchor. Doing so, I nailed a kingfish on the way up. Around eight o'clock a full moon set in the southeast. We're anchored some mile from where we had dove, prepping for night fishing. "We gonna catch maneee feeesh," proclaimed the captain. I knocked the fillets off

351

the grouper and hogs. Steaked the king. Sensi, Debbie and Cathy began cooking in the galley.

Dad, Mike and the captain began catching yellowtail on cut bait. A half hour later, sharks. Dad yanked them in. I clubbed the blacktips on the head with a tire tool. "Jeeeus Christ! Ah Sheeet!" yelled the captain.

As the sky darkened the breeze increased. Rolling swells. "I think we now have a leedle reefreshmunts," spoke the captain. BYE Y'ALL tugged hard at the anchor line. Debbie left the gallery, seasick, climbing to the bridge. Dad poured another round of vodka. Sensi and Cathy did all they could to stand without falling while serving fish. I finished my fourth rum and climbed up to see Debbie, smelling marijuana. Charlie and Mike were burning one. The approaching storm was being received with a smile. Below, the captain spoke to Sensi and Cathy. "You pussycats fix guuud feeesh." Cathy, the captain's ex, had a boy's hair cut, gold bracelets and cute smile.

The captain ordered the anchor be pulled. At ten o'clock, Mike Charlie and I struggled on the slippery bow. Nothing was giving. Finally, Charlie spoke. "Let's twist one." The wind whistled. Black engulfed us. Cold rain. Waves were getting larger, irregular. Around midnight, a new half gallon of vodka was opened by the captain. Everyone was laying on the floor inside the cabin trying to hold on. "What de sheeet wee do?" he asked.

"I don't care," I said.

"We have two choices. Wee cun try to move dee boat an dee anchor may go free. Or wee might break dee rope. If dat happens, we must go for home. Deeeze Gulf stream, Sheez no guud tonight. Sheeet!"

"Go for it. We ain't doing any good anchored here. I'll do about anything. But I aint junpin' for the anchor. Got no lights. Fins are breaking the surface. My tank is reading zero. The storm is getting worse."

"We need to take a konsinsueeeus."

"Aint no consensus to be took. Everyone is sick or passed out."

"Sheet!"

"Yeah."

"Dat Charlie, heez drunk on dee bow. I'm afraid heez fall off and drown."

"He won't have time to drown. The sharks will eat him before he can drown."

Dad raised. Poured the captain and himself another drink. Just the way the captain liked. Add nothing. Straight. He wanted as little air mixed in with the vodka as possible.

Straighter than straight.

Around two AM, the storm lowered and raised BYE Y'ALL nearly capsizing. Everyone clung to the floor. There was no consistency to the jerking.

At three AM I was sure that I was hearing water coming into the hull. Any given wave was our end. Dishes tossed. Bottles of rum rolled. No one tried to stand. a coffee pot flew off, pouring over Cathy. I looked at the Dad and Sensi's BCs with reverence.

Around six, the sky lightened. Headaches. Whitecaps surrounded us. A fresh glass of vodka. The captain looked at me. "We need for dee anchor to be lifted."

Checking all the tanks they read, "O". I tried each of them. Sensi's still had a few breaths. Ninety feet. Strong current. Big waves. Sharks. Damn headache. Nobody else can do it.

"You going down?" asked Sensi.

"Yeah," I said, gearing up. "I may have trouble coming up."

"Remember, let your air out."

"What air? Just hope the sharks have gone." Looking over the side, I jumped. Sharks. Eight. Get on down. Damn anchor. Damn captain. Look at the fish. Get on down. Anchor.

Pulling. Hung. Pulling. Gotcha. They know.
They're pulling me up. Going too fast. Hanging
on. Feeling lighter. Another sucked breath. Not
going too fast. Surface. Made it.

Back at The West End. Sea legs. Shower
and shave. Tanks refilled.

Around noon we anchor in green fifteen
foot water.

"Theeez place she guud. I catch many
grouper."

An hour later we head for Singer Island.
Rum all around. Night falls. Stiff frozen fish are
cleaned.

Wide Eyes is OK.

Mother lays drunk on the bed. Sores are
all over her arms and legs. Says it's hives.

Sleep comes easy.

The trip fades.

Dreaming.

Night and day.

"Alan and I had been the first to excavate the officer's headquarters, the hospital complex, the smallpox hospital, the confederate prison, the largest cookhouse, the pumphouse that pumped water up to a reservoir, the refugee camp, the church where the slaves worshiped, the blacksmith's shop, the machine shop, the bakery, several of the forts and numerous small camps, gun emplacements, sentry posts and garbage dumps. During one of our metal detecting excursions at Abe Lincoln's experimental city, Camp Nelson, Kentucky, I told him if the law began to chase us that I knew a good ground hog hole that I would go down in. Alan said that if they captured him then he would strike a deal that if he could make them laugh then they would have to let him go. His ploy was to direct them to my position."

NS

Journal Entry 76 – LOVER COME BACK TO ME

July 24, 1983

Sometimes you stop and see them.
You say,
In a way
They aren't gone.
But you know that's a lie.

Being alive is some strange divorce.
But whatever happens
You don't join them.
They are gone. Gone absolutely.

Death is not being more than alive.
It's not being part of it all.
It's being gone in fever.
Gone in laugh.
Gone.

Spirit and memory are one thing.
Flesh another. And horror
Champion of all. Don't kid
Yourself.

"Guy Davenport told me that I would have to have the hide of a rhino to be the kind of writer I was dreaming to be."

NS

Journal Entry 77 – **DEEP SONG**
For Earla

August 6, 1983.

Scorcher. Saturday afternoon
Left out fishin'. Plenty booze.
Pink crashing the heavens.
Mellow fiction.

Now we are a comin' back from 20 miles
Out.
Night.
Phantasy heavens.
Secret ocean.

Look, condo row. Like Miami.
No. Miami's are closer.
Palm Beach, Singer Island, Jupiter,
Gasping.
Here you go. Eight hundred square feet.
For the rest of your life.
Give me Papa's shotgun.
Can't crowd this raw stranger.
Even though we try, and more.
Drunks and dad know it.

My ol' man, he's plenty drunk.
Sings jazz. Cries '44 sandstorm on the Red
Sea.
"No land was in sight."
Sings Lena. He's plenty drunk.

The "Ah Sheet" Swiss captain nurses
warm vodka.
He's no captain. He's plenty drunk.
He loves this shimmering Gulf stream.
So contagious.

In the pink I saw...

Sailfish dancing. Dolphins laughing.

Charlie, pirate, wears shades.
His curly head dreams on the bridge.
Marijuana. He's plenty drunk.
Dreams inside the dream.

Dark lies port.
The Breakers off the bow.
Every three seconds a red light blinks.

Out here. Lifted. Opiate breeze.
Shoreline stretches forever.

20 miles out we were.
Now, just one.
Three souls are plenty drunk.
The worst possible drunk.

We're a-comin' back.
Back.
Back from 20 miles out.

"Charlie, Bo and I dove off Big Pine Key all one summer. The limit was six legal sized and legally caught lobsters per person per boat per day. Most every day we caught well over a hundred lobsters. We'd bring in our eighteen lobsters and then dump them in a submerged fifty gallon holding drum. Every time we headed back out we sang but one song, *TAKE IT TO THE LIMIT ONE MORE TIME*."

NS

"I always divided lobsters as evenly best as I could. You get the heads, I'll take the tails. I once caught by 289 of them by hand in four hours. And the biggest I ever caught was a 13 pounder measuring 51" from the tip of its antennae to the end of its tail. Cooked him like a turkey."

NS

Journal Entry 78 – **HE AIN'T GOT RHYTHM**

August 9, 1983

Five AM.

Charlie and his stepson, Clark, picked dad and I up for a three tank dive at Stuart. Clark, a stout sergeant on leave. Special Forces. Delta something or other.

"What happened to your hands?"

"Rappelling. Drop racing from a chopper."

Sprit Park Dock. Stuart Inlet. Fifteen white caught yesterday. Bigger one came around some boat.

Noon. Nil visibility. Icy water. Gray sky. Whitecaps. Lobster buoys pitch up and down. Swells. Pissed lobster trawler bearing down on us.

First dive. Fish, three lobsters. Moving farther south and out deeper. Waterspouts. Black heavens approach. Storm. Rain sprinkles.

Back in the water. Snook busted. Second tank. The surface churns, is being pelted. Lightning flashes. Fish dart. Concert light show at forty four feet.

Surfacing. Rain stings. Surreal arena. Shrouded. Wind cries. Suspended.

Cannot pull anchor. No compass. Hello storm. An hour passes. Lightning horrifies. Quiver. Chill. Wet suit jacket covers head. Scooping. Bilge not enough. Swells smack, toss. Lightning cracks close. Dad and Clark scared. Lightning targets. Jump overboard with BCs. Hang off the bow. Bobbing. Tied. Bailing. What's your pleasure? Drowning, sharks, or lightning?

Eerie. Lost. At fate's mercy. Giant swell frees anchor. Drifting. Dragging anchor. Won't hook. Dad and Clark stream. Where in hell are we going? Boat all but flips. How long can this storm maintain? The Gulf stream runs north. Are we going to hit something? Stuart Inlet. Riptides. Lobster trawler? Freighter?

Screaming. Must shout. "DAD, LOOK ON THE BRIGHT SIDE!"

Bobbing. Hanging for mercy. "WHAT?"

Bent over the bow. *Voit* jacket wrapped over my head. "I SAID, LOOK ON THE BRIGHT SIDE!"

"WHAT?"

"WE DON'T HAVE TO SWEAT THE MAN TODAY!"

"Dad hears. Can't look up. Rain wounds eyes. Stings scalp.

"IT'S ONLY ROCK AND ROLL BUT I LIKE IT!"

Clark hollers. "I HOPE WHEN YOU PULL US IN WE HAVE OUR BOTTOM HALVES!"

Rain eases.

Now, just a hard rain.

Coastline unveils.

Light at the end of the cave.

Rain stops. Armistice. No wind. Blue sky.

Did anything happen?

Repose.

Night.

Twenty over for snook and lobster. Florida pigeon friend, divers, family. Clean fingernails. Storm stories.

I've got more friends here than in Aopehh."

Silence

"You don't have to go in outer space to know this world is blue."
NS

Journal Entry 79 – **LOVELESS LOVE**

August 15, 1983

Dark Star and I on South Fork. South Fork comes from Aopehh's hollows. Feeds into The Wagersville Creek. Wagersville goes into The Kentucky River. Somewhere at the end goes my soul.

South Fork is a secret. Kentucky red agate. Wild turkeys. Marijuana growers. Getting there, jeep and good legs. Can't be afraid of snakes.

Or being alone.

Surfer's trunks and sandals fade to camouflage and boots.

I'm home.

"It ain't easy coming back."

"Ain't easy staying."

"Heard Tanya Tucker sing 'Baby I'm Yours.' She's got that right. 'Till the sun don't shine.'"

"Got no shine no how."

"You're telling me."

"Why do you stay?"

"They asked me that on Singer Island. Don't know why. Maybe I'm afraid. Maybe it's the mountains."

"This is our last wild spot left. Choppers combed my hollow ten times the last two weeks. No telling what that cost."

"The government says parquet won't hurt the environment. If parquet won't hurt anything, why do they spend millions on it? Black Hole said there's a Mrs. God. Can't be no other reason God would do this."

"The man that owned Delta 9 hadn't been there in years. Took some potential buyer over his land. That's how our patch got found."

Walking for miles in the seclusion of a deep hollow a jay moved in the shade along a shale streambed. I picked up a geode inspecting it for color. Calcite. No good. Coming to a gravel bar flanked by poplars, sunshine filtered through the geometric leaves down to the silver pool surrounded by thousands of butterflies. Black and tiger swallowtails. Bad thick. As if Fall had dumped the creek with black and yellow leaves.

Bending over. I pinched one by its wings bringing it to eye level. Two tiny black antenna shaped like golf clubs. Iridescent scales overlapping, shingles on a roof. Slender body. Teardrop tails. Letting it go it joined thousands and thousands in flight. A hundred thousand lined the creek. Sunflower yellows and tuxedo blacks. Filtering, waving, landing, rising. Garish hues.

"Butterfly Summer," said Dark Star. "I've never seen anything like it. Must be a lot of marijuana this year. The butterflies are stoned. Easy to pick up."

"Like that hummingbird that was in our patch. Too bad things so beautiful die so quick. Birds don't like black and yellow. Reminds them of bees. Usually, any bug black and yellow, stinks." Taking a few more steps I bent over stirring myriads of wings. Thousands brushed against me leaving faint, dusty reminders of color. Walking more we stood in the midst of a butterfly fantasy.

"Stop and look back."

Surrounding us were masses of butterflies blanketing the greens of the forest in a whirlish downpour of yellow and black snow. Farther down, stands of walnut stood untouched. "When the choppers stop we'll check The Triangle and ES #1. Pull males. Salvage something."

"Both are hot."

"What place ain't?"

"I want you to go down to Delta. See what happened. We'll get the 10-10-10 and the hoes we hid."

"Let's go next week. By then we'll know more on the choppers. Squirrel and dove season are coming. That'll heat up the scene. I always get back at the wrong time."

"There's a right one?"

"I hated spelling.
I hated writing.
I hated typing.
I hated English.
I hated reading
I hated literature.
I hated computers.
I loved telling stories."

NS

Journal Entry 80 – **SUMMERTIME**

August 18, 1983

Sweat stings eyes. Grimy hands. Swollen feet. Thick air. One hundred and three degrees. Briars. Vines. Poison ivy. Cudjold. Pollen. Grey mountains. Friday afternoon. Regan's D.E.A, Army paraquating Aopehh. Governor Sanders recouping from triple by-pass. Too many secret herbs and spices.

Dark Star didn't want to drive. Afraid jeep recognized. Two o'clock. Delta-9. Dried -up. Grey. Barren. Lifting flat rock. Dig out hidden bag of 10-10-10. Cedar. Hidden hoe.

Es#1. Next destination.

Yellow dust.

River valley.

Big-eyed grasshoppers ride hood. Elms slap windshield. Shriek.

Parking.

Green swamps. Humid. Itchy. Copperheady.

Mile later.

Familiar whistle. Dark Star. Backing through briars. Pausing. Whisper. Scene, good. Fifty ten footers. Bushy. Purple polk surrounds. Only one male. Two females, red hairing.

"Back in three weeks. Cool nights should bring out sex."

Pale blue and white morning glories entwine three plants. Innocence and evil embraced. Forked limbs support. Yellow sun leaves suckered. 10-10-10.

"Next time, I might swim the river."

Re-situate briars. No trail. No talk.

In van.

"It's costing a million dollars to spray one hundred plants. Reaganomics should handle us like wheat farmers. Pay us not to grow."

"Mom said that during WW2 her brothers were in The Civil Air Patrol. Patrolled for Germans and Japanese over Aopehh. Dad said they did a damn fine job, neither attacked."

NS

Journal Entry 81 – **YOU'RE SO DESIRABLE**

August 23, 1983

Black Hole's back yard. My thirty second birthday. Afternoon. 101 degrees. Dogs at our feet.

"Guess you read about the spraying?"

"Domestic Agent Orange."

"Dark Star and I are the Cong. Half this country is spraying and praying. The other half, growing and toking."

"America confuses pleasure with progress. Napoleon said, in battle, the moral is to the physical as ten is to one."

"The Fed in charge of spraying the paraguat is the same man owning its patent."

"Shades of Nam. People think they can buy the truth. Truth is horror. This nation is going to learn that. All this patriotism. All these bumper stickers proclaiming faith. We're headed to Fascism. Complete rule. We'll all be, not on the wings of an angel, but World War Three. There's never been a nation so full of cowards. More worshiping death. Did you know, Kentucky prohibits certain sexual positions you may have with your wife? This nation once made it part of its constitution not to allow drink. All on God's behalf. We're the only country that puts God on its currency."

"Less than 1% of humans are redheaded. The percentage grows less every moment."

NS

Journal Entry 82 – **THIS YEAR'S KISSES**

August 25, 1983

Ocher mane.
There's no red but hers.
Vibrant hair laughing at one end.
Aopehh's filth at the other.

God knows torture.
Virgin. Freckle to freckle.
Giver of Wide eyes.
Old green-eyed soul.

I'm always drunk around you.

"Gonzales was Aopehh. Only more mosquitoes. Between Baton Rouge and New Orleans. Fried squash and onions. I got there by taking a yellow cab from the airport. The sun glassed cabbie had been a prison guard until he got caught stealing a truck load of marijuana from the prison. Was supposed to have helped burned thirty tons of the stuff that night. When we pulled up to the Gonzales Police Station the law told me about recovering my van. It had been stolen in Palm Beach a month back. They'd caught some hippy putting gas in it on the interstate. The plates were off a stolen pick-up. License was his dead brother's. Inspection sticker was done with a crayon. My van was at a nearby garage. The hippy had been extradited back to Palm Beach. Ten eighty pound bales had been found inside. I then understood why my van had been chosen over the parked Mercedes which had been beside it when it was stolen. I told the law, just give me the bales, you can keep the van. They thought I was joking. At the garage I owed for the wrecker service and storage. The Creole that owned the garage was upset I showed up. Another month and the van would've been legally his. The bill was sixty dollars for AH. After hours. There was also a charge of ten dollars for storage. I looked at the bill and told the man that my van had been recovered on July 22nd and not on the 21rst as his bill stated. I also pointed out that he had me down for 14 days in July. Twenty-two from thirty-one wasn't fourteen. The man very plainly told me, who was running his business, him or me. He had me there. Paying for the fourteen July days and twenty-one August days I left on August 20th wishing him well. My radio and speakers had been stolen. My van was in fair condition. A good buy at $650.00. Inside, a few of the thief's items survived the clutches of the police and the garage owner. A Rod Mckuen poetry book. Hemingway's **TO HAVE AND TO HAVE NOT**. A braided leather belt with an inscribed brass buckle: *THE RIGHT TO BEAR ARMS*. A newspaper classifieds with a job circled: *WANTED, DELIVERY PERSON, CARPETS. MUST OWN VAN*. There was a receipt showing where my dive gear had been sold in St. Augustine the day after my van had been stolen. Both parties badly lying to each other. And last, a can of unopened Budweiser. This Bud was for me. On my drive back I picked up two West Germans hitchhiking from The World's Fair headed back to New York. University of Munich students. We talked Goethe, Mann and Hesse, drinking wine all the way back to Kentucky."

NS

Journal Entry 83 – **I'M GONNA LOCK MY HEART**

September 8, 1983

Wide Eyes dropped for school. Dark Star and I drive on to the Lexington Airport. Shipping pigeons. Twenty five hundred dollars. Dark Star carries food stamps. Russians shooting Korean 747 still news.

Returning. Wide Eyes brought home. Dark Star and I leave. Headed to Es #1.

"The weather going from forty five at night to a hundred in the day is bound to be getting the females to swell and the males to show."

"Think you and Rollanotherone could go down to Mammoth Cave with Sensi and I this Friday and Saturday?"

"Got no money. Rollanotherone is six months along."

Country grocery. Bologna. Royal Crown Cola. Doors slam. Dark Star's jeep. Willie sings. EXCUSE ME FOR LIVING. Moving. Dust. LOUIE LOUIE. Bodies bounce.

"It's been quiet this year."

"Too quiet."

"We're fools going up her with no shirts on."

"Shirts don't affect our fool status."

377

ES#1.

Half the plants, brown. Dead. Fallen over. Wilted into the dirt. Leaf dissolving to dust. Fifty pounds of 10-10-10 with three straight rainless 100 degree days. Burned the plants. 10-10-10 killed their roots. Radio said, hottest summer in the century. A few plants, turning from green to rust, get propped. Forked branches. Clorox jugs taken to the river. Plants watered. 10-10-10 kicked away.

Chopper.

Flying low. Moving slow.

Hiding.

Chopper searching up the river. Checking the bottoms. On other side.

"We need to come back, Monday. Bring hoes and buckets."

"I can't believe we killed our own plants."

"I said, shirts didn't make a difference."

"Just as well. We can't sell it anyhow. Word is, you are a narc. Your haircut and college."

"What about True making the papers? Doesn't that help my image."

"Doesn't matter. You're too mysterious."

"Let's go up to the Triangle. Haven't been there in a while."

"It's a good hike."

"We've got nothing else to do."

As the jeep trudges around a bend leaving Es#1 we find two women asleep in the ruts of the road in the shade of a beech.

"Hello ladies! How do you get to Staten Island from here?"

The girls stood, dusting themselves. "Our car is up yonder. You can't get around it. I'll holler for our husband. SHELBEE!"

From the woods. "WHAT!"

"Shelbee, Thar's some fellars hyur a-wantin' you to move yor car."

"Ok!"

Minutes later, Shelbee. Lean. Bristly. Poor. Mature. Grimy cap has marijuana emblem.

"Whatcha doin' in the woods? Sang huntin'?"

"Newww. We're-a-huntin' to stick our noses into somethin'. Y'know what I mean?"

"Yep."

Shelbee's ancient Dodge wouldn't start. I hollered to Dark Star who was conversing with the women. "Come on through! You can go around."

Again on our way.

"What did those girls say?"

"Claimed they were squirrel hunting."

"They didn't have any guns. Were they going to catch them with their hands? Or throw rocks?"

"Growers, probably."

Deciding to scale the cliff at The Triangle we took the shortest way to the patch. Finally, we reached a familiar crack in the mountain, California Cave. Putting our faces to the crack we enjoyed the cave's cool air. We paused to rest our backs against the steep fall to the woods below.

"Somebody has slapped blue paint over your dad's name."

"Nothing is sacred," spoke Dark Star. At the entrance, dripped blue paint now covered where his father had painted his name in red over fifty years ago.

Disgusted, we left for The Triangle. A half hour passed before we came to thirty scraggly plants intermingled with mint, sumac, locust, grasses and goldenrod. Most were males. I touched the dirt.

Dead dry.

After weeding the few females and uprooting the males we listened to a chopper slowly closing in. Crouched low, we held motionless. The thumping monster disappeared into the grey mountains.

"No Sweat, look, insects have worked this plant."

"That ain't insect. That's human. Stripped just like that before."

"Mrx."

"We can chalk off The Triangle."

"Again."

"He'll be back. Some things are certain."

"They don't need traffic signs or signals in Aopehh. Everyone knows when and where everyone is going."

NS

Journal Entry 84 – **SWING, BROTHER, SWING**

516 Poplar
Aopehh, Kentucky
September 15, 1983

Dear Swallowtail,

Have you seen yesterday's front page of
THE CITIZEN'S BLADDER? Lips claims he
dropped the Buckeye's charges because the
Buckeye stood a chance of being murdered.

Supposedly, the discovered ledger
contained names and addresses of Irish
Terrorists. Lips calls Dunlopper a psychopathic
liar. He states that he has been secretly
cooperating with the FBI on the case. No
mention of the missing cocaine or sinsemilla.

Revisiting. Possibly around Christmas?
Maybe goose hunting?

No Sweat

"Dad wanted me to be an attorney. His brother wanted me to be a jazz trumpet player. Dad's mother wanted me to be a preacher. Fred Marcum wanted me to be Indiana Jones. Mom said I could be anything. Miss Winn, my high school guidance counselor, said I should join the Navy."

    NS

Journal Entry 85 – **LONG GONE BLUES**

September 19, 1983

True's fat face sweats. Mouth twitches. A jerk-twitch. Just like mom's nervous politician brother. Mom blames the spasm on drugs. Dad doesn't notice. True is giving dance lessons. Little girls wait in mom's basement.

Blue eyes, red.

True believes she's got everyone fooled.

Drugged.

What is it this time? Demerol? Delaudin?

Spaghetti stains. She sits alone at the kitchen counter. Avoids eye contact. Laughing. Mouth open, eating. Food spilling. Pink leotard. White stockings. Bulge. Fat. Hide needle marks. Dance is all she has.

Mom gives her that.

The doorbell rings.

"Doc!" Hands, pale and puffy. Long sleeved cuffs cut into swollen wrists. "Did you get my letter?"

"No."

"I sent you a long letter. Knew you were in jail on your birthday. Wonder what happened to the letter?"

"Mom got me out early. Fed 'em the doctor routine. Don't worry about the letter. None of them can read." Lighting cigarette from inlaid teak box normally carrying joints. Blonde hair, grey-blue eyes, dull.

"I wrote telling you about a good dove hunting spot over in Richmond."

"Can I use your phone? I'm getting a divorce."

"Divorce?"

"Yeah. Blackwidow ain't draining me any longer. She's been in bed with everybody in Aopehh."

"If you're calling a lawyer, get Ibold. She'll be lucky if she doesn't have to pay you when he gets through."

"That's who I'm getting. His phone is still busy."

"Wanna run up Cobhill? Out past Sally Ann's. Some guy is growing grapes. Makes wine. We'll fetch Dark Star."

Dark Star's. He's swinging on his front porch. Van radios YOU'RE NO GOOD.

"We need another disciple to spread the word on Cobhill. Wanna go?"

"Those heathens need converting!"

"Praise Be!"

Inside van.

"Doc! When did they let you out?"

"Some scum came up to me and unlocked the door. Declared I was a free man. Said the Judge himself was getting busted for marijuana."

"They captured the ex-governor's nephew with ten pounds of cocaine and a bale of marijuana. Lips fined him for improper auto registration. Stated The Irish Terrorist made him do everything."

"Let's go see Swallowtail."

"He's gone. Ain't nothing left there but a field of rotten peppers, molested women and cold checks. He snuck off to Wickliffe pretending to be an upstanding attorney. I don't blame him. Can you imagine? Him bringing a case under Lips."

Vineyard.

Gravel Road. Dirt road. Oak ridge. Hillside. Grape vines.

"Listen! Beethoven!"

"Loudspeakers in the trees."

Stopping. Block building. Parked vehicles.

"Hello."

"Hello."

"My name is, No Sweat. This is Doc and Dark Star. We came here yesterday. Nobody was around. You don't mind us drinking, do ya?"

"No. Get out. These dogs won't bother you."

"Them's awful big poodles. We were hoping to buy some grapes."

"To eat? Or for wine?"

"To eat. But we'd love a taste of your wine."

"I've got a few grapes I'll give you. But I won't sell them. I won't have any wine until March."

"This is supposed to be a great year for grapes."

"Best ever. They thrive in dry weather."

"Love your set up. Out in the woods."

"You need a good hillside for the best grapes. I don't care for apples. And this isn't peach country."

"How many acres have you got?"

"A hundred."

Hey, I like that Hudson. What would you take for it?"

"It's not for sale."

"They made good autos in the forties."

"She's low to the ground."

"What year is she?"

"Forty-nine."

"Are you from around here?"

"No. Louisville. Spent fourteen years in Nam."

"How long have you been in Aopehh?"

"Since seventy--seven. I sold my land in Louisville and Islamorada and moved here. Here's your grapes." Whole basket load taken from a walk-in-cooler inside a dug--out shed.

"Wish you'd let me pay."

"Enjoy."

"We'll be back in March."

"Sounds good."

"You ain't allergic to lobster, are you?"

"You ain't allergic to wine, are you? What kind of wine do you like? I only make very dry red wines. Point seven."

"Point seven just happens to be my absolute favorite."

"Marijuana has a queer way of adding time while
taking it."
NS

Journal Entry 86 – **DREAM OF LIFE**

September 21, 1983

Bitter rain from Gray

Beating down upon the

Fog quietly smoldering in

The hollow. First hurt of fall.

Who loves this season

Of death.

Who could love verdant mountains

Above madness. Love

Them sweeter than the

Kiss of blues. Who loves such

Death.

And that unseen rose. Wild.

Cursing blood in every way. The

Dead rose. Meaningless. Gone.

Who loves a dead rose.

"My mother's father loved me more than any of his grandchildren. Whatever mother's brothers stole, they couldn't steal that."

NS

Journal Entry 87 – **BODY AND SOUL**

September 22, 1983

Aopehh. Thursday. Noon. Sixty degrees. Main Street. Behind the clinic. Doc's Door. Knocking.

"Who is it?"

"The law. Open up. We have warrants."

The door opens. Blackwidow stands in a satin robe that is open down the front showing her nude figure. "The door was open." she said, smiling. We follow her up the steps. Wild black hair. She stops at the top. Silence. She smiles, stretches, yawns, wipes sleep from her painted face. She is opiate. We pass by ten Gibsons and two banjos before coming to Doc. Grey image turning yellow. He's asleep, breathing slow, sprawled on maroon silk sheets. Beside his bed, draped on a Victorian marble stand, is a new wardrobe of camo, boots and three boxes of high powered sixes. A new Fox double barrel lays atop the gear. "Should I wake him," asks Blackwidow, grinning.

"You can try."

"Come on, Doc," I said, nudging.

Doc stirred. Bleary eyed. Blackwidow's dark eyes prance among my countenance as she smiles. I smile. So does Dark Star. We stand around the bed.

Blackwidow walked away opening a double wide closet. Dark Star and I sat down on a black leather couch looking at the porno. Blackwidow inspects rows of clothes. Then sits down across from us in a leather chair lighting a joint. Passing it to me she asks, "Y'all want a coke or something?"

"To snort or drink?"

"I wish. I'm out. You don't know where to get any, do you?"

"No."

Blackwidow stood and walked to a new stereo, dropping in a tape. ME AND BOBBY MAGEE. Bending over she turned offering a most nefarious view. Straightening up, she went back to her closet. "No Sweat, have you seen my black leather pants?"

"No."

"I love them. They were three hundred dollars. I got them for two." She held them up.

"They look pretty tough," I said. "You ain't got any old Beatle stuff, do ya?"

Blackwidow's hands were swollen. Her slender figure was due to pills. She looked perfectly Cuban. Cubans thought she was Cuban. I'M A LOSER filled the room.

"Clown wearing a frown," I said.

Blackwidow stared. Then burst into laughter.

MONEY CAN'T BUY LOVE comes next. Blackwidow lights another joint, takes a hit, passing it to me. "I'm twenty two since last week. I can't believe that's all I am."

"Twenty two and what to do."

"Try Doc again," asked Dark Star.

At the bed. "Eh, Doc, get up."

"My side hurts," muttered Doc, pulling a sheet over his head. One of his sketches of a stork hangs on the wall behind him.

"What's wrong with his side?"

"I probably broke his ribs last night. We had it out. I'm going downstairs. You all wait a little longer. I know he wants to go. That's all he's talked about."

Dark Star and I sat back down. A fat billfold, a thousand dollar watch, three Nikons and a half gallon vase of marijuana seeds rest beside us.

Blackwidow topped the stairway to heaven. "Is he ever gonna get up?"

"Doesn't appear so."

"No Sweat, isn't your birthday in August?"

"Yes."

"You, Doc and I are all Virgos."

"The planets had to be spinnin' when we popped on the scene. Reckon we'll cut out. Tell Doc we're going hunting, Saturday. And maybe next Thursday."

"I'm sorry."

"What for?"

"Would you like for me to go? I've never shot a shotgun. But you could teach me.

"Better not, today."

Back in the van. Dark Star and I drove through the rolling hills where Aopehheans were spotting UFOs.

"Why didn't you ask her?"

"Are you kidding? Marijuana, beer, shotguns, Blackwidow and the woods."

Hold the thought.

The best Kentucky agate hunter that there ever
was, was one of the truest friends I ever owned.
He was someone you would never want to get
into a fight with. I was always the best digger
until he'd show up. Then he'd quickly put me to
shame. He loved finding Kentucky's rare state
rock. Most of the fun of finding such was finding
it with him. He owned this inner joy about the
rock and when it was cut open for examination
it was like some kid getting his first bike. He
taught me about agate and I taught him about
Indian relics. Between the two of us we kept
ourselves fascinated with possibilities. One
wintry afternoon he went alone to shoot a coyote
that was bothering his neighbor's cows. Never
returned. His wife found him. His leg was
tangled up in a bob wire fence. He was laying
partly on the ground. The rifle he was carrying
had accidentally discharged. His foot had
somehow slipped on the fence. The bullet went
straight into his head. In his will he instructed
that his wife and I were to take his ashes and
place them at the site where he and I had dug
the finest and rarest agates ever found."

                                                    NS

Journal Entry 88 – **SAY IT WITH A KISS**

October 2, 1983

I'm lying cradled in the rut of a dirt road. I'm alone. The rut is dusty. Its contour fits my tired back. It allows my head and feet elevation. My feet are crossed. Down my body beyond my legs I wear Converse. Four years ago they were white with blue stars. Now they are grey with thin soles. Dirt comes through their cracks. My feet form a "V. "Open sights. Through the sights is a pink sunset of familiar dream.

Not far is the woods and river. A hundred yards away are two hidden duffel bags of marijuana that are growing warm with decay. There were a few small females showing hairs. They're in the bags. Had to take them. They were laying over, rotting. Beyond help.

When I awoke this morning it was already ninety degrees. The day had been a scorcher. Aopehh's worst drought, ever. But it's not bad, now. I feel good in the rut. A crow disappears in the distance. Maybe a snake would like to rest with me? Not far, I caught a 60" rattler.

Camo covers my lower half. Day is dying. Patterns are growing dark. The pink sunset is fading. Leaves above my head mark oak outlines. Oaks have spirit. IN THE GOLDEN BOUGH oaks were worshiped. Close by, a sycamore's large leaf falls. A blossom unto death. Another falls. Curled, brown, brittle. Floating down. Cascading through the branches. Joining the grave of accumulation.

Three or four hours ago Dark Star was with me. He had to leave. Somebody was promising firewood. When we made this trip into ES#1 we were shocked. Never dreamed that this late into the year that our largest plants would turn out to be males. Males everywhere. Fortunately, no released pollen. Our females were still virgins. Sensemillia. There had been too many plants to drag through the briars. Lose half their value. Field stripped. Our job became my job when Dark Star left.

I stripped for hours. The green, fibry limbs cut my fingers, caused blisters. I nibbled on the sticky hash. I quit for a while, tending the virgins. Hoed. Weeded. Carried buckets of water from the river. Cut limbs for propping. Taped split branches.

As I sat cross-legged, stripping, a bass broke the water for bugs. A ruby-throated hummingbird sucked nectar from tiny orange

and black spotted, horn-shaped touch-me-nots.
A squirrel barked. Leaves fell imitating the
sounds of someone stalking. Fishing boats went
by. Then, a chopper and a low flying plane. I
continued stripping. My index finger grew black.

Black Hole called last night. Wanted me to
accompany him at a dinner meeting of the newly
formed Lexington Chapter Air Force Association.
Told me to wear a tie. I didn't. When we got there
some hundred men were either in tie or uniform.
Black Hole called me an arrogant bastard. B-47,
B-52, and B-1B filled the air. I nodded, finished
nine gimlets. Generals watched. One of the men
at the bar was, General Ralph Daughtery. He
was the big cheese. Black Hole told me
Daughtery was a Kentucky boy. Wrangled
Commander-In-Chief of SAC once out of
Louisville's Law School.

Daughtery was easy to spot. Groomed.
Manly. A magnet. I shook his hand. Applauded
his anti-Russian speech. He said that we must
be number one. The arms race is a poker hand.
A good hand is not enough. The long linen table
held pitchers of dry wine. My salvation.

On our way home, Black Hole raced his
Delta 88, ranting, telling me that for the first
time, he saw me. Said my Aopehh was Ashville.
Told me I had it to prove. That the Jews would
sort me out. He hung sharp curves between
ninety and one hundred miles an hour. Refused
to hit his brakes. Left his speed on auto cruise.
No fear of death. The shadows raced.

"Audry."

"What about Audry?"

"She'd been taking stellazine."

"Stellazine?"

"For psychotics."

"I thought she shot herself?"

"She tried. She tried everything. Finally, I just told her to go on. I didn't care anymore. I was flying a B-47. I saw man. I wanted to black the world. None of this talk matters. Audry was so much like you. Full of rage. Yet, she smiled. She hated with your hate."

What could it be like for my wife to commit suicide with my twin baby sons at her feet? For those sons to be taken away. Told that I was the murderer.

There was only one cure.

When pink mixes with black, black is the result. The light of the pink sunset was being consumed by night. I lay in the rut looking up. Dark hues. The crows were roosting in nearby pines. The caws settled. An odd silence reigned. Then, a vehicle. It had to be Dark Star. Raising out of the rut headlights hit my face. I was wrong. It was Jimmy. An old High School drinking buddy I hadn't seen in years. One that use to dig relics with me. Jimmy's brother had some problem that caused him to be owl-eyed. There was a girl with Jimmy that I'd never seen.

"No Sweat, would you like a cold one!"

"How did you ever find me?"

"We didn't know we were hunting for ya!"

"I was just lying in that rut. Give up on the whole stinkin' world. Now, you've come with Budweiser."

"What are you doing up in here?"

"Reminiscin'. Remembering how good it use to be."

"You mushrooming?"

"Mushrooming is in the Spring. Nah. Dark Star and I were hunting agate. Got separated. I figured he'd come back. He knew where I'd come out."

"You talking about niggerheads?"

"These are a rare kind. Solid. Smooth on the outside. Red and black on the inside."

The three of us walked around Jimmy's truck getting beer out of the back cooler. Fifty feet away toward the river ran the railroad

tracks. Long stretches. Coal trains flew by.
Getting a joint from the glove compartment we
toked. I hadn't eaten all day. Water had been
sipped from the river. The beer and the
marijuana went quickly. Soothing. On my third
beer and second joint Jimmy began talking.

"No Sweat caught a big rattler up here one
time, remember?"

"Yeah."

"He put it in a pigeon carrier and set it on
the desk of our science teacher. She sent him
home."

The tracks started vibrating. In the
distance was a circling light. Jimmy got his
girlfriend to put some coins on the tracks. After
we found the flattened coins we drove on out the
dirt road until we hit such dense foliation that
Jimmy had to park. Darkness and silence.
Turning on the lights we continued to smoke,
drink and laugh. "I better try to turn around,"
spoke Jimmy. "You never know, I might run
smack into somebody's marijuana patch."
LUNATIC FRINGE was playing on the radio.
Jimmy's girlfriend was biting him on his neck.

"Here comes a light," I said. The lights
paused, blinking on dim and bright. I turned up
the radio. Hanging my head and sixth Budweiser
out the window I yelled.

"Dark Star! Join the party!"

"No Sweat, is that you!"

"This Bud's for you!"

"I passed a dozen coal trucks on the wrong side of the road to get up here! Figured the night creatures devoured you."

"If you'd known this was going on, you'd've passed fifty trucks."

"You're right."

"When I opened the door, Vicky stood smiling. Her leopard bikini was microscopic. She stepped in, got bad close. Looked into my eyes. We were alone. Asked if she could light a joint. Dad's brother had told her, no. She fired up. Smiled. Then spoke. They call me, Five Minute Vicky. Know why? I held ground. Silence reigned. She smiled again, explaining, If I'm gone longer than five minutes, your dad's brother comes looking. Took three big draws. Put out the joint, leaving. She'd been there about four minutes. A minute later, a knock. Dad's brother. Asked had I seen Vicky. Blood was in his eyes. No. Not me. I absolutely haven't seen her. I'm gonna blow that Lifeguard to Hell if I catch him with her, he declared. Honesty in spades. He pulled out a joint. Asked if t was ok to fire it up. Don't tell Vicky, he said. I told her she couldn't smoke this stuff."

NS

Journal Entry 89---**AS TIME GOES BY**

October 16 thru 18, 1983

For the past hour Sensi and I have been straightening our cluttered attic. Stacks of funny books, National Geographic's, term papers, notebooks, boxes of letters. In one corner on its side, a thirteen point buck. There's a wooden framed cage on wheels, Screened sides. A screened lid top that locks, 'KIDDIE KOOP." My baby bed. Sweaty remembrances in confined gray. A treasure. Two dressers out of my grandfather's hotel are filled with cancelled checks and tax records. Sensi's 60's clothes hang. Purple mini. Dive gear in revered space. A six gallon Adena jug I dug in 1968 lays on its side. Piles of army clothes lay near the fan. Sensi sits at the top of the narrow steps reading in the dim light.

"What's that?"

"An old love letter of yours."

"Read it."

"Mom has been drunk all week. Dad hit and smacked me telling me what all he's done for me. True lies every breath. You cannot believe my life. I'll be so glad to leave these people. You'll never know."

"Hold old was I when I wrote that?"

"Sixteen. It's a letter you sent me from Florida."

"Nothing has changed."

As Sensi continued reading I sat looking at the stack of bagged marijuana sitting in one corner. At first I never noticed anything wrong. Then, did. Something was missing. Four half pound bags of seeded buds. The only buds. Gone.

It had been four days since I had last been in the attic.

"Sensi, someone has been up here." Two pounds of buds are gone."

"Are you sure?"

"I haven't lost my mind. Not yet. Whoever did it knows marijuana. They left the leaf and took the buds."

"I've told you not to leave the house unlocked."

"There's only two people that knew. Dark Star and Mike. Someone Annie trusted."

"Mike?"

"Yeah. He was here last Saturday. You were gone. He could've done it. He screwed me taking care of the birds this summer. He's been wanting marijuana."

"Do you think he'd rip you off after all you've done for him?"

"I don't want to think about it. I've given money to get his brother out of jail. I've given him tires for his car. I paid for his Florida trip last summer. I've always given him anything he's asked for."

"You can't be nice when it comes to marijuana."

"I can't find the seeds. They're gone, too. That leaves Mike out. Dark Star has been acting strange the past two weeks. Every call made, I made. Can't believe he'd rip me off. Take all the buds. Take all seeds for next year. Leave me with nothing. That's it for us."

"Funny, he never asked you to go to County Court day, today."

"He knew I wanted to go. Last night he asked me about those seeds. Was seeing if I knew they were gone. I'll bet you he's ripped off Es#1. I'm going up there right now. If it's gone, I'll know."

At Es#1.

There's females.

My temper subsides. I'm puzzled. Dark Star lied about those seeds he had from Custer. Threw them away. Hardly. The other day when he pulled up part of a fresh male was sticking out under his seat. Doesn't he know? Ripping me off is ripping himself. Any way it's told, I'm screwed. If Dark Star did it, he'll act innocent. If he didn't, I'm responsible. He's got fifteen pounds of shake. Ours. Don't forget that. We've got a crop still standing. What should I do?

Back home.

"Was it there?"

"Yeah. But it's too young to take. Or it might've been gone."

Checking my jewelry box on my bedroom dresser I discovered one hundred dollars gone. My Louisville Pigeon Show money.

"I'm sorry this happened to you. I really am. I know how much you trusted Dark Star."

"And Mike. The whole summer Dark Star barely wrote. Back in the spring he'd rush me around. For someone unemployed he sure had deadlines."

"What are you going to tell Dark Star?"

"What I know."

"You might want to give that a thought."

"Maybe I'll play dumb. He might hang himself."

"I would. I don't believe Mike did it. He wouldn't do that to you. True could've done it."

"She didn't know I had it. Besides, she'd've taken it all."

"I hope this teaches you never to fool with the stuff again."

"How can I? The seeds are gone."

"What about NDN? Would he have done it?"

"Nah. He's got a job. He wouldn't know leaf from bud."

The next day. October 17, 1983. Gray sky. Rain. Noon.

"Hello?"

"Rollanotherone?"

411

"Yes?"

"What's going on?"

"Not much. Dark Star has been trying to find you. He wants a few bags of bud. He's got it all sold."

"Tell Dark Star, there ain't no bags. I've been ripped."

"What?"

"Someone came into my house. Stole all the buds and seeds. Plus a hundred dollars."

"When?"

"Sometime between Wednesday and Saturday. I think, Saturday. I spent that day washing and waxing the van. Sensi and Wide Eyes were gone to a Daughters Of The American Revolution meeting. Anyone from noon until six could've walked in."

"I can't believe you leave your door unlocked."

"Always have."

"Even after you got broken into?"

"That was seven years ago. True's boyfriend. Don't worry. The doors have new locks."

"Who could've got it?"

"Only two people. Dark Star or Mike."

"Dark Star didn't do it. He would never do you like that. This dissolves all partnerships."

"Tell me about it."

"I'm gonna call Dark Star."

"Fine. If you don't, I will."

Five PM. Dark Star at my front door.

"Rollanotherone told me you had some trouble. What happened?"

"There's an omen on the Triangle."

"Omen?"

"Ever contemplated the failure of reverse psychology?"

"No?"

"It's called, Aopehh."

"I didn't get the marijuana. I wish you wouldn't think I did."

413

"I don't want to think it. God, I wish I couldn't think at all."

"Rollanotherone said you checked ES#1. Were there any buds?"

"Nothing noteworthy."

"Have you talked to Mike?"

"Not yet. I've tried. There's nothing I can do. I can't whip him. That would bring the law. Not to mention his heathen clan."

Seven thirty PM. Home with Sensi.

"What's wrong?"

"You're not going to Mike's."

"Alright."

"How dare Dark Star start that stuff in front of Wide Eyes."

"What did he say?"

"You heard him. Don't you think Wide Eyes takes this in. She listens. Are you wanting to raise her like you were raised?"

"You're leaving out something. I happen to love her."

"You've done all this to us."

"Done what?"

"Jeopardize our lives."

"I was trying to help."

"That's a joke."

"What is it you want me to do? Kill myself?"

"That's right. The ultimate selfishness. Kill yourself and you'll kill Wide Eyes. I'm so sick of this. I wish to God I had never seen Dark Star. There was never any marijuana until him. That's all he knows. All he talks. Out of all the risks--- you've gotten nothing."

"Cause I was ripped. My life has been ripped. Dad ripped the heart out of me the day I was born."

"There's no money in this."

"It's a dangerous game. That's all."

"When you are murdered or thrown in jail, what happens to Wide Eyes and me?"

"You don't want to move. I can't make enough with the pigeons. I'll never get hired as a teacher. There's no work here unless you know somebody. And even then, it's nothing. What am I suppose to do? Lay down and die?"

"You are insane."

"Yes."

"If I had a hundred people here and took a poll they'd vote you mad."

"They'd be correct. Very mad."

"I don't want to go to the pigeon show with you this weekend."

"That's it. Fill the room with hate. That's the sane way. I've not liked it any more than you. I'm not apologizing. If you are so blind as to think that I've done something to you or Wide Eyes, then you scare me. I really don't know you at all. I must be truly insane."

October 18, 1983.

Mike sitting in my living room.

"Did you want to see me?"

"I don't know how to put this. Some of my marijuana sprouted legs and walked out of my attic. You and Dark Star are the only ones that knew. I ain't mad. If you got it, I understand. You remember me giving all that camping gear? You remember me giving you money when you graduated? Haven't I always given you anything you wanted?"

"Yes. I didn't get it. I wouldn't steal any of your stuff."

Long pause. Mike is scared. Cupped hands. Fingers going round and round. I don't know why but I feel bad. Embarrassed like Mike. I wanted no more rips. Mike or Dark Star. Both Aopehheans. Marvelous actors. I sensed Mike's guilt.

"This theft has caused me a lot of problems. It's ruined Dark Star's and my friendship. Not to mention a lot of sweat and risks down the drain. I hope that you understand all that I am saying. You can go now. That's all I wanted."

417

"The word, Aopehh. It didn't matter. You knew where it was."
NS

Journal Entry 90—**DO NOTHING TILL YOU HEAR FROM ME**

October 18, 1983

In time still Aopehh, Medieval county,
Frightened, scurrilous, earthbound wolf mud
heads.

Trudge lug their crush-consuming crucifix.

Hate.

Aopehh's rust steel drawbridge at Kentucky
moat
Remains lock-raised for investitured fief
peasantry
And its smirking, castle, cold, golden justice.

Worms.

Overalled, mercenary- eyed, hook-beaks
hypocritically scurry
With squirrel-tailed-CB-antenna moonshined in
dim fog lost.
And tearless, drawn, sag jaws hide serrated
fangs.

Lonely.

Gray, I don't know but faces, sneak in Sunday
hats.
Desolate, patriotic, Appalachian hearts curse
April.
Only the groundhog sees his shadow.

Plastic flowers.

Aopehheans dream-worship The Black Death.
God's punishment.
Flagellants wander raped country sides
whipping babies
As atonement for their sins.

Frightened.

A Hundred Years War.
Ha.
A Billion.
Do Nothing.

"My mother worshiped dad. When they took the dance floor the brightest star in the heavens beaconed upon them. Every motion telling their story. Hillbillies and Palm Beachers stood blank. When mom died, dad's new wife had him concrete over her name and mine by the front door to mom's dream house."

NS

Journal Entry 91—**WALKING MY BABY BACK HOME**

October 20, 1983.

Black Hole's.

Late.

"Last night I dreamed a flow of words poured into a grave. Mine. I was lying in the dirt. No coffin. Staring up at friends peering down. Everything became black. The words crushed. Then, I woke up."

"Someone in the business after six or seven years might tell you what that means. I can't. I'm not sure anyone knows."

"Freud?"

"People always want a success story. Life is not a success story. Not since The Garden. We are all lost. To be alive is to be depressed. To know the truth is to be depressed a little more."

"Did Eng diagnose you with bipolar depression?"

"Yes. That's why my lithium must be monitored. Eng believes Heraclitus. When gods die they become men. When men die they become Gods."

"Do you believe Freud hated sex?"

"Yes. Freud was primarily a writer. Any real writer hates man. Writers can take what they want. Do what they want. But they must pay for it. Dostoyevsky said, if there is no God then anything is possible. Say that ten times to yourself. See if that doesn't scare you."

"I excavated Fort Boonesborough for 30 straight days. Dug with the University of Kentucky. Dug BLOCK C. Despite the fact that the person in charge of the dig didn't appreciate my honest remarks about Daniel Boone's life and asked me to dig out away from the main group where I could no longer be heard, I dug into a hearth that produced a particular piece of redware that we were all desperately searching for. This particular pottery proved that we were in the actual fort site. And because of this there might be a chance of receiving future grants for more intensive excavations. TV stations came down to film our digging. So did others including Eastern Kentucky University. For several weeks after the dig I gave talks about the dig to anthropology classes. Many years later when the leader of the dig was asked if she remembered my digging with her she stated that no such thing had ever occurred."

NS

Journal Entry 92 – **SAYS MY HEART**

October 29, 1983

Dawn.

Atop Pilot Knob. Boone's lookout point. Appalachian panorama.

Sandstone. Ancient beach. God's sentenced beach for my eternity. Jack rocks weathering. Fossil molds.

Dark Star sits smoking a ten gauger, looking. Passive.

A strong wind.

7:00 PM. Showered. Shaved. Jumbo margaritas sit on opposite sides of guacamole dip. Chi Chi's. Norman Vincent Peale's version of a Mexican restaurant. Sensi and I chomp. Her cinnamon mane drapes across a black coat. Emerald eyes. Each freckle sparkles.

"I'll give you one thousand dollars for that coat," says a stranger.

Sensi passes a pigeon smile.

Midway into third margaritas we are seated to a booth.

"It's not gone like we dreamed."

"No. Your life has gone well. You earned it. Mine, well."

"If you had gone to The University of New Mexico you'd've been an archeologist."

"An archeologist without Sensi would've been nothing. I'm sorry I haven't given you and Wide Eyes more. I was always afraid I'd turn out to be just what I am. Thank God for pigeons. They're buying the drinks tonight."

Two fresh margaritas appear. Compliments of a girl we met at the bar. I ask the Mexican waiter to ask the girl and her friends to join us. In a few minutes four girls sit, two on each side of Sensi and I. Short haired. Mention P.E. and lacrosse.

"You two married?"

"We were married long before we ever met. Somewhere in the cosmos."

"Have you done much nightlifing in Lexington?"

"Nothing of consequence."

"Ever been to JA's?"

"Yeah. I hear it's about twenty percent straight."

"I wouldn't go that high."

"Did you like it there?"

"No."

"What do you do for a living?"

"She's a teacher. I raise pigeons."

"Pigeons?"

"The kind that go, coo."

"Wanna hear a something that'll blow your mind? She's gay. She's gay. She's gay. I'm gay. What do you think?"

"I'm glad everyone is happy. Happiness is elusive."

"I've been all over the United States. There's more gays in eastern Kentucky than any place. Does that shock you?"

"No."

"Really! How do you feel about gays?"

"They've got their hell, I've got mine."

"Do you go to church?"

"I raise pigeons."

"One of the proudest moments in my grandmother's life was my being awarded a pen for having never missed a Sunday in church for thirteen straight years. Later on someone in my family stole it."

NS

Journal Entry 93 – **ME, MYSELF AND I**

November 5th thru 7th, 1983

Air rushes through my window. I'm drifting. Open tunnel. Down the snake. Wheels spin. Music thumps. Tree shadows meet. Fall afternoon. Narrow rows. Van and I are shadow. Moving. Zebra patterns. Rib patterns. Jail patterns. Shadow wind sweeps. I flow. Aopehh's mountains, bridge and cornfields disappear. *JESUS DONE LEFT CHICAGO* sirens. Wonder which friend stole my billfold? Only Mike knew I hid it under my van seat. Three hundred dollars. THC and ZZ Top combine. High and down. Alone. Heading for another Mike friend. A Jack Daniels Musket Mike.

Angie, Mike's wife, hugs. Smoke and sip.

"Hope this pigeon show doesn't bore you."

"As long as there is Jack."

Rebel Yell sits between us. My driver's license was inside my billfold. One rear light is out. I-75 North. Buckeyes. Catholic Cincinnati. Spirals.

"Pour another."

"What's with the duffel bags?"

"Dirty laundry."

Midnight rendezvous. Enon, Ohio. Thick eye glasses greet. A wounded Nam marine. Jack Daniels smiles. Pizza rings at the door.

Van moves. Two Mikes and me. Images back off from ten gauge. Lights. House. Parked. Five hundred dollars. I'm back. Purple Heart stares. Black hearts kiss Jack. Beacons catch mating rabbits.

Back in Purple Heart's kitchen.

"I'll kill that son of a bitch!"

Drinks.

"What?"

"If your Purple Heart ever puts another knife to my neck---he's dead."

"He's just drunk."

"I'll kill him!"

"Yeah. You'll kill him. OK."

Fifths vanish.

"I got it here."

Chest bared.

5:45 AM. Hot shower. Red eyes. We're off.

VFW Hall. Six hundred racing homers on stance. One hundred expectant glares. Friends. Most have my blood.

Big I and I lab coated. Strobes. Metallic shades.

"Hackle," spouts Big I. "Body first. Beauty second."

I disagree.

Birds shuffle.

Open vents. Deep keels. Too much pocket. Tunneling. Neck cuts. Eleven flights. Split tail. Pearl eyes. Too much back skull. Rangy.

Show breaks. Lunch. One o'clock. Hippies stance door. Earrings. Grinning. Braids. "Eh! No Sweat!"

Van. Ten pounds. Eleven hundred. Musket Mike counts.

Window knocks. Mr. Ten Per Cent. "No Sweat, they need you inside."

Showroom. Smoke droops wings. Open backs open. Big I sits to my left. Audience observes our judging. Listens to our comments. Big I knows the score.

Best In Show announced. Mr. Ten Per Cent's racer. He's drunk. Confused. Suffering the loss of a stolen entry.

Losers re-shuffle birds to crates. Crates to cars. Cars to lofts.

Purple Heart settles up. Eighteen hundred. The pigeon auction. My birds. Half for me. Bills wad blue jeans.

"Mike, money isn't the root of evil. It's the love of money."

Getting gas and six packed. Jeans feel the ocean in the dark snowfall. Spews. JESUS DONE LEFT CHICAGO. And Enon.

Dawn.

Aopehh.

"When my father's brother's lock box was opened seven of his nine wives were in attendance. All it contained was an 8" x 10" black and white photo of him nude with an erection."

NS

Journal Entry 94 – **LET'S CALL A HEART A HEART**

November 9, 1983

Dreamy harvest.

A mockingbird stripes the breeze.

Crinkly leaves.

A sky beyond forgotten leaves.

Winter whispers.

I trail flashing.

Dark Star's jaunt into reticent ES #1.

All is pearl.

Such depth.

Leaves sigh.

Smells woo.

Dark Star's camo winks.

Briars re-mingle.

Dark Star studies. Beyond limpid grasses pouts virgins.

Slash.

Defiant plants weep. Ancient plants lay piled in unzipped sleeping bags. Plant and man pose. Nectarous spearmint cloys. Regal sens. Jasmine. Luring dirge. Bags zip. Machetes secured. Groundhog gets hoe. Stalks spear the air. Spartans at Thermopile spearing the river. Polk is scattered. Purple berries stain. Es#1 total in nature. Undetectable.

Silence. Nothing happened. The river sweeps. That degage river.

Into the jeep. The attic. Sens was hung by the chimney with care.

Ten gauge burns. From a camo pocket comes a Bladder story:

"LIPS PLEADS INOCENT!"

District Judge Lips waived a formal arraignment and pled not guilty to official misconduct charges during proceedings in Aopehh last Wednesday.

Lips was recently indicted by the Aopehh Grand Jury on charges that allege mishandling of drug charges in a case last fall.

At the arraignment last week, special prosecutor Trueman Deny said the tapes of the

Grand Jury discussions concerning the indictments were either completely missing or did not exist and now, no one seemed to have any idea of the tapes whereabouts or what could have possibly happened to them.

Special Judge, Rebecca Oversight, inferred the tapes were very crucial to the Commonwealth's defense against Lips. Because the facts given at the time of the indictment were not very specific.

Oversight termed the disappearance most unusual. And said she was bothered very much that the court was put in an unusual position because of this.

Richmond attorney, Shy, Lip's council, requested the charges be dropped after learning of the missing tapes. Because 'the effectiveness of Lip's court is being greatly impaired and a real urgency exists for speedy disposition of the matter.'

Oversight gave Deny ten days to either produce the tapes or affidavits from the jury and foreman and others in contact with the tapes.

Dark Star released smoke, smiling.

The wind swept across the water

"Slap me if I don't put flowers on my father's grave. Plastic flowers."
NS

Journal Entry 95 – **THE MOON LOOKS DOWN AND LAUGHS**

November 24, 1983

Doc. Hands swollen. Wantin' huntin'.

Gauger smoked.

Parley.

Old road.

Laughing. No sense crying.

Doc's been screwin' True.

And she ripped him for four hundred.

Laughin'. No sense cryin'.

Blackwidow wrecked one of her lover's cars.

She told the law, SEIZURE.

"I get them seizures sometimes, don't you?"

Laughin'. No sense cryin'.

Long drive down to the river.

Rattlin' pick up smells like high school.

"That Chops! Did you catch his dinner drift?"

"The Judge said, thirty flat years or castration.

The otherns had to take impudent pills."

Laughin'. No sense cryin'.

The cracked mirror hangs wounded.

I glimpse a cryin' stranger.

I'm drivin'.

They took Doc's liscense.

That mouth tells stories.

God's hands are swollen.

They gotta be."

"Good writing is frying a mountain of onions. A lot of crying. And the longer the words simmer the less they become."

NS

Journal Entry 96 – **SADDEST TALE**

December 6, 1983

Sensi, Black Hole and I. Heading to Richmond to see a portrayal of Twain at Model's school auditorium.

A gorgeous redhead and a dark knight. Ballast. I was lucky. One pushing for life. The other, opposite. Black Hole warned me, never lose her.

He loved her, too.

Her freckles brightened Aopehh.

Black Hole's Air Force monthly retirement money all went for the care of his invalid mother and to his two sons. There was nothing he wanted. But out. When I had first moved to be the neighbor of Black Hole's mother she'd gone to The City Council complaining that my pigeons were eating her chimney and tulips. I typed a response explaining that racing homers had little such notions. Until Black Hole arrived, she spent most her time throwing empty cans. Doing all she could to addle anything avian invading her space. Developed a good arm. The Reds needed her.

How proud she must have been when he graduated from West Point. The only Aopehhean ever to do so. Beautiful pianist. How desperate she must have been when her husband died the year before he graduated. Black Hole became all.

Handsome was nothing.

How horrible emotionally in debt he was to all he had ever loved. Inside a body fighting him at every turn.

Yes, out.

Parking.

EKU's lot is full. Basketball.

Snowing. Bitter wind. Black Hole's favorite weather.

Inside the Model's auditorium. Eight people total. Four are children.

Twain sits cave quiet in his opposing white attire in front of maroon curtains. Shocked hair. Walrus mustache. Stammering voice. Striking matches. Trying to light a cigar:

"You perceive, now, that these things are all impossible except in a dream. You perceive that they are pure and puerile insanities, the silly creations of an imagination that is not conscious of its freaks--in a world, that they are a dream, and you the maker of it. The dream marks are all present; you should have recognized earlier.

It is true, that which I have revealed to you: There is no God, no universe, no human race, no earthly life, no heaven, no hell. It is all dream--a grotesque and foolish dream. Nothing exists but you. And you are but a thought--a vagrant thought, a useless thought, a homeless thought, wandering forlorn among empty eternities."

Performance ended.

We three stand applauding.

Twain winks. Points in our direction.

Minutes later. Conversing.

"Europeans loved him. He sold more in Europe than in America."

Interruption. From the only other adult in attendance.

"I imagine they did like him. Especially the Russians. He was an atheist."

Twain and we three stare. The man attacking the performance is acclaimed to be one of Richmond's best doctors.

Black Hole ignores the doctor. Continues talking with Twain.

"His family was enveloped by him."

"Only one daughter survived him. She had only one child, that died. He has no living heirs."

"You," stated Black Hole.

The doctor re-interrupted. "Twain lost all of his money. That's why he hated everything and was so bitter."

It was time to leave.

Loosening my tie, we talked on the drive home.

"I don't believe Twain could foresee mega death."

"Or Cabbage Patch Dolls."

"Our nation is Fantasia."

"For nine dollars New York will give your Cabbage Patch Doll an astrological reading."

"Know what Caudill said about Lexington?"

"No?"

"Aopehh took Lexington without firing a shot. Do you see any artistry in an eight foot black man dropping a ball through a hole?"

"I couldn't believe it was possible that dad was worse to mom after she died than when she was alive."

NS

"If you can't cry and write, don't."

NS

Journal Entry 97 – **GOD BLESS THE CHILD**

December 16, 1983

Rollanotherone, long overdue, had Simon. Dark Star waxed. We looked through the hospital window. I bragged. Rollanotherone's parents were suspicious. Bad spoke of Aopehh's School Board. Upset their only child's husband had been terminated. Never to teach again.

Simon came home below zero. Frozen well. Rollanotherone's requests. Fetch wood for pot bellies. Axe out creek. Tote sixty gallons. Pour some water in pans. Put them on the stoves. The three grandparents hovered. Dark Star and I put on a wonderful performance. Discussed Conrad and caving. Rollanotherone's father peered at me with my bucket and axe.

We left out. Stayed on the creek a long time. When we got back all the parents were gone. As we warmed our hands I spoke about my Buckeye call. Marijuana certain sold.

Upstairs, Dark Star went to a door leading to a walled eve, squeezing through. Cellophane half pound bags of marijuana accumulated on the floor. Two years labor. The marijuana had faded from cane break green to brown and gray. The bags were still air tight. Filled with leaf.

Downstairs, we sat on the floor. A mounted grouse was on the wall. Dark Star rolled a purple joint next to his stove. The one carpeted floor was a patchwork of samples. Plants surrounded us. An elephant's ear touched my head.

It was late. Simon and Rollanotherone were bedded down. Dark Star and I and third joint. Custer's Afghan. The stove door was open. Fire shot into my face.

"Burning must be the worst way to die."

"No. living in Aopehh."

Making two trips, I carried four double lined garbage bags tightly filled with half pound bags of marijuana. I left the hollow. Marijuana in van. I felt all was a dark dream. Oblivious to the intense cold. Purple Afghan. The radio thumped. *I HEAR THE SECRETS YOU KEEP WHEN YOU'RE TALKING IN YOUR SLEEP.* Deserted highway. Then, double bright headlights. For two miles, the law.

The next morning. Saturday. Up early. Showered. Beige suit. White shirt. Kelly tie with fox on the end. Kissed both girls. Suitcase. Be home Sunday night.

Headed over Aopehh's Bridge. Wind rippling half froze Kentucky. Marijuana in the back. I-75 North. Bible on the dash. Bootlegger's trick.

Passing Lexington, Cincinnati, Dayton. Finally, Springfield, Ohio. Gas station. Noon. Calling, Rick. Next, Bob, Ten Percent's buddy.

At Bob's.

"Where's Ten Percent?"

"He was drunk all night. Be over. Noon."

Changing clothes. Boots. Torn jeans. T-shirt. Black leather Harley jacket. Heavy belt. Heavier knife.

Ten Percent showed. Head for bar. Fifth beer evolves into tequila. Ten Percent makes calls. Speaks low. Rendezvous at Boots Bar. Nine.

Drunk at Boots. Looks like Sloppy Joe's. Band destroying country. Eerie eye looks me over. Whiskers buys me a drink. "The law is after me," he says. "Slapped the ol' lady. Ain't been to bed in four days."

"The band wants some of your smoke."

"How much?"

"A hundred dollars."

One AM. No rendezvous with Rick.

Back to Bob's. Kitchen table. Two pot bellies blaze. Low ceiling. Farmhouse. One room, a shrine to Elvis. Hawk-eyed Bob. 105 pounds. 5'1". Black hair, straight Elvis. Cigarette welded to fingers.

"I was a sergeant in the War. Fought about on every island. Ran a still in the

Philippines. The MPs knew I had mines laid out Left me alone. Made shine from the cavalry's horse feed. Captured a Jap officer. Still have his pistol. I was the first to walk into the prison camp holding The Bataan Death March survivors. I got a Jap whore's bar graveled. Boy, did we make out. I was also the first to walk into Hiroshima after the bomb. My father got killed on an Indian inside a circle rink. My grandparents raised me."

Bob stretched. Walked to a hutch. Got out a notebook. Handed it to me. Paintings. Sketches. His father's. Talent. Putting it up. Placed between Hawthorne, Dickens and Melville.

A foot of snow fell during the night. Sunday morning. Bob's kitchen table. Fourth cup of tea. Phone ringing.

"Hey! This is Pete. Are you, the No Sweat with the Kentucky blue grass?"

"The grass ain't blue."

"Ten Percent told me about you. I'll be over."

An hour later. Bob's garage. Motorcycles and machinery. Bob stoking. Ten Percent's contacts. Strangers. Chopper types. Bob's buddies. Two Cheech and Chongers, Rick being one. Pete a clean cut pilot. And a gypsy in a black Dodge van with hex signed windows.

450

Caution. Select talk. Rick's Michelob and my joints help.

First the buds. Five pounds. Manicured. One thousand a pound.

Next, fifteen pounds of shake. Old. Starting to crumble. A lot of seeds. Asked two fifty a pound. Got, two.

Last, straight leaf. Twenty pounds. Pete triple beamed. Gave two thousand.

The beer vanished. Everyone would double. Once they left I gave Ten Percent a thousand dollars. Bob got a half pound of shake. We ate boiled pork chops. I headed home.

It was late when I came back across Aopehh's Bridge. I leaned over kissing my two girls as they slept. Their long red hairs dark. Entwined together.

Two blankets from the closet. I lay at the foot of the bed. Piled Hell's Angel gear beside me. Tomorrow, Dark Star would get his half. You fool. You could have been busted. Oh well, Florida.

"I once had one of the finest Indian relic
collections in Kentucky. Forty Clovis points.
Forty dovetails. And much more. My life was
wrapped in them. Each a story. One summer
while my family was in Florida my sister's
boyfriend stole everything. Sold it all for a little
cash and drugs. I laid awake nights thinking.
But never did anything. Never got a single piece
returned. The loss taught me a lot about
material possessions. Was one of the best things
that ever happened."

NS

Journal Entry 98 **WHAT IS THIS THING
CALLED LOVE**

516 Poplar

Aopehh, Kentucky

December 24, 1983

Dear Doug,

Received your letter. Thank your family for scouring England for a Cabbage Patch Doll. Please inform them that Santa did manage to acquire one. There will be joy on Christmas morning for Wide Eyes.

You inquired about getting to judge at The National Young Bird Show. In the end it will be up to Big I. He's not keen about the way Europeans view racing pigeons. But rest assured that I will write on your behalf. I have to be careful in what I say as you may appreciate.

I am assuming you've seen the journals and read about my winning my sixth Southern Racing Pigeon Association Show. I remain undefeated in what is actually the largest show in The United States. No one has ever come close to this record. A powder blue hen earned the victory. The Convention was in Ashville, North Carolina. I was asked to give a seminar on the sport. When I began with Thomas Wolfe's *LOOK HOMEWARD ANGEL* the crowd scratched their heads. I discussed not the showing of racing homers but rather how for some strange reason romance had always failed to play any part of pigeon literature. I then read a story about an insecure boy living in the Kentucky mountains next to a pigeon-filled bridge. And how those pigeons lifted his soul and held him together. In the end they were all crying.

Poor Roy has been banned from The Chicago Combine and The American Racing Pigeon Union. He was caught cheating on The American Racing Pigeon Union Convention Race. It's a wonder he wasn't done in. Found on the ground from an accidental fall from high above. Remember, Brando has pigeons in ON THE WATFRONT. Roy also sold a stolen bird at a show. And his checks have been bouncing. Despite his errors there is a child in him that I like. Maybe I shouldn't say such as I understand he still owes you for imports.

My breeding program is primarily a few select pairs line breeding for powder blues and blood red velvets. We're enduring the coldest December on record. Always testy for raising babies. Last year it was 70 degrees warmer on this date.

The next time Scotland Yard assigns you to guard Princess Diana, give her a little pinch for No Sweat.

No Sweat

"When I was fifteen I was placed in Aopehh's dungeon jail for Breach Of Peace. Officers Riddell and Ward were most proud. After a darksome night with my cellmate, Mitch Neal, Aopehh's singular bridge painter, I plead guilty. Paid a $6.50 fine."

NS

Journal Entry 99 – **FOGGY DAY**

December 31, 1983

North Aopehh. Cobhill. Snow scares school buses. Over on the backside, another mountain, Sally Ann. There's a hollow back in there with hemlocks Boone thick. Off that hollow shoots other hollows where sun is precious. Whims of fern. Lichens. Moss. Partridge berry. Stillness. A pathless place. Tonic for troubles. Warblers flit. Sunflower yellow with satin-black hoods. What road is near is creek rock and mud. Come winter, jeeps can't make it.

Dark Star and I left the women. All the way I prayed his brakes would hold. Blinding snow. Keen air. We were dressed warm and rough. Going caving with Custer. Our four best cola tops rested between us. Peanuts were in our RCs.

"Slow down."

"Get some sens burning."

I lit our calumet. Strange whispers began. Several tokes later. All is apparition. Another bowl tamped. I'm half dead, half alive. Images speed. Perfection. Color. Angelic. Imaginary. Beneath the delicate flakes mute grasses cry. Along the frozen cliffs, immense icicles aim. A beech flexes its muscle, tossing snow. Who am I? I grow distant. Floating beyond the jeep into the sky. The calumet warmed my hand.

"Put some more sens in the caluuuumetttt."

"Yeahhhhh."

Mouth fog. Fire breathing simians. Lost in mystery. Romance in white hell. Parking. Crystal Creek. Upstream, Custer's. Miles. Numb cheeks. A droopy oak sleeps on a tiny island ice surrounded. Bracket fungus trails upward gnawing.

Frozen landscape. Murmuring water. Ice. The last day of 1983. Lungs hold all bearable. Dark Star copies desperation. Demure folly.

Still another mile. Sitting. Ten below. Content. Creamy foam glistens. Calico towee hop-scratches backward. Cascading mountains overlap into Vs. Silver poplars. A half moon hangs facing the sun.

"What's this pipe made of?"

"Persimmon roots. Kentucky's finest pipe wood. Nothing else harder. Or blacker."

"For black souls."

Moving further. Footprints. Fox. Rabbit. Coon. Birds.

Dead shadows.

Solid creek. Frozen. Heaving chunks of flint. Nothing cracks.

Moving. Snow swirls leave S patterns. Dark Star and I pause. Pipe. Eat snow. Woodsy. Pure.

"Look."

Beneath the ice, liverwort. Beside it, a terrapin. Brown and gold. Complete. A short haired dog meets us. Custer's.

"What kind is he?"

"Cur. Carob's been all over. During Nam he protested in Washington. Bit the police. He's been jailed, shot, poisoned, caught in traps, run over, stole and whipped."

Juncos flitted among the cedar tops. Leaving the creek we moved to a forested rise. Below, through the symmetry of maple branches was Custer's. Off from his double log cabin connected by a dog-walk was a pyramid.

"He's been talking about a pyramid ever since moving here," spoke Dark Star. Then, behind us, out of the belly of a sycamore, appeared a grinning Custer holding a Winchester.

"I could-a blown you away."

"Too bad you didn't."

"Like my pyramid?

"Yeah."

"You said you were going to build one."

"I say a lot of things," said Custer. He was wearing overalls. Thin red hair trailed from his toboggan to his hips. A Nordic hillbilly. The clone of General Armstrong Custer. He had fled to Aopehh living under a false name. Secretive. Mouse was the name of the girl that lived with him. Her brown hair wasn't as long as Custer's. And her blue eyes, more relaxed. Mouse was a beaten down earth child. Loved cooking. She'd been the wife of a DC DJ. Had a son by BJ the

DJ. Everyone lived with Custer. BJ was fifteen. Stephen Crane handsome.

Entering the cabin the smell of good food filled the air. The kitchen table was loaded. At the table with BJ were three maidens rolling marijuana. A green and white friendship quilt hung down the wall behind them.

"Hope you're hungry," said Mouse, sitting next to a stove. BJ gave us hugs before we got our jackets off.

"Was the walk in, bad?"

"It was beautiful."

"Take long?"

"Three pipes of sens."

"Got any left?"

"Do pigeons coo in their dreams?"

Open chestnut beams ran over our heads. On the kitchen wall above the wooden icebox and straight over the stove was a framed 1927 New York Times. I walked over and read aloud." Mexican party go insane. Five said to be stricken by eating marijuana. Mexico City, July 5. A widow and her six children have been driven insane by eating the marijuana plant, according to doctors, who say there is no hope of saving the children's lives and that the mother will be insane for the rest of her life. The horrible tragedy occurred while the body of the father, who had been killed, was still in the hospital. The mother without money to buy other food for the children, whose ages range from 14 to 19, so they gathered some herbs and vegetables growing in the yard for their dinner. Two hours after the mother and children had eaten the plants, they were stricken. Neighbors, hearing outbursts of insane laughter, rushed to the house to find the entire family insane. Examination revealed that the narcotic marijuana was growing among the garden vegetables."

A cut glass sphere hung from one window. In a door less hutch next to the icebox were shelves of honey, blackberry preserves, Mason jars of beans, pears, okra, apples, tomatoes, squash, kraut, beets and moonshine. One whole shelf held bread and butter pickles.

At the table set a cut glass lamp and two blackberry cobblers, a block of cheese, a sweet potato pie, a basket of apples and a gallon of Custer's cherry wine. A cola nearly two feet in length as fat as a coke bottle, rested in a wooden bowl. Four high backed Shaker chairs held the women as they passed the pie. Something was bubbling on the stove.

"What's cooking?"

"Stuff to smell up the place."

"Making me hungry."

"You boil three cinnamon sticks, orange and grapefruit peel, clove and some pine needles. Would you like some tea? Strawberry, sassafras and marijuana. It's good for your blood."

Behind me was a stained glass window. Running down it was a string of peppers and Indian corn. On the other side ran leather breeches beans down to a red agate I had given them two years ago.

The dog walk led to another two-story cabin. "1784 was written in the root cellar," said Custer. "Wanna try my shine?"

"Check the blubber."

"Blubber?"

"The bead."

Dark Star shook the jar. The shine spun round and round.

"Look at that goose eye," spoke BJ. The bubbles popped and disappeared.

"Won't be long till '84," said Dark Star, lifting the jar to his lips.

"To George Orwell," I stated, having a taste. "Ain't no hog died in this batch."

One of the maidens, blonde, willowy, tight jeaned, agate breasted, moved to the window, reading as we fought moonshine and marijuana." What-cha reading?" I asked.

"Nothing."

"Must be a Kentucky author."

Lighting a lantern we proceeded to follow Custer down some steps. The blonde stepped behind me. Mouse brought up the rear carrying another lamp. We stepped down into a cold room where Custer was grinning. "Paradise," he claimed. Two walls were lined with gallon jugs of moonshine. A third wall held jars of vegetables, fruit and gallons of wine. In the middle of the fourth wall blank shelves rested against a rock laid foundation. "Hold the lamp," spoke Custer. Strawberry scent came from the globe. Custer disassembled the section of the shelved area of the rock wall. Then, he exposed a secret door. Beyond the door was a dark corridor.

"Where's the tunnel go?" asked Dark Star.

"To the pyramid," answered Custer. "You wanted to go caving, how's this?" Taking the lamp, he stooped and walked. We followed. "We're just a few feet from the surface through here." Coming to another door, Custer opened it. Everyone went through the door stepping down several steps, entering inside the pyramid. Inside was a table and four chairs, a bunk bed, a Jim Morrison poster and a moonshine still with water lines feeding to and from the room. On the table sat a circular brass container, oriental in design. We sat as Custer undid the lid. "More paradise," he said lifting a resinous bud.

I was sitting on top of the copper still watching the blonde. "What's that?" I asked, pointing to a wooden barrel with copper arms running in and out of it.

Custer glanced. His red eyes continued pinching the bud. "Thumper keg. Puts the thump to the corn."

I got down off the still. "We ought ta have a smoke-off. See whose marijuana is the best."

The blonde looked at me, then spoke. "You two give me the marijuana you want judged. Give me some time. Then, everyone come back to the cabin. I'll have the joints rolled. No one but me will know which marijuana is which."

"I'm game," I said, reaching into my paratrooper pants, handing her a cellophane bag of buds.

"Here's this," said Custer, handing her part of his bud.

The blonde lifted a lamp, disappearing up the steps and through the door.

When we all regrouped in the kitchen the warmth felt great. Four joints of equal size lay on the table. Each joint was to be smoked one at a time. Each would be given a grade from 1 to 100. Aroma, taste and effect.

The first joint smelled like a skunk and was quickly consumed.

The second joint smelled like spearmint.

By the last joint night had fallen. While the blonde tabulated the results the blackberry cobblers were devoured. BJ sat next to a window with a green-eyed maiden in his lap. Pure hippy. They stared at frozen snowflakes.

"It's a tie," announced the blonde.

We all laughed.

"Let's get wood for the cabins," said Custer. The guys went outside to the woodpile. "You all stay over tonight. We'll hit the cave in the morning."

As midnight approached the guys stood outside shooting the Winchester at the moon.

"Wilde said it was awful how so many fine people wind up in some useful profession."

"Think the blonde would like to shoot the moon?"

"No Sweat, you ask her. She likes you."

In the kitchen everyone was stoned to the max. "Would you like to shoot the moon?" I asked.

"I'd love to shoot the moon," replied the blonde.

Outside. Alone.

"I've never shot a gun before."

"All you do is cock this lever. Put it up to your shoulder. Aim at the moon. Squeeze the trigger."

"Would you get me a glass of cherry wine before I do this. Find out how many minutes it is before midnight."

"I'll be right back," I said. As I touched the door a shot fired.

In the snow the blonde lay motionless.

"In the middle of the apartment that I grew up in there was a room where mom kept the record player. I'd stack up Gershwin, Billie Holiday, Sinatra, Ella Fitzgerald and Nat King Cole. The old player just barely held them. Mom sang as she prepped supper. I sat in a corner writing one page stories. For over an hour our grey confines were wondrous. Mom's deer roast. Fried rabbit. Frog legs. Duck. Food from the heart. It didn't matter that the skylight leaked. Or that roaches crawled in from the theatre. I never fret about heaven. I've been there."

NS

Journal Entry 100 – **IF YOU WERE MINE**

January 21, 1984

Minus thirty below. No wind chill factor. Saturday. Six AM. Two foot of snow concretes Aopehh. Starlings mob. Water lines burst. Iced windows. Stillness. Baby pigeons die in a minute if parents leave for food. White hell.

Dark Star, Quarterback, Badwhite and I are headed to Sally Ann. Grouse hunt. Rusty jeep is igloo. Cramped.

"Get-cha a swaller of this. Warm you up."

"Alcohol gives a false---"

"Drink. I went through Bahamian storm just so you could share this moment."

Quarterback took a hit. Shook his head. Handed it back.

"Puts summer in your belly."

Badwhite rolls a gauger of purple. Quarterback and I burn one in the back. Dark Star maneuvers. Slides in IT WAS TWENTY YEARS AGO TODAY. Chug holes. Thermos. Cinnamon spiced rum. Sticky slosh. Numb feet. Guns fresh scratch. I'm wearing two toboggans, five T-shirts, two long underwear, sweat pants, insulated pants, two pair of socks, insulated boots and two pair of gloves.

Parked.

Out. Paired. Quarterback and I. One side of Crystal Creek. Badwhite and Dark Star, the other. Slow pace. Hard snow. Woods are postcard.

Miles and hours later.

We covey. Abandon cabin.

"Won't be many like this in a few more years."

"Once the roof goes, she's gone."

"Time for breakfast, ain't it?"

"What's on the menu?"

"Sardines in mustard sauce. Rum and marijuana."

Joint passes. Rum follows. Quarterback pulls out a quart of Asti.

"Better drink fast before it freezes."

Last sip. Feet numb hurt. Standing at the back door. Snow light.

Leaving.

A valley. Five hundred yards of clear. Corn stalks. Yellow-gray. Log cabin. Barn.

Inside.

Wall chart describing the effects of drugs. HIGH TIMES. Packs of rolling papers. Strewn post cards from France, Key West, Washington, DC, California.

Outside.

"Buds!" cries Quarterback from barn's loft.

"Don't get it all!"

Scramble. Laughing. Quarterback sits. Smiles. Half pound of tops. Thousands of stripped stalks crisscross. Empty garbage bags. Tape on side reads, AFGAN.

"Wonder where they are?"

"French Riviera."

"What do you think, No Sweat?"

"Death shadowed Vicky closer than any girl I ever knew. Judges were quandrified punishing such an enchantress. She was Elvis handsome. Elvis paced. Smoked marijuana. Snorted coke. Shot up. A sexual panther. Had lived with my friends before marrying my best. They were rich with little to do. Champagne kisser. Aopehh's sultress. In the end was prison. Then, cancer. What a divine mystery. I miss her so."

NS

Journal Entry 101--- **TWENTY-FOUR HOURS A
DAY**

February 13, 1984

Parking my van I went to see Doc. I hadn't seen him since Thanksgiving. He'd grown recluse since his divorce. Aopehh canonized him. Thought he had it made. Satin sheet waterbed. Leather couches. Thousand dollar watches. Diamonds. Drugs. Strife was on R and R. Ringing the doorbell I got no reply. It was one in the afternoon. I went around to the side of the house and threw pebbles against the upstairs window near his bed. On my seventh throw the curtains moved. A window opened. "What the hell is it?" he said.

"It's No Sweat. It's raining. Open the door."

Fifteen minutes later Doc opened the door. He was pale and drowsy. "Can you take me up to Mamalade's. Mom's got my scripts up there."

Doc got in my van and we headed through Aopehh. "Dad gave my family what he always gives for Christmas. Nothing. You get use to it. I've seen him tip Keeneland whores hundred dollar bills. Mom was supposed to see a specialist about her skin. Have you seen her?"

"No."

"She's wearing long sleeves and pants trying to hide the sores. Her liver has gone to hell. Says it's nerves. She was supposed to go see the specialist today. But she's so drunk she can't move. Dad didn't try to take her. He won't quit drinking to help. Says she's weak. There's nothing he can do. Real love. He doesn't think

471

about mom. Just himself. He doesn't want to deal with mom being an alcoholic. He won't make any sacrifices. He keeps saying that mom's family owes him. What has he ever given them?"

"Blackwidow is de-toxing in Lexington. But, ahh, that's all a bunch of talk. She'll get more over there than she got off me."

Parking at Marmalade's drugstore, Doc stepped out entering the heavy wood and glass door setting off a bell. The Venetian blinds swayed. Outside, faceless Aopehheans disappeared into the surrounding colorless mountains. Rain formed pools in the potholes. A filling station waves good bye to a bootlegged six pack.

Ten minutes later Doc got back in my van. *TEENAGE JAIL* was playing. Ten minutes more we were at the bottom of Doc's stairs that led up to his part of the house. A sketch of a vulture by him was on the wall. It had a hole ripped through it. "What happened?"

"Shrapnel."

I remembered. Doc caught Blackwidow in bed with one of his friends. Emptied his pistol through the house. Going up the newly carpeted steps we were soon in Doc's den of darkness. A long, open, spacious room. I stepped across guitars making my way over to a black leather couch smothered in cameras and porn.

"Here you go," spoke Doc, handing me a joint. "There's Budweiser down stairs. Excuse me while I shoot up."

"Don't mind me, Doc." The lurid image entered his doorless, yellow bathroom reflecting faint shadows. Doc moved near the medicine cabinet.

"Check out my new sound system and speakers---Santa."

"Bet that cost."

"Four thousand," answered Doc. Then something popped. A few seconds later there was another pop. "Damn!"

"What is it?"

"Can't find a vein."

I took a hit off the joint. "What-cha shooting?"

"Demerol."

"How's this sens compare to Demerol?"

Silence.

When Doc stepped out there were pink dots on his swollen hands. Those hands had been like that for years. He had lost himself in that bathroom. It comforted him. He had been lost since birth. Once he came out I went. He began testing his microphone and amplifiers. Throaty echoes. The Afghan was settling over me. Drops of fresh blood were on the on the tile. In the sink was a bent spoon, needle and a piece of surgical rubber. "I'm going to call Bullet. My pistol was stolen last night. I know who got it. That bootlegger, Troy." Doc sang something Mexican for a half hour. When we were kids we use to slide over the hills on cardboard. Walked the tracks, swam the river, hunted, camped, shot fireworks, formed clubs. I drew another hit of Afghan. The doorbell rang. Two Aopehhean High Schoolers.

"Doc, did-ja hear what just happened to Littleman? The law blew out his brains."

"He's laying on the street right now."

"After Lindy committed suicide his twin sons
flew in. Stayed with me. One a MD. The other, a
rodeo rider. For five nights we spoke of nothing
but. His body was donated to science. I never
went to the memorial. When the twins decided to
leave they chose to sell his house. Was going to
let a realtor have it for $15,000. I offered
$16,000. They took it. They only took a Boy
Scout Award belonging to their grandfather.
Nothing else. During the weeks that followed I
caught a half dozen people in the house. All had
keys that Lindy had given. All wanted
something. And got it. I sat for days alone in the
house. Totally haunted. Thompson and Riley
auctioneers offered me $1,000 for the contents
and got them. I took his West Point brass and
blanket, SAC uniform, photos, grey bathrobe
and a box that his mother had cherished. Inside
it were his baby things, a lock of hair, a silver
spoon, notes. What a dark force. A Black Hole.
Not all angels have wings."

NS

Journal Entry 102– **YOU GO TO MY HEAD**

March 11, 1984

The long winter again covered Aopehh. Pale Aopehheans hid in dark hollows. Lonely. Gazing into mirrors. Praying for Joe B.'s Wildcats to win the NCAA.

Dark Star got in my van. For a mile we straddled ruts before stopping at a farm house. Rust. Gray sky. A small boat sat on two flat tires. Sanctuary for guineas. I stepped out into a pack of dogs. A worn figure appeared on the porch calling them off. I kicked mud before entering the bleak refuge.

"Mrx told me you might sell your boat and motor?"

Standing next to her pot belly stove the woman fondled a baby hog in a blanket. The hog's mother roamed calmly through the house. "Five hundred dollars," she said.

Hitting blacktop. Noon. Aopehh. Off River Drive. Briary shanty. Mutts sound intrusion. Primitive figure appears from shed. Head the size of a baseball. Arch. He knows of my interest in his twelve foot green aluminum boat leaning

against a corroding fence. Arch talked World
War One. Germany. Trenches. Pepper Gas.
Bombs. Strewn bodies. Sometimes, old cowboy
days in Texas at ten dollars a month. No one
listened. Gleaming yellow-black teeth. Black
spotted pores. Leathered veneer. "She's a good-
urn. Coast Guard Boat. Read them words on it."

"Can I see the motor?"

Inside Arch's house. Getting a key to a
room inside the tool shed.

Bedroom. A hump deathly reposed. Gazing
expressionlessly toward the low ceiling. Greasy
machine parts lay at the foot of an 11" x 14" of
Jesus.

"The ol' woman and me are feeling poorly.
Here's the key. Look all you want. It's new. Ain't
used but twice. Went from the boat dock to the
locks. Don't use no gas."

In Arch's shed.

"She looks good."

"Listen! I work for The Man Above. I
wouldn't lie to a person. I wouldn't hurt nobody.
But let me tell you something. You gonna be on
that river this summer?"

"I guess."

"Well, don't go down there a-lessen you've got a good pistol. That river is a queer place. There's hoodlums down there. Last year, I was fishing at the Locks and catching a string of perch when some feller on the bank took to cussing. He was jealous cause I was catching them fish. I shut his mouth then and there. Got my pistol. Emptied it into the son of a bitch. Hit him a few rounds. I never checked. Never was sure. You should-a seen him kick up sand along the bank."

"And you think you might-a got him?"

"Don't know. He might be a-layin' in the high weeds this moment. No matter. A mean bastard like that. Jealous. Talkin' filthy. Outta be shot."

"Hopefully, a Buckeye."

"What you needing this boat for anyway? You ain't got marijuana growin' on your mind, do ya?"

"Lord no. I just want to run a trotline."

"She'll be good fer that."

"How much for everything?"

"Three hundred. I ain't taking a penny less."

Another stop. Fighting Branch. A shoddy fourteen footer leaned against a diseased water maple. Under it, a motor molded to the mud. Knocking on a torn screen door. A woman sitting in the window. Waves, come in.

Inside. House no bigger than a jail cell. Glass chickens rest next to Dish barn lamp. Pictures. An angel and three children walking through a forest. A hand-painted photo in a bronze frame of a young, mustached man. Her husband. Half century past. Crochet covers. Withered figure holds quiet. Wheel chair. Multi colored yarns. Two needles in her lap. Close by, a flesh-colored wooden leg. Just like Black Hole's mother's. Grey hair tied in a knot behind her head.

"You Rosy?"

"Yes."

"I'm No Sweat. I called over the boat on the radio."

"I thought I'd get rid of that ol' thing. It belonged to my husband. We use to use it on the creek before he died up at the quarry. That hole. He used to say he lived in a rock pile. Never figured he'd die there."

"You do any reading?"

"Can't read."

"Watch TV?"

"Don't want one."

"Radio?"

"I listen to WMAR. Just sit here. I'd like to get rid of everything and go on and die."

"All of us are lonely. Be glad you aren't a writer. They are the loneliest. They have to live twice."

"If the Lord loved me, he wouldn't have done this."

"Who knows what He knows."

"Oh, I know Him."

"Death nicks reality until reality becomes death."
NS

Journal Entry 103 – **LAUGHING AT LIFE**

April 8, 1984

Last night I stood at my back door. The porch light beamed behind me. A veil of clouds covered the moon. The mountain was dark. My shadow cast onto a fog. A glow of light surrounded the specter.

A week earlier I had taken Wide Eyes on her first camp out. Her face, short a tooth, reflected in the camp's fire as she gazed upward through the trees towards the sky. She seemed lost. The day of the camp out I paused by a waterfall down from the same hemlocks to photograph Sensi. Two strands of gray.

The day before the camp out Wide Eyes and I went to my old home. I showed her the dark apartment. We walked down the back steps and over to a hill looking at the coal spilt tracks below. Across the tracks a damp widow weed field entangled in cud weed and cane ran parallel the river. To our right was the bridge. I'd grown up under that bridge. Had known its colors. It had given me my first pigeons. The storm swollen river appeared with shores so spectral. At the base of the bank was a lone apple tree consumed in vines, leaned in death. When Doc and I were boys we tasted her sourness. Beyond the long stretch of brown water and the mud fields were gray mountains.

Earlier that same day I had emerged from my backdoor, kneeling, holding Annie's head. She wagged, looking into my eyes. Trotting alongside, she entered the wired porch section of my loft resting at her spot as I fed my pigeons. It was the first day of April. Life was cooing. My birds told me they were hungry as they flapped their wings above their heads.

Rook, a royal red check cock, left his day shift on the uppermost nest joining in the lineup already rapidly pecking. Rook was no accident. He was my living art. I had bred every bird in his pedigree for seven generations. He gorged his craw before returning to two eggs, seventeen days old, beginning to hatch. Other doweled rooms were fed before I returned. Rook was staggering on the floor. I lifted him. What's wrong, ol' boy? You aren't sick, are you? Running my hand along his chest, I felt firm muscle through his thick feathering. His wattle was white. I was puzzled.

I placed Rook on his top roost. The one he'd fought so bloody hard to win. Rook stood. Then, gradually, he slumped, half shutting his eyes. The smart face tilted over. Feathers flared. Body rose and puffed. Then quivered. The slumped body grew from relaxed to motionless.

Rook died.

I couldn't lift him. I stared the longest of time. The other birds were indifferent. Finally, I picked him up. Was it a heart attack? Inside his mouth, already fading to death's submission, there was a slit that allowed air to his lungs. There, lodged, stuck two sunflower seeds. I buried him with my hands. Annie looked on. A mossy grave at the foot of the mountain where he had spent his entire life, near a branchless oak diseased and dying. For some time I stared up past the pines. I thought of summer. What kept me in Estill county? Beguiled, I looked into the sky's crepuscular rays. I was so alone.

I could not go back to Black Hole's.

I turned, bent over, looking at the fresh grave.

I could not escape the phone call received from Sensi before I had gone to the loft. Black Hole had gone to Lexington. Rented a room. Bought a pistol. Placed a mattress in the middle of his room. Locked the door and sat down on the mattress. Shot four times. One in each wall. The fifth was his. Barrel in mouth and pulled the trigger.

Black Hole finally got out.

He left me here.

In a place where he told me there was nothing to write about.

"That Christmas card sent to me from my stepmother was like the thank you note Butch Cassidy sent to that bank."

NS

"I couldn't retreat from *THESE PRECIOUS DAYS*, ghosts and mirrors wouldn't allow it."

NS

"You just think you are touching the ocean. Really, she's touching you."

NS

I LOVE MY MAN

August, 2010

The ocean talks, breathes, listens.

You can leave the ocean.

Not really.

You can love the ocean.

No love in return.

Send a love letter to her.

No address.

Dream and be lost.

Mainlining the Gulf Stream.

Needing a fix.

Driving hard.

Left before sun snuck.

Racing.

Gotta make Bo before dark.

A day earlier Sensi and I were on Caicos on Provo Island, 600 miles below Miami. Before that, a month diving off Singer Island with Wide Eyes our son-in law and our two grandsons.

"Pops, I don't want to grow up."

"Pops, I love you."

(I hear you).

Summer had been crying oil spill.

But my waters were heaven.

As soon as we flew back into Kentucky kissed bye. Grabbed dive gear. Loaded a wicker crate of racing homers. Headed south, van. Something called.

Where was Palm Coast?

No fret, cell phone would guide.

Hadn't seen Bo in years.

When I did it had been nothing.

There he was that evening, just the two of us, him standing in the middle of the street where the old Colonnades Beach Hotel once was, his hand at his side, facing me, the imaginary gunslinger, ready to draw.

He'd been doing coke all week and fishing in the interior of Florida; catching cheap fish; most still inside the cooler in his old caddy, rotting.

The next day we dove the Palm Beach inlet;
Came out with a barnacled golf club.

He'd had a lot of ups and downs.

The worst, his forced leaving Turneffe Island,
forty miles off the coast of Belize; that simply
murdered him.

Bo had been a fish guide and dive master
while there; lived in those particularly clear
waters and sun for ten years until his uncle sold
the island.

That's when he and Angel sorta died, sorta
went to hell; sorta nothing came back.

Neither owned education.

He wound up working construction. She
pitched her tiger patterned bikinis; became a
doctor's receptionist.

A long time they disappeared from No Sweat.
Dead or in prison, I supposed.

Bo once looked like Gregory Peck. We'd
caught thousands of lobsters and shot world
record snook; laughed at sharks. We'd lived in a
world of tan, clear water, melted butter and no
authority.

"HEY NIGGER!" shouted someone across the Palm Coast McDonald's parking lot.

I was bent over inspecting my crate of racing homers.

It was Bo; hanging half out of his pick-up.

Drunk.

He turned his reddened face and saw two black families eying him, upset as they walked in.

He laughed. "Follow me to Mom's," he instructed.

He was still thin. Not healthy; there were ugly dark places scattered on the pale skin of his arms; his black hair now turning grey.

Pulling up. Surprised. A fine home. Inter-coastal canal. Complete with coconut palms.

Into the spacious interior. Bo's mother. Off alone. Quiet bedroom. She was sitting half up in bed breathing oxygen from a tube going into her nose, a cigarette was burning in an ashtray beside her as she poured cheap vodka into an empty glass from a plastic, half-gallon jug. Near the lamp next to her was a frame of mounted Confederate money made up of different denominations. "So, you're the famous

No Sweat?" she spoke in an effete
southern drawl. "I've given Bo money for this
trip. Besides you, it's all he's been talking about.
Make yourself at home. Pour a drink. I've got
some ribs and fried okra in the kitchen. Eat all
you want."

"The Gulf Stream is a tramp. She doesn't run
north. She runs through your soul."

Starved, I walked back into the kitchen
looking at the food in this rich lair. Near that
pile of ribs were two garbage cans filled with
empty beer cans and rib bones. The dried out
food was yesterday's; had been left out over
night among the stacks of dirty dishes. If tasted
it would destroy my stomach. I had to stay
healthy. In two days lobster season would open
and it was still a long way on down to Big Pine
Key.

"I need to get my pigeons on over to Bill. We'll
eat when we get back."

"I'll drive, you rest. Put the pigeons in my
truck."

Bo poured himself a large cup of vodka, lit a
cigarette and turned up heavy metal on his
radio.

Down the road.

"Can you crack the window and turn down the volume?"

Bo laughed. Weaving bad. ENOUGH! No Sweat took control.

More vodka; "Obama has ruined me. And that stripper I lived with, damn bitch stole my house. Had me arrested for stalking."

Near Orlando; at Bill's "WINSTORM LOFTS." Bill judged the birds I had brought. They would have to fly over 700 straight air miles to make it back to my home. "You'll be lucky if you get a single one back," he said. "The birds are down in weight from the trip. I'll fatten them for a few days before releasing them."

Walking through his loft he selected four racers that were just learning to fly, giving them to me. "I haven't been feeling well. You have them. Money can't buy these birds."

"What do I owe you?"

"Don't worry. Tell everyone where you got the blood when they win."

Bo staggered out of his truck and into the loft. "Man, look at that pretty one," he commented, wanting to grab roosting champions.

491

Bill was amazed. "Is this guy acting?"

"Bo is suffering from the clutches of ocean melancholy and a double dose of society. Free things have to be free or they're nothing."

Bill caught a pigeon. "Here is how you hold a bird," he explained to Bo. "You place the wings behind the bird and at the same time with the same hand hold its legs with two fingers. The rest of the bird is maintained with the other hand helping to control the bird's body."

Bo was Bo drunk. The only thing his hands felt comfortable in holding was another cup of vodka. He clasped the poor bird as one might a blowfish in the process of it blowing up. As the pigeon struggled to get loose Bill took the bird back and shook his head in disgust.

Late at night; driving north back to Bo's.

"Angel has been undergoing operations, battling throat cancer for two years; Chemo. Now down to eighty pounds, looks bad. She wants to see you. When we get back we'll go over to her place. It's not much but it's on the water."

"Not tonight, Bo. I'm tired. We'll have to leave at dawn to make it to Charlie's on time to be ready for opening day. We'll go see her when we come back."

Sunrise.

Bo in his mother's garage, loading gear; same duffel bag we had put speared snook in thirty years ago along with flippers and mask equally dilapidated.

"My spear-gun that I stole off Francis Ford Coppola in Belize, some asshole stole off me. I hate a damn thief. Do you still have your boat, NANCY LOU?"

"Yeah, Can't get rid of her, too many memories. Every time I'm on her, Larry, mom and Luisa ride with me. Right now, she's perfect, new motor and steering; had to get the new steering where she was made, in Miami."

Since Bo chain-smoked we took his truck. It wasn't long before we were all over the interstate, bypassing every toll booth. For breakfast he had substituted bacon and eggs for vodka and vodka. He kept rambling about his recent stalking imprisonment. It was no prison compared to the one he owned; ball and chain; only a matter of time before his lungs would go black or his eyes would turn yellow. When you are so far down inside a bottle it's impossible to climb out.

Mom couldn't.

Sensi had discovered her body. She'd been

dead for three days; half-slumped over the mohair couch in the den; heart attack.

My heart stopped, too.

Now I was glad she was dead; gone beyond dad's hell cell.

I was now sorry I had gone out of my way to take Bo with me down to the Keys to catch lobsters. I realized my old memories were of another Bo; Of a Bo that I once believed wanted to live.

Even then I was probably blind.

Bo began professing the best way to catch lobster; some friend used a net. The pretentious discourse soon reached a saturation point.

Changing subjects.

"Charlie's wife died of cancer last October. She was one of Sensi's best friends. We were supposed to go diving on opening day last year but never made it. Charlie stayed by her side the whole way."

Islamorada.

"Look at that lobster statue! Stop! Get a picture of me!" A van owning two black families piled out and scattered about the statue. Bo frowned. "Forget it."

Driving.

"In Eleuthera I caught a 13 pound lobster. Measured 53" long from the tip of its antennae to the end of its tail. That was my last summer with dad. Caught an eight pounder ten minutes before that."

"Thirteen pounds!"

"His legs were the same length as my arms. Cooked him like a turkey. The big ones are just as good as the little ones, maybe better."

"How is your dad?"

"Ain't seen him in eight years."

"How come?"

"If you whip a dog long enough it'll leave."

"Are you the dog?"

"I feel like one, a cur that nobody wants when it comes to dad. He has always owned this urge to beat something. Now that something is gone. It's gotta tear him up. A life wasted in his own sunshine. He married some woman that crawled out of a hollow eight years ago. She knew what she was doing, robbing a bank without using a gun. She'd been married twice before; one time to an attorney, the last time to another old man; when that old man died she spit on his two sons, got their inheritances. Dad wanted to know what I thought of her. I said, if you lived in a trailer out on some ridge, do you think she'd be after you? That's when he hung up. It ain't love when you are seventy-seven and she's fifty. Didn't take her a year to take control of everything he owned. True allows he has some kind of clot in the veins that go to his brain and that he has trouble remembering or communicating. Eight years ago when he was staying with me in Eleuthera, on about the fourth day he'd been in my house we were in his bedroom and he asked where was he? I said, dad, this is your room. This is where you have been staying the last three days. He stood there and stared at everything totally lost. I knew then something was wrong. Now, everything he ever stole and worked for, including my inheritance, is gone. This makes two times in my family that my inheritance has been stolen; nothing to pass down to my grandsons. He always boasted that he was the smartest man in the world. But it's like my old swim coach always said, talk is cheap. I'd hate to be like him and realize that I hated my father, brother, father-in-law, brother-in-laws and my only son. When that woman moved in she had him concrete over mom's name that was by the doorway of the house that I helped build. She had a yard sale and sold everything that belonged to mom, never told me a word. Dad told True that mom was gone. I told her to tell him that as long as I lived she would always be alive. I didn't think it was possible for him to be more cruel to mom when she was dead than when she was alive. He has never seen my grandchildren. I've sent word to him to come see them and that he is welcomed but he has never come."

"Those pigeons you got off that guy, we're partners, right?"

"Tell you what. You keep the birds up in a good loft and keep them watered and fed and healthy and mate them exactly the way they should be mated. You select the races their young birds should go in. You pay all the entry fees. You pay the shipping to the race. You pay for the box it cost for them to be shipped in. You pool the birds before the race. You win the race against men that have devoted their lives to the sport. You do all that and then we'll be partners."

"What's it cost to get in a race?"

"Depends on what kind of race you want in. There are races that pay ten grand and there are races that pay out a million dollars. In South Africa they're supposed to have a race that has two million dollars in it. If you want to get in it you have to cough up a few thousand in entry fees and fly against several thousand of the best from all over the world. Y'know, I've handled a lot of great pigeons but none of them compare to holding the hands of either of my grandsons."

"How do they find home?"

"Like us, they follow the sun."

GIMME SHELTER snuck out on the radio. I cranked it up. We needed that song.

Bo needed it bad. "Do you still love your dad?"

"I've disappointed him. His dream was for me to be some attorney that was a jazz trumpet player. Do I love him? Yeah. Despite everything, I do love him. I'm lucky he is my father, or was. Even a gorilla can be loved. I love dad but I can't go over to his house. I can't be around anyone that spits on mom and my family. That day I caught those 289 lobsters in the inlet he was my bag man. I've hit a crawl two times in my life, both after storms. How do you erase memories like that?"

I thought of Sensi; my Caribbean Sea forever, P.S. I love you. P.S. and P.S. again. Our 2010 summer had been one lost in blue. We were in awe when we first saw the waters of Iguana Island off Providence Island in the Turks and

Caicos; was water so possible? Water electrified
with blue. As though blue were on fire. Blue as if
blue were on trial for murder and pleading for its
life with all the color blue could ever be. Beneath
the island's clouds reflecting turquoise bottoms
she found a conch in the surf; On the
inside, pearlish. But dull compared to
her. Whatever love had been denied when I was
growing up she had more than replaced.
She owned no qualms in my leaving, the Gulf
Stream was everyone's mistress; All my life I had
sacrificed security to be near whatever that
stream was. Sensi had stepped out of a dream
rescuing me and the rescue had always held
steady. I took solace remembering our
summer's last dive, us hovering hand in hand
120' deep along the wall of the 6,000 feet drop
off along the world's third largest barrier
reef; our underwater honeymoon. I loved her the
first moment I saw her and always would.
Without her I was nothing, the world was
nothing.

The toil of traveling held me in a certain
languor. My mind fell back to that morning by
the Palm Beach pump house; a surreal memory
that so often and oddly came to me. Why did it
do so? I was nine years old. Dad and I had pole
guns. It was the summer of 1960, when there
were no laws about spearfishing around the
inlet. There weren't but a handful of us divers to
be found. Somewhere, dad had bought those
guns in one of the few places that had any dive
gear; powerful guns especially made for eastern
Kentucky's Tarzan and Boy. We always routinely

checked the iron rail that ran underwater out into the ocean some twenty yards north of the pump house when we would first dive. Any lobsters hiding there were easy pickings. But that morning when we entered into the water there was no time for that rail. Before us was a massive school of striped fish, most were larger than myself. So many that you could not see anything but them; Scared expressions on their faces as though they were being chased. I began looking for a shark. And then I saw dad bust one of the striped fish behind the gills and it began to pull him through the water. I found myself doing the same. My heart raced inside a swirl of madness. That afternoon dad and I grilled the fish as he sang and drank and told war stories of his days in the merchant marines. How could you not love all that?

Strange indeed our dreams, why hide so within us? When we die why must they disappear? Carol had told Charlie that she looked forward to seeing her dead father.

I envied her.

Bo had no job. And from the looks of what I could see, would never have another. All his talk was of the past, not one word about the future. He wanted me to feel sorry for him, a typical Machiavellian ploy. I had hoped this trip would revive the old days but one look at him, no.

I didn't know what I was going to say to Charlie. He had to be lonely, too, but not Bo lonely.

"There's the seven mile bridge," spoke Bo. While he poured more vodka. "I use my ganoe to hit the traps. The owners grease them. You don't want a lobster boat seeing that grease on your arms."

I said nothing. Any decent lobster thief always worked in an old disposable sweatshirt. We were still north of the seven mile bridge. Bo would see that soon enough. But he wouldn't admit it. The world was wrong, not him. If he recognized the seven mile bridge he'd just take another drink and pretend it wasn't there.

And did.

"What did you say you did to your boat?"

"Put a new motor and new steering in her last year. Sure wish I could take her to Cuba, stay there about a year, lots of wrecks still untouched, the women are good looking, too. I guess I'm the only fool on the face of the earth that can honestly say that Ernest Hemingway bought him his boat. Y'know, they've got a half-sister to Hemingway's boat, the 'PILAR,' back in Islamorada. We'll stop and look at her when we go back. Every time I watch that movie, KEY LARGO, with Bogart, I look for her. She's got SANTANA painted on her hull. Pilar was Hemingway's second wife's nickname; the rich one, the same one that had her uncle give them the home in Key West as a wedding present. Hemingway used that name on a part-gypsy woman in For Whom the Bell tolls. Well enough. Any good boat is part gypsy. Tell me somethin', do you have your fishing license and lobster stamp? If you don't, we'll have to stop and get 'em. We're getting' too old to go to jail."

"They've gotta be three inches in the head, right?"

"No, Bo, they've gotta be OVER three; If you are one one hundredth of an inch off they'll write you up. You have to have a gage on you at all times. You have to leave them whole. You can't spear 'em or puncture 'em in any way. They check for all that, and no eggs. If they see one with eggs, there'll be no sunshine again."

When we got to Big Pine Key we found Charlie's white, two story block and stucco house and Charlie there busy at work; he had been gone for several weeks having just arrived before us and was going through his routine of unbattening the house's hatches; In his yard was a bright green iguana giving us the reptile eye as a small deer across the street

rummaged through a garbage can; air plants
were growing along the side of his house
and there by his mailbox was a wooden lobster
trap.

"You all have the basement. Mark, his wife
and son will be here in a couple of days. We
always go diving on his birthday. I'm
reserving the other upstairs bedroom for them.
Get your gear unloaded. We're going fishing
tonight; Seven miles out on the ocean side;
Snappers. Probably the last good shot we'll have
at 'em for a while. They start hitting when it gets
dark."

Bo and I found our blue bedroom with two
single beds; there was AC and a large floor fan.
Say it isn't so but I am permanently bewitched
by the strange weight of three blue shades: The
Blue Bar's umbrellas on Harbour Island creating
their blue shade; seeing my redheaded Sensi
and Wide Eyes in a blue cast beneath them;
their feet on a blue floor sitting at a table of blue,
a blue drink in hand and a blue sky above and a
blue sea still beyond. And next, that blue shade
reflecting a magical blue as if a blue fire were
somehow dancing, casting it's spell up from the
pink ocean floor and onto the craggy
Neanderthal walls of an eerie grotto hidden in
Eleuthera; a wild place illuminating the Gulf
blue eyes of my daughter, Wide Eyes; she and I
alone; a day forever where I made the luckiest
shot in my life, stopping a seven foot cuda

making a it's straight run at my leg; A lie, no. A fish that was more wolf than fish; A fish that I would say, liar, if you said the same to me; Now, forever, Wide Eyes' and I our secret. And last, the blue shade coming down on Carol on our last dive day together; miles out into the quiet Gulf at high noon and her sitting there, fish hawk comfortable with Sensi in Charlie's anchored Mako; a warm, cat-like smile covering her face, monitoring the marine patrol and captured lobsters and by the day's end owning tired arms from throwing back the under 3" shorts.

Bo was thrilled we were going fishing, dragging out his old tackle. "Some of these lures are worth a lot of money," he boasted. "They're about all I got when my uncle died."

"You won't need any of your fishing stuff. Charlie has everything."

"I use to take the L.L. Bean people fly fishing; made my own flies. We'd hit the flats. Biggest bone fish you ever saw."

I went upstairs and there was Charlie's green conure perched on his shoulder cuddling next to his chin, making some intimate noise interpretable only between him and Charlie; there they were, Hemingway and Robinson Crusoe's parrot.

Blue.

Blue turned to black. I was one with a starry night. Found myself in the boat with Bo, Charlie and Charlie's friend. We went a few hundred yards out into the bay and pulled in Charlie's bait-fish cage-like traps, unloaded them into his live well and continued.

Night fishing arouses. I discovered myself once again some fifty years ago, that freckled redheaded boy under Aopehh's bridge cutting down a cane pole getting ready to go to the Kentucky River dreaming of a giant catfish. Charlie's polite friend was in good condition and about my age. I sensed he was a yankee with some kind of authority by the way he elevated himself and when he spoke I knew it for certain, some place in the north east, so many people, god help him. And God had, as there he was.

Bo owned a splendid smile on his beleaguered face as we headed twelve miles out toward the Atlantic side; each jolting bump into a swelled wave jarring life into old memories. Charlie kept monitoring his GPS while the rest of us yelled out, helping him dodge the lobster buoys. Off in far the distance we began to see specks of light; small boats already anchored over our targeted reef. After a few attempts to anchor we were soon chumming the water and then baiting our hooks. I wished for Sensi and my grandsons. Back in June, while on Singer Island, every evening after supper Sensi and I had taken our oldest grandson on a walk around the perimeter of the island. Sensi and I had been doing this for years long before our grandson. Over a half of a century had passed and in that time the island had changed from its simple sandy days to its high rises with uniformed attendants, pass cards and computers. There were a still a few places on the island that had not been developed and when we came to those places I would stop and tell my grandson about how when I was a boy I played at that place or another, catching the green lizards that changed color and sometimes the baby turtles that had hatched on the beach during the night and had wandered off in the wrong direction. And here and there I would point out a pigeon. I had always had pigeons; It was good knowing that Picasso had painted a woman with a pigeon and that Cezanne had done likewise with his sister's loft. And that Darwin changed man's image of himself because of them. I had always been a writer viscerally knowing memory is everything. I had an eye for pigeons. Marlon Brando cleaned his teeth with the end of a pigeon feather in *ONE EYED JACKS* and spoke softly in his loft about his dream to be a prize fighter while tending pigeons and running errands at the docks for Johnny Friendly, the corrupt boss of the dockers union in *ON THE WATERFRONT*; it seemed only I knew that. My loft was like the ocean, a place where words died. At nights I would fall asleep and the ocean and my loft would fill my dreams, waves and wings. A week ago, Sensi had informed me about our oldest grandson slipping off to be alone and writing stories. What was there to say? He knew I was always there for him; Knew even now with me so far away. Knew it as much as I knew my dead grandfather was still here for me. It was a strong feeling and good. But then I thought of my grandson's name and I felt poor. His name was the name of my father and his brother. Dad was still alive and didn't know that; didn't know the name of either of his only two grandsons, when they were born, or cared. The ocean at night allows you to lose everything but I couldn't lose the thoughts of my father. Charlie was fast pulling in a snapper attempting to keep it from the sharks.

The next sunrise we stood at Charlie's dock filleting fish. The Gulf side was pond flat and the water was aching to be invaded. Once we had the fillets on ice we headed out in Charlie's Mako to scout for lobsters, daybreak tomorrow, I would be grabbing those bugs. I had phoned Bill to learn more about my racing pigeons that he was supposed to release, discovering that he had suffered a heart attack and was now in intensive care. That left me blank. I remembered Bill telling me that he gave me those four young racing homers in part because he hadn't been feeling well.

"What's that damn 'BP' doing on your boat? That's not BRITISH PETROLEUM, is it?" asked

507

Bo, bent over in the cooler, adding and mixing in a half of case of Budweiser in with the water and sodas; he was referring to the painted letters showing on the bow of Charlie's Mako.

"It doesn't have anything to do with the oil company," explained Charlie. "Boaters on Big Pine Key mark their boat with those initials. If your boat gets lost its easier to trace."

Charlie's old Mako ran sweet. Even better than she did on the day Charlie had bought her. That was more than twenty years ago. I'd been on her that day, too. We hit the four mile reef off Stuart. The water was cold and dirty and sharky. It also produced Florida's biggest lobsters.

"I call this place, The Current," spoke Charlie, looking at his GPS and watching as I dove in with my cocked arbelette; in the near distance the bridges were running along A-1A hooking Key to Key.

The moment I hit the water I felt like mom was close, and dad, too. I was home. For this time of year in the Keys the water was cooler than usual and the visibility better, at least 60 feet visibility. Holding onto coral at the shallow bottom I saw nearly a hundred shed lobster hulls, many sprawled one on top of another. I had been diving for half of a century and I had never seen so many. If cared for properly, they could be made into attractive lobster mounts. I collected three and brought them to the boat making sure not to damage them in any way."I know season is out but I don't think they'll say anything over these. Their worth a hundred bucks each if you want to spend some time messing with them."

Charlie neatly lined the bugs along the side of the boat. "Did you see any lobsters?"

"There's probably a hundred down there. We gotta be back here before daylight, tomorrow."

How can you go from being fifty nine back to seventeen?

The Gulf Stream owned that power.

How can you forget every single problem you have?

Bo handed me a beer and smiled.

Charlie put his Mako in gear. "For supper, I'm going to fix snapper using my secret recipe," he boasted.

END